THE DEVIL'S TRIANGLE

Also by Mark Robson

Imperial Spy
Imperial Assassin
Imperial Traitor

The Dragon Orb series
Firestorm
Shadow
Longfang
Aurora

For more information on Mark Robson and news on
upcoming books, visit: www.markrobsonauthor.com

THE DEVIL'S TRIANGLE

MARK ROBSON

SIMON AND SCHUSTER

First published in Great Britain in 2011 by Simon
and Schuster UK Ltd, a CBS company.
Simon & Schuster UK Ltd
1st Floor, 222 Gray's Inn Road, London WC1X 8HB

www.simonandschuster.co.uk

A CIP catalogue record for this book is available from the British Library.

ISBN 978-1-84738-978-7

1 3 5 7 9 10 8 6 4 2

Typeset by Hewer Text UK Ltd, Edinburgh
Printed in the UK by CPI Cox & Wyman, Reading RG1 8EX

For Sam and Neve.
A special reading adventure for you.

And for Katharina (Kitty),
who has been like an extra daughter this year.

CHAPTER ONE

'Row 41. These are ours.' Niamh dumped her little backpack on the nearest of the three seats and reached up to open the overhead locker. 'Bags I get the window seat.'

'It's yours,' Sam replied, leaning forward to look out through the little porthole window. 'It's a naff view anyway. All you can see is the wing. Do you mind if I have the aisle seat, Cal?'

'Sure,' Callum replied amiably. 'Fine by me.'

And it was. At this moment he didn't care where he sat. It was just exciting to be here. Sam and Niamh might be casual about heading out to the Florida Keys for the summer holidays, but this was the trip of a lifetime for Callum. The furthest he'd ever been from home before was to Paris on a school trip. He could still hardly believe he was about to fly to America.

'Cool!' Sam exclaimed as he settled into his seat. 'This is one of the jets with the new entertainment systems. Not all the 747s have these. Loads of films and games on demand. It helps the time pass no end, Cal. The flight takes forever without it. If you'd come with us a few years ago . . . aw, Dad! Do you have to?'

Callum leaned forward and instinctively pushed his glasses up his nose. Curious to see what had put the exasperated note into his friend's voice, he looked across the aisle at Mr Cutler. Matthew Cutler did not seem in the slightest bit bothered by his son's outburst.

'Yes, Sam,' he replied calmly, glancing across the aisle and then returning his attention to finding his page in the book he was holding. 'As a matter of fact, I do.'

'But you must have read that book a dozen times already,' Sam grumbled. 'You'll freak out the other passengers. Haven't you got anything else in your bag?'

'I've got my old friends Berlitz and Kusche. Would you rather I read one of those? Besides, you exaggerate. I've only read this one a couple of times and while Quasar is something of a sensationalist, his work is much more recent than the others. Some of the stuff he's dug up is very interesting.'

'Can I have a look, sir?' Callum asked, intrigued to see what they were talking about and keen to ingratiate himself with the man who was paying for his holiday.

'Certainly, Callum,' he replied, leaning across the aisle and passing the book. 'But please, call me Matt or Matthew. I have enough of being "sir" during the school term time.'

'OK ... Matt,' Callum agreed hesitantly. After the formality of St George's Grammar School for Boys, where all adults were 'sir' or 'miss', it seemed strange to be calling Mr Cutler by his first name, but the smile he received for using the familiar form immediately made him feel more comfortable with it.

The book had a dark cover picture of a stormy sea with a map of the North Atlantic Ocean superimposed over it. A line of dashes joined Bermuda to Puerto Rico and Miami, and the title read *Into the Bermuda Triangle* in bold red type.

'Is this true?' Callum asked, pointing at the statement in smaller white type at the bottom of the front cover that declared 'More than 1,000 ship and airplane disappearances in the past 25 years'. 'I mean, I thought the Triangle was a sort of modern-day myth.'

'Well, as I said, Gian Quasar, the author, appears

3

to be a bit of a sensationalist,' Mr Cutler replied carefully. 'He's probably right about the total, but not all of those ships and planes vanished without trace – far from it. The vast majority of the incidents are perfectly explainable, with little mystery about them. The Triangle is renowned for its unpredictable weather. It's had a bad reputation with sailors since the time of the early explorers. Of course it wasn't called the Bermuda Triangle then. It's been given many dramatic names over the years: the Hoodoo Sea, the Twilight Zone, the Port of Missing Ships, the Limbo of the Lost. My favourite is the Devil's Triangle. Perhaps that's because the name implies an *intent* behind the disappearances.'

There was a strange note in Mr Cutler's voice as he spoke.

'So you think there might be something more to it than just weather,' Callum suggested thoughtfully, turning the book over and skimming his eyes across the blurb. 'Is the Triangle a hobby of yours?'

Something dug sharply into his right side. He twisted to get comfortable only to discover Niamh was jabbing him with her fingers. He opened his mouth to ask her why, but stopped. Her expression was full of warning. She was using him as a shield to keep from being in her father's line of sight.

The slightest shake of her head was enough to tell Callum this conversation was not one he should be pursuing.

'I suppose it could be called a hobby,' Mr Cutler said, oblivious to his daughter's intervention and his voice sounding suddenly grim. 'Do I believe the Triangle holds some strange mysterious force that causes ships and planes to disappear?' He paused. 'My head tells me no . . . but then my heart . . . well, let's just say that I'm not sure quite what to believe any more.'

'Give the book back,' Niamh whispered softly to Callum. 'And change the subject.'

Callum didn't need any further hints. He handed the book across the aisle just as a stewardess in her red and white uniform approached on her seatbelt check. She twisted her head to glance at the title of the book and chuckled as she read it.

'Oh, you don't want to read that today, sir,' she said, her blue eyes twinkling with amusement. 'We're going to be flying right through there, you know.'

'Are we?' Callum asked, surprised. A nervous knot tightened in his stomach. 'I hadn't realised.'

'I shouldn't worry too much,' the stewardess said, her smile clearly genuine. 'Our pilots today have a pretty good track record of finding their way to Miami.'

Almost as if he had heard the comment, the aircraft's public address system burst into life and the pilot began his welcome to the passengers.

'Good morning, ladies and gentlemen. My name is Phil Hanson and I'm going to be your captain today. Together with my first officer, Mark Gillies, I'll be flying you out to sunny Miami. Our estimated flight time today is eight hours and fifty minutes and we'll be cruising at an altitude of . . .'

'Eight hours fifty!' Sam groaned.

'Is that longer than usual?' Callum asked, the feeling of tension in his stomach twisting a little tighter.

'Not much,' Niamh said calmly, flicking through the in-flight entertainment magazine she had pulled from the seat pocket in front of her. 'Ignore Sam's moaning. What's a few minutes here and there when you're going to be stuck in this seat for the best part of the day anyway?'

The captain finished his announcement by requesting all passengers to watch the safety video and the demonstration of the location of the nearest emergency exits by cabin staff. Callum was happy to comply, though he saw that Sam and Niamh weren't paying the slightest attention, and Mr Cutler was already lost in his book. There was a buzz of happy excitement in the aircraft. Young children were chattering excitedly and parents were trying to keep them in their seats and amused while the cabin crew began their final checks.

Callum failed to notice the movement at first, but then he did a double take as his eyes glanced around at the window.

'We're rolling backwards!' he gasped.

'Relax!' Niamh chuckled. 'It's totally normal. We're being pushed back away from the terminal building, that's all. Haven't you flown before?'

'No. Never,' Callum replied, doing his best to look casual about it. 'Does it show?'

'Only a lot!'

'Well, I guess I'll just have to live with that,' he muttered.

Taking off was the most exhilarating experience Callum had ever felt. As the powerful engines of the enormous Boeing jet accelerated them down the runway, he could not help wondering how such an enormous machine could ever climb into the air. It didn't seem right that air could support something that weighed so much. Just as he felt sure the laws of nature were agreeing with him and the runway must be running out, the front of the aircraft tipped upwards. Much of the vibration ceased instantly, and the dominant sound changed from the deep rumble of wheels on tarmac to the clean roar of the jet engines driving them away from the ground. They had been airborne for more than a minute before Callum realised his fingers were clasping the seat arms in a white-knuckled death grip.

'Wow!' he breathed, relaxing his fingers and wiggling them to release the tension.

Niamh glanced down at Callum's hands as he interlocked his fingers and flexed them back and forth. 'So did you squeeze us into the air today?' she asked, affording him a knowing smile.

Callum could feel his face flushing. 'I'd have thought you'd be thanking me,' he replied quickly. 'We'd be sitting in a smoking wreck halfway to Windsor if I hadn't squeezed at the critical moment.'

Niamh laughed. 'I can't wait to see how you intend to get us down again,' she said.

Callum didn't notice when the aircraft stop climbing. They had still been rocketing skywards when a stewardess worked her way along the aisle handing out little plastic bags containing headsets. Sam showed him where to plug the jack into the armrest and Callum spent the next couple of hours happily watching a film on the small screen that was set into the headrest of the seat in front. Sam, he noted, was watching a different film, but Callum didn't recognise it from the little he saw out of the corner of his eye.

When both their films had finished, Sam challenged him to various computer games and, before Callum realised it, another hour had passed. After being beaten for the umpteenth time at 'Who Wants to be a Millionaire?' Callum had to admit that Sam had better general knowledge than he did.

'So much for my reputation as a geek!' he said. 'That's enough thrashings for now, Sam. I need to pee and stretch my legs. Try Niamh. Maybe she'll give you more of a game.'

'You mean, you need the *rest room*,' Niamh corrected. 'We're going to the US. You might as well start getting used to their terminology.'

'Fair enough,' Callum replied, squeezing past Sam and into the aisle. 'I'll see you in a minute, y'all. I'm just off to the *rest room* . . . for a pee.'

Sam gave a bark of laughter. Niamh shook her head, but smiled as she did so. Callum looked a total nerd, but his appearance was deceptive. When he had first appeared at the house with Sam after school one day, she had found it hard to hide her surprise. He seemed an unlikely friend for her brother. Sam was tall, athletic and trendy, with a sharp haircut and clean-cut features, while Callum was a full head shorter, comparatively weedy-looking, with an unruly mop of hair and glasses straight from Austin Powers' shelf. But Niamh had quickly warmed to his self-deprecating nature and sharp sense of humour.

When Callum returned, Sam had started watching another film. Callum didn't fancy staring at the little screen again for a while so, settling into his seat, he reached down into his hand-luggage and pulled out a book. Niamh was also reading. Callum glanced across at Mr Cutler; he was still totally absorbed in his book.

'So what's with your dad and the Triangle?' Callum whispered to Niamh. 'All that rib-digging earlier has me curious.'

'Didn't Sam tell you?' she replied softly, surreptitiously peeping round him to check for herself that her father was not listening.

'Tell me what?'

'Why we go to the Keys every year.'

'No. Should he have?'

'Typical! Sam hates talking about anything emotional.'

Niamh took another furtive look across at her father and then leaned right back into the seat to make sure she was as shielded as she could be by the two boys. 'It's where Mum disappeared nine years ago.'

'Disappeared? You mean she just left?'

'No,' Niamh breathed. 'She disappeared. Vanished.'

'How?' Callum asked.

'Who knows?' Niamh replied, her eyes wary and her voice sounding suddenly tight. 'Dad's pretty obsessed with finding the answer to that question, but aside from learning a lot of history, he doesn't seem to have achieved a lot. To be honest, I don't remember much about what happened. Sam and me were only five at the time, so all I can tell you is what Dad's told us. Apparently, Mum was out in a boat with her dive partner studying nurse sharks. She was a marine biologist. Dad says she was involved in a project with a private marine research lab. One day, her boat didn't return to the lab. The circumstances were so strange that Dad's been haunted by the Bermuda Triangle phenomenon ever since.'

'I'm sorry. That must have been tough.'

'Yeah,' Niamh said, unable to totally conceal the bitterness in her voice. 'You could say that. Dad went through a really tough time with the police investigation,'

'I didn't realise the Keys were inside the Triangle,' Callum admitted, not fooled for one moment by the dispassionate front Niamh was displaying. The pain in her eyes was obvious and although she was trying to sound cool and detached as she talked about it, hints of emotion kept leaking through. Although he didn't want to pry and upset his best friend's sister

11

further, he found he couldn't curb his curiosity. He had often wondered why Sam and Niamh lived alone with their dad. He had assumed it had been the result of a divorce. The idea that their mother had disappeared under mysterious circumstances was horribly fascinating.

'The boundaries of the Triangle seem to vary depending on which book you read, but inside or out is a bit irrelevant really,' she explained, her eyes distant.

'Could the boat have sunk?' Callum asked gently.

'Mum and her partner were supposed to be working in shallow water. That's where nurse sharks breed, so most of the research was being done in water that was only a couple of metres deep. If the boat had sunk, it should have been found. And even if they had gone out into deeper water, they had masses of emergency equipment: radios, emergency locator beacons and flares. They should've had no problems raising the alarm with the coastguard at the first sign of trouble.'

'Maybe they were kidnapped,' Callum whispered, lowering his voice still further.

'Dad suggested that to the local Sheriff's Office. But why would anyone want to kidnap two marine biologists?' Niamh asked. 'And if they had, then surely the kidnappers would have sent a ransom note or something. No. It was very strange. The two of them just vanished. There was a search of course. But after a few days it was called off, and Mum became a statistic. Just another missing person.'

The hollowness in her voice as she said those final four words sent a shiver down Callum's spine. He knew he couldn't ask any more.

'I'm really sorry,' Callum said, trying to think of something comforting to say. There didn't seem to be any adequate words. 'It must have been horrible for all of you,' he added, knowing how lame his sympathy sounded.

Niamh nodded and gave him a weak smile.

Callum pushed his glasses up his nose again before stealing another glance across at Mr Cutler. He seemed so ordinary. How was it that something so extraordinary could happen to a man like him? It was like something out of a Marvel comic. He could almost see the blurb:

Meet mild-mannered teacher, Matthew Cutler, forty-something father of two by day – paranormal investigator by night.

What superpowers would he have? Callum nearly laughed aloud as he momentarily pictured Mr Cutler wearing a spandex suit, cape and mask. The image was ridiculous. The science teacher had a receding hairline, a few too many pounds round his middle and little rectangular reading glasses that were clearly not for show.

'Dad has never truly given up on Mum,' Niamh volunteered suddenly, breaking his ludicrous train of thought. 'I'm pretty certain he still believes there's a chance she's alive somewhere, but I doubt he would ever admit that out loud. The life insurance company was slow to pay up after the coastguard called off the search, but when they did, Dad spent all the money he got on buying our house in the Keys and on kitting out a boat that he could use to search the waters there for clues. He gave up his career with Lloyds Bank and took up a teaching job so that he could use the long holidays to continue looking. I guess it's nice to know that he loved Mum so much, but it's also a bit sad that he can't let her go.'

'I'm just glad that I didn't offer to lend him my book when Sam made that fuss earlier,' Callum said.

'Why?'

Callum closed his book and turned it face up on his lap to reveal the distinctive black cover. It was a copy of *Gone* by Michael Grant.

14

CHAPTER TWO

Sam Cutler was quietly amused at his friend's reaction to the turbulent approach into Miami. Callum's face turned a deathly shade of grey as the pilots wove between the worst of the heavy showers and battled their way down towards the runway. The majority of the flight had been smooth and predictably dull, but it was clear that Sam's friend did not share the benefits of his travel experience.

Callum's fingers were white with the ferocity of his grip on the armrests, and the muscles in his arms and shoulders looked bunched and tight. For the final ten minutes the aircraft bumped and bucked like a wild horse before a clattering *thump* announced their landing onto the wet tarmac of Miami International Airport.

A spontaneous ripple of applause from other passengers around the cabin was punctuated with the sound of relieved laughter. Sam had felt none of the nervousness displayed by many during the turbulence of the last few minutes. It had felt rather like the lurching, rolling simulator rides at Disney World, and he could remember far worse trips. Niamh had looked similarly calm, reading her book throughout the approach.

'It's OK, Cal. You can relax now,' Sam said, giving Callum a friendly nudge with his elbow as the aircraft began to slow. 'We're down. The only thing you have left to worry about is whether you'll be allowed through customs. The Americans are quite particular about who they let in, you know.'

'Ha, ha, Sam! Very funny. If they let you in, then I sure won't have anything to worry about.'

Sam grinned. This holiday looked set to be the best he'd had in years. It would be so good to have Callum along. He was a good mate. Their friendship had begun on the first day of secondary school when they had both earned three days of detention and a reputation with the form teacher before even getting through registration.

Sam had started it, of course, but Callum had been quick to join in, spraying the boys in front of them with water from the high-pressure taps in

16

the chemistry lab, which happened to be their form room. Those three days of lunchtime detention had sealed their friendship. Cal could be a bit serious and sensible at times, but he didn't take much persuading to join in with some of Sam's wilder escapades.

It had been something of a surprise to Sam that his dad had agreed so readily to Callum coming on holiday with them and, according to Cal, an even bigger surprise that *his* mum and dad had allowed it.

'If it'll keep you from getting bored and irritable, then great,' Sam's dad had said. 'But if you have someone along this year, it's only fair that it'll be Niamh's turn to bring a friend next time. Deal?'

Agreeing to that had been easy. Some of Niamh's friends were pretty hot. All Sam had to do was to guide her a little in her choice and he stood to win both ways. He smiled at the thought.

It took about an hour and a half to get through immigration, collect their bags and clear customs. Sam's father spoke to the man at the car-hire desk and picked up the keys to the car he had leased for the summer.

Moments later, they were out of the cool, air-conditioned airport building and into the hot, muggy depths of the dimly-lit multi-storey car park, their bags piled high on the airport trolley. The combination of the close heat and trapped exhaust fumes in the busy car park was horrid. Sam could taste the oily tang of diesel on the back of his tongue. It tickled, causing him to cough several times before they found their car.

The red SUV was comfortably big enough for the four of them and all their bags. The boys piled the cases into the boot and Niamh climbed into the front passenger seat, leaving the back to Sam and Callum.

Sam could feel trickles of sweat running down the middle of his back as he tried to get comfortable. His shirt was sticking to his body in several places. He lifted the front of it and wafted air up inside just as a loud rumble of thunder rolled around the car park.

'Can you hurry up and get the air con on, please, Dad? I'm melting here.' Sam turned to his friend. 'Don't worry, Cal. This rain won't last long. We often have thunderstorms late afternoon when we're here, but they rarely hang around. By the time we get to the house we should be able to chill out in the pool. I can't wait. It's just so hot! What are you doing, Niamh?'

'Just texting my friend Beth.'

'Already? What could you possibly have to tell her? We've only just landed.'

'Stuff,' she said cryptically, and after poking her tongue out at him for a second, she returned to tapping at the screen on her mobile.

'How long will it take to get to the house?' Callum asked, looking as uncomfortable in the heat as Sam felt.

'It normally takes a couple of hours from here, Callum,' Mr Cutler answered. 'But we have to make our traditional stop at Denny's on the way. What do you think, kids?'

Sam rolled his eyes at his father's use of 'kids', but was quick to add his 'yes' to Niamh's.

Callum looked confused. 'Denny's?' he asked. 'What's that?'

'It's an American diner,' Niamh told him. 'There are loads of different diner chains over here, way more than in the UK. Denny's is sort of an all-day breakfast place, but there's Red Lobster, Chili's, Dunkin' Donuts, Frankie & Benny's, TGI Fridays . . .'

'We've got TGI Fridays in the UK,' Callum interrupted.

'Yeah, but nowhere near as many as they have out here,' said Niamh.

'And IHOP,' Sam said. 'Don't forget IHOP.'

'IHOP?' Callum asked, feeling more confused than ever.

'International House of Pancakes,' Sam explained, licking his lips. 'Mmmm! It's a shame our house is so out in the sticks. The nearest IHOP to Summerland Key is nearly twenty miles away at Key West.'

'Key West has most things,' Niamh agreed.

'OK, OK, kids. Cut it out,' Mr Cutler warned. 'I'm sorry if Summerland Key doesn't fit your idea of civilisation, but I didn't buy the house for its proximity to American diners, or shopping malls, or anything else commercial for that matter.'

'We weren't complaining, Dad,' Niamh protested. 'We were . . .'

'Well, perhaps it would be better to change the subject before I begin to think you are,' he interjected, giving Niamh and Sam a pointed look. He put the car into gear and swung out of the parking bay. 'Do you think Callum will be up to the Denny's challenge?'

Sam and Niamh both instinctively looked at Callum and then burst out laughing.

'Not a hope!' Sam said, grinning as he looked across at his friend.

'Denny's challenge?' Callum asked. 'Is this something else I should have heard of?'

'It's something we started years ago for a bit of fun,' Sam told him. 'The challenge is to get through ordering your food and drink without the waitress asking you a single question.'

'That doesn't sound too hard.'

Sam exchanged knowing glances with Niamh and his dad.

'We'll see,' Sam said. 'We'll see.'

*   *   *

The roads around the airport were busy, but they made steady progress southwards until they started seeing signs for the Overseas Highway. Sam inwardly marvelled that it felt so natural for his father to be driving on the right-hand side of the road again. It was as if he had flipped a switch in his head from left to right. No sooner had they joined the dual carriageway that would take them hopping from island to island for the next one hundred and sixty miles to Summerland Key than the sun came out from behind the clouds and the tall yellow and red Denny's sign became visible on the left. Mr Cutler eased the car into the slip lane and crossed the opposite carriageway. The car park outside Denny's was about half full.

As they climbed out of the car, the air felt thick with moisture and even the few paces from the car to the door were almost unbearable.

'Is it always like this?' Callum asked, goosebumps instantly rising on his arms as they entered the comparatively cold, air-conditioned environment inside.

'Pretty much,' Sam replied. 'Don't worry. You'll get used to it.'

A stern-faced waitress showed them to a table by the window. Sam glanced at her name badge, which identified her as Delores. Something about the way she moved around the restaurant told him she had worked here a while, which would make the challenge all the more difficult. Delores would know all the questions to ask.

'Good afternoon,' she said, her voice bland. 'Can I get you any drinks before you order?'

'Regular coffee for me,' Mr Cutler said. 'With plenty of creamer.'

'A large orange juice, please,' Niamh said.

'Two,' Sam added.

'Make that three, please,' Callum said.

The waitress nodded, thanked them and moved away.

'Playing it safe?' Sam teased.

'Totally,' Callum replied, turning his attention to the menu. Sam knew what he was going to order, but he scanned through the pages of his menu anyway, curious to see if there was anything new that might tempt him away from ordering his favourite. There were a vast number of choices on offer with typically hyped-up descriptions.

'Oh, look,' he said, pointing at the menu. 'The Grand Slam just got grander!' he read, doing his best impression of a southern drawl. 'Don't you just love the descriptions? How about a "New Super Grand Sandwich"? Two scrambled eggs, sausage, crispy bacon, shaved ham, mayonnaise and American

22

cheese on potato bread grilled with a maple spice spread. Served with crispy hash browns. Sounds amazing, doesn't it? The problem is I've always found the reality behind the description a bit of a disappointment.'

'So are you going to break the habit of a lifetime then, Sam?' Niamh asked.

'Nope,' he replied. 'It's steak and eggs for me. One of the best things about coming to America is the meat. The steak over here just tastes better somehow. How about you, Cal? Seen anything that grabs you?'

'Think I'll try the "Awl A-mare-ican Slam"!' Callum said, making a reasonable attempt at copying Sam's previous drawling accent.

'It's ten o'clock at night back home!' Sam protested. 'How can you eat bacon and eggs at this time of day?'

'It's never too late for bacon and eggs.'

'Fair enough.'

The waitress returned bearing a tray of drinks. 'Are y'all ready to order?' she asked.

'I think so,' Mr Cutler said. 'Go on, Callum. You first.'

'I'd like the All American Slam, please,' Callum said, pointing at the picture on the menu.

'And how would you like your eggs today?'

Sam could barely keep from laughing at the confused expression on Callum's face.

'Medium?' Callum offered tentatively.

Sam, Niamh and Mr Cutler all burst out laughing. The waitress looked on, clearly bemused by the hilarity.

'Sunny side up? Scrambled? Over easy?' Sam offered, giving his friend a few options that the waitress would understand.

'Oh, sunny side up, please,' Callum said, flushing red with embarrassment.

'Hash browns or grits?'

'I'd go for hash browns if I were you,' Sam suggested, delighted to see his friend fall for the usual question generators. 'I don't know how anyone can eat grits.'

'Hash browns then, please.'

'White or brown toast?'

'White, please,' he replied.

Sam raised three fingers on his right hand. Callum ignored him.

'Any sauces?'

Sam raised another finger.

'Ketchup will be fine, thanks.'

'That's great,' the waitress said. 'And will there be anything else at all?'

'No, that's it, thanks,' Callum said.

Mr Cutler was smiling openly. Niamh had her hands over her mouth to hide her grin, but her eyes were laughing louder than any smile.

'Nice one, Cal,' Sam chuckled. He turned to face the waitress. 'I'll have the steak and eggs, please. Steak medium rare, eggs over easy. No toast. Ketchup and a side of mushrooms, thanks.'

The waitress nodded. 'Anything else at all?' she asked, seemingly by reflex.

'No, that's it, thanks,' he said, pursing his lips and shaking his head as the others all took obvious delight in his failure.

The only person who managed to order without being asked a single question was Niamh. Sam noted she looked suitably smug as she sipped her orange juice afterwards. 'So what's it to be, sis?'

'Oh, any soft rock station will be fine,' she said.

'The winner of the Denny's challenge gets to choose the radio station for the rest of the journey,' Sam explained to Callum. 'It could have been worse. If Dad had won, we'd have been subjected to Mozart, Bach and Handel for the next two hours.'

The food came quickly and it was not long before they were back on the road. Once off the mainland and out on to the Keys, mangrove trees lined both sides of the road for much of the route between the more densely inhabited islands. Occasional views

25

of the sea became progressively more frequent the further they drove. Just seeing the turquoise shallow waters and the darker blue beyond brought a forgotten excitement to Sam.

To his surprise, he found he was looking forward to his summer holiday here with eager anticipation. It would be good to show off what the Keys had to offer to Callum. Just having him along brought a feeling of freshness to the place. Sam hadn't felt this way about their summer holiday in the Keys for ages.

The mood in the car was light, with much laughter at the advertisements, both on billboards and on the radio.

'Avoid scurvy – eat Key lime pie,' read Callum, laughing and pointing at a sign.

'Don't miss out on this amazing offer. Be shoppertunistic!' urged an advert on the radio.

'Shoppertunistic? What sort of a word is that?' Mr Cutler asked, shaking his head with apparent disbelief. 'As you can see, Callum, people on this side of the Atlantic have little regard for the Queen's English. What do you think, Niamh? Are you going to be shoppertunistic while we're here?'

'Of course I am, Dad. It's top of my priority list,' she replied. 'Right above having a tantastic time.'

They all laughed, and for the next ten minutes everyone took turns in making up words that ranged from outrageous to ridiculous, and, as they found more and more things to laugh at, the journey to the house seemed to fly by. Sam was genuinely surprised when he saw the sign for Summerland Key ahead.

'Wow!' he said. 'That was a quick run.'

'No traffic to speak of,' his dad agreed, turning the car into the road that led to the house. 'Here we are, Callum. Welcome to our home from home.'

CHAPTER THREE

The first few days had been fun. Sam had enjoyed showing off the house to Callum. Compared to the average house in the UK, it had plenty of 'wow' factor. The open-plan living area was enormous. A luxurious, cream-coloured carpet covered the main floor area, giving way to similar-coloured floor tiles in the kitchen area. There were two soft leather sofas, a large glass-topped dining table, a gigantic flat-screen TV, a breakfast bar and a kitchen area with every convenience imaginable.

Each of the three large bedrooms had their own en suite bathroom. Sam and Callum were sharing one bedroom, while Niamh and Mr Cutler had a bedroom each. Two sets of patio doors opened from the main living area on to the poolside. The kidney-shaped swimming pool was not enormous, being about ten metres by four, but it was clean, inviting and plenty big enough for the four of them to enjoy splashing around in. After the long journey, the three teenagers had barely got through the door before they were changing into their swimming gear and racing to relax in the refreshingly cool water.

Later, Sam had shown Callum around properly. His friend had wandered after him as if in a daze, trying to take it all in.

'Wow!' Callum had exclaimed on entering their en suite for the first time. His eyes were wide as he took in the huge sunken corner bath and the large separate shower cubicle. 'This bathroom's bigger than my bedroom back home! Is your dad one of those secret millionaires or something?'

'Kind of makes you realise why some Americans are inclined to go on about things being bigger and better out here,' Sam agreed, dodging the question. He grinned at his friend. 'You've got to hand it to them. They know how to make their homes comfortable.'

'You're not kidding!'

Not five paces from the poolside was the canal that led out to the Atlantic side of the Key. Apparently, the boat moored there had even more 'wow' factor to Callum than the house. It was a beauty: nearly ten metres long with twin Yamaha 225cc engines.

'Jeez!' Callum had exclaimed, leaning over to look into the cuddy cabin. 'How far do you go in this thing? Satnav, VHF radio, an autopilot . . . and I don't even know what that screen is for.'

'It's a side-scanning sonar,' Sam had told him, unable to keep from smiling at his friend's enthusiasm. 'They're normally used for finding fish, but Dad's always been more intent on looking for other things.'

Callum had not asked what sort of things, but Sam had overheard some of Niamh's conversation with Callum during the flight out and he was certain his friend was sharp enough to work out what he was talking about.

The temperature was steaming hot – in the thirties every day. Clear blue skies in the mornings became studded with white puffy clouds around midday that bloomed rapidly into huge scattered thunderstorms by late afternoon. Although the storms did not always hit Summerland Key, flashes of lightning and the grumbling of thunder became an expected part of the late afternoon.

To Sam's surprise and delight, his dad had been more fun than usual. He had taken them out in the boat several times to go snorkelling, fishing and waterskiing. He had even taken them across to the little airstrip on Summerland Key one morning, hired a light aeroplane and taken them on a flight along the Keys. The moody behaviour that Sam had come to expect from his father when they came here had remained hidden for the most part. The only strange outburst occurred after a shopping trip to Key West.

'What's *that* doing in here? You two should know better. Get it out of the house! Now!'

'What's the matter, Dad?' Niamh asked, getting up from the sofa at the sound of his raised voice.

Matthew Cutler stabbed a finger towards a conch shell on the breakfast bar, his face red with anger.

'Oh, sorry, Matt,' Callum said, rushing to pick it up. 'That's mine. I bought it today as a gift for my mother. Is there a problem with it?'

'They bring bad luck, Callum,' he replied, his tone more civilised, but still tight with anger.

'Oh, Dad, that's just an old superstition,' Niamh said, looking at him reproachfully.

'Tell that to the Queen,' he told her, his eyes hard. 'Callum, I'd very much appreciate it if you stored it somewhere outside, please. There's a lockable cupboard on the boat if you want to secure it. Personally, I'd sell it to another tourist and buy a different gift for your mum if I were you.'

'No problem, sir. I'll do it right away.'

After Callum had taken the shell out and locked it in the boat, the atmosphere in the living area remained awkward for a while. Sam and Niamh tried to make light of their father's strange reaction, but the incident left an uncomfortable feeling in the room that was difficult to dispel.

'What was that all about?' Callum asked Sam a bit later when they had slipped back outside to the poolside. 'Your dad really freaked out when he saw the conch.'

'Conk,' Sam replied.

'Sorry?'

'It's pronounced *con-k*, not con-ch.'

'That could cause some interesting misunderstandings,' Callum observed. 'Oh, my! That's a big conk you've got there.'

They both laughed.

'So why did your dad flip? And what did he mean by "Tell that to the Queen?" '

'Well, Dad's always been a bit superstitious and according to local folklore, it's bad luck to bring a conch shell into your home. There's a story he heard from the local historian down in the library at Key West about the Queen that he's told us a few times, but it's been a while since I've heard it. It supposedly happened before we were born, back in about 91, I think. The Queen visited the Dry Tortugas – they're a group of islands off the end of the main line of inhabited Keys. Believe it or not, the nearest thing to royalty here in the Keys is the position of Queen Conch . . .'

'You're havin' a laugh! Queen Conk!'

'No,' Sam said, shaking his head. 'Dead serious. Ask Niamh if you like. She probably remembers more about this stuff than me. Anyway, from what I remember, the reigning Queen Conch met Queen Elizabeth at the Dry Tortugas and presented her with a conch shell. Within about a year of the Queen's return to the UK, a whole load of bad stuff happened.' Sam closed his eyes as he recalled the list of misfortunes and ticked them off on his fingers. 'First Prince Andrew and Fergie separated in early 92,' he began, 'Then the next month Princess Anne and Mark got divorced. A couple of months later, the tell-all book about Diana was published and then, to top it all, Windsor Castle burned down.'

'Really? But the castle's still there! I saw it from the M4 only a few weeks ago.'

'Yeah. Well, I guess they must have rebuilt it. Apparently, it was a local joke in the Keys that Queen Conch's gift caused all the bad luck. Some of the locals were more than a bit serious.'

When they went back inside after their dip, Callum sat and wrote a postcard to his parents.

Chuckling, he waved Sam over to look at what he had written.

'You can't send that!' Sam exclaimed, his eyes widening as he read the card.

'It's a joke, Sam. Lighten up!'

'I know it's a joke, but what will your mum and dad do?'

'They won't do anything,' Callum laughed. 'They know what I'm like. I'm always fooling around. Don't worry, I'll send them another one in a couple of days spelling it out as a joke if you like.'

'Yeah you'd better,' Sam said. 'For goodness' sake don't let my dad see it though. You saw what he was like about the shell. He'd really do his nut if he saw this!'

There was a haunted look in Matthew Cutler's eyes that afternoon. Sam recognised it immediately, as he had seen it all too often during past trips. To his frustration, the next morning his dad went off on his own for much of the day, leaving the three teenagers to their own devices. It was the beginning of a familiar pattern. Just when Sam had begun to think this holiday was going to be different, his father appeared to be slipping back into the old routine that had soured Sam's feelings towards coming here.

Sam found it hard to understand why his dad could not let his missing wife go and move on with his life. For Sam, losing his mum had been a terrible thing. He still vividly remembered how upset he had felt immediately after she had disappeared. But that was nine years ago. Over time his pain had dulled and life had swept him along too fast to allow him to get caught in the same emotional eddy as his father. He still felt sad, but he had learned to live with the feeling. At least this year there hadn't been the added insult of a childminder, Sam thought.

Several days passed and the three teenagers saw less and less of Mr Cutler. He left most mornings after breakfast and did not return until after sunset. Sometimes he took the boat. Sometimes he took the car. Every time he went alone.

Even given his father's recent behaviour, Sam was surprised when he was woken by the sound of the hire car backing out on to the gravel driveway. Despite the bright sunshine outside, the blinds kept the room quite dark. He squinted at the luminous display of the alarm clock through blurry, sleep-filled eyes. It read 07:30.

'Where's he going at this time in the morning?' he groaned.

'What's that?' Callum mumbled from the other side of the room.

'It's Dad,' Sam said, pulling back the light duvet and rolling over to sit on the side of the bed. 'He's going out on his own again. Just before we went to bed last night he promised to take you and me out to chase some big game fish this morning, but it looks like he's forgotten all about it. Knowing Dad, by the time he gets back, it'll be too late and the weather will be closing in!'

'Shame,' Callum agreed sleepily. 'Still, we can always chill out by the pool.'

'That's the problem,' Sam grumbled, padding across to the window in his boxers and tweaking one of the slats of the blind aside with a finger. He was just in time to catch a glimpse of the SUV driving out on to the road. 'When Dad gets like this, chilling out by the pool is all we *can* do. I wish he would let this Triangle mystery thing go. It's all a load of superstitious nonsense anyway.'

Callum mumbled something unintelligible and rolled over, pulling the duvet up over his head. Sam decided to leave him to sleep. Stepping lightly out into the kitchen, he opened the fridge and pulled out the gallon container that was two-thirds full of Tropicana orange juice. Armed with this and a tall glass from the cupboard, he headed out to the poolside. Even at this time in the morning it was warmer outside than it was in the air-conditioned environment of the house.

Sam downed the first glass of orange juice in one long draft, delighting in the icy-cold wetness of it.

That was one of the biggest problems with the air conditioning, he thought – waking up with a dry mouth and throat. Taking a deep breath, he poured another.

Not in the slightest bit self-conscious about sitting outside in his boxers, Sam watched as a boat cruised past along the canal. He recognised the owner immediately. It was Mr Mitchell, the ex-US Air Force colonel who owned the villa two doors down. Mr Mitchell gave a jaunty wave, which Sam returned. Inside, though, Sam could not quell the pang of jealousy he felt on seeing the sport fishing rods set up at the back of the passing boat.

It was the sight of Mr Mitchell's rods that triggered Sam's sudden decision. Downing his second glass of orange juice, he got to his feet with a new sense of purpose.

'I'm not going to let Dad ruin this holiday,' he vowed under his breath. 'I'm going fishing today whether he's here or not.'

Half an hour later, Sam had topped up the boat's fuel tanks with the spare jerrycans of petrol from the back of the garage. He checked the bilge as he had seen his father do many times and gathered the fishing rods and lures, stowing them neatly inside the boat. Sam knew his dad kept the ignition keys for the boat in his bedside cabinet. Getting them would be easy.

To his surprise, Sam felt an intense wave of guilt heat his gut as he entered his father's room. Matthew Cutler had never been a particularly private person. Indeed, his bedroom door had been left wide open today. Surely that was an invitation to enter? So why was it Sam felt an overwhelming urge to creep across to the bedside cabinet like a cat burglar?

Sam didn't notice he was holding his breath until he opened the top drawer of the cabinet and saw the keys to the boat exactly where they normally were. A thrill of excitement ran through him as he picked them up. This was going to be so much fun.

His father had let him drive the boat plenty of times in recent years, but always under supervision. He knew his way around the waters in the immediate vicinity of Summerland Key well, and having a satellite navigation system onboard meant that it would be hard to get lost even if they did go further afield. All Sam had to do was tell the navigation system to take him home and follow the line that appeared on the screen. It was hardly rocket science.

'Sam?'

Sam jumped. Even though he recognised Niamh's voice instantly, his reaction was instinctive.

'What are you doing in Dad's room?'

'Just getting the keys to the boat,' Sam said, trying to make it sound as casual as he could. 'You going to come fishing with us?'

'I thought Dad went out this morning,' she said, her brows drawing together in a thoughtful frown.

'Yeah, well, I'm not going to just sit around and wait for Dad any more. You know what he's like. He probably won't come back till this evening now, and I don't want to hang about here all day again.'

'Why don't you take the bikes along to the beach and go snorkelling then?' Niamh suggested. 'Dad'll be furious if he finds out you've been out in the boat.'

'Well, don't tell him then. There's no reason for him to find out, is there? I can drive it as well as he can. You know that. And it's not like I'm going to take it far, Niamh. Just beyond the reef, to have a chance at catching something bigger than a snapper.'

'And Callum's going along with this?' Niamh asked. 'I thought he had more sense.'

'He doesn't know yet,' Sam admitted. 'But he'll be cool with it.'

'Please don't do it, Sam. Dad's bound to catch you and then there'll be hell to pay.'

'What's he going to do? Restrict me to the house? Big deal! He's pretty much done that already. Maybe if he does find out, it'll be a wake-up call for him.

Maybe he'll finally realise that we're growing up and bored with hanging around here all the time.'

'In your dreams, Sam,' Niamh said. 'If Dad wants to find a punishment that'll hit where it hurts, he will. Don't be a fool. Go snorkelling or jump on a bus to Key West if you have to. Anything.'

'I'm *going* fishing,' Sam said. Then, in a louder voice, he called, '*Cal?* Are you dressed yet? Come on. We're going out fishing on the boat.'

'Is your dad back already?' Callum asked, emerging from the bedroom in shorts and flip-flops. 'That was quick.'

'No. We're going without him.'

'Are you sure that's a good idea?'

'See!' Niamh said. 'I told you Callum would have more sense.'

'Don't listen to her, Cal. She's bein' a wuss. We don't need to go far. Just far enough to get into big game water. I don't want to hang around here all day . . . again!'

'Well, if you think it'll be OK.'

'Of course it will.'

'Of course it won't!'

Niamh and Sam contradicted each other at the same time, leaving Callum looking from one to the other, clearly unsure of who to listen to. Loyalty to his friend won.

'Am I alright dressed like this?' he asked.

Niamh looked up at the ceiling and shook her head. 'I don't believe this,' she said and stomped off into the kitchen.

'Don't worry about her, Cal,' Sam said, placing a hand on his friend's shoulder. 'I'd grab a T-shirt, shades and a pair of deck shoes or trainers. If we catch anything big, you won't want to be barefoot.'

'Fair enough. I'll be back in a minute.'

'Meet me at the boat,' Sam directed. 'I'll get the engines running. The fish are waiting for us. I can hear them calling.'

CHAPTER FOUR

The throaty growl of the engines sent a warm rush of adrenalin racing through Sam's stomach. It had taken longer than he had expected before he felt sure he was ready to go, but they still had plenty of time before his dad was likely to return. He eased the throttles forward and swung the boat away from the mooring and out into the canal. He had driven the boat from here to the ocean many times, but doing it without his father's watchful eyes looking over his shoulder was a whole new experience.

Niamh was standing by the mooring post. Her arms were folded tightly across her chest and her eyebrows were drawn together in a worried frown. Sam was rather surprised that she didn't shout at him as he steered the boat out into the centre of the waterway. It was unlike her to miss a chance at having the final word.

'You do know what you're doing, don't you?' Callum asked, looking back at Niamh. His expression and voice mirrored her concern.

'Of course I do. Relax. We've got life jackets on. Everything's cool. We won't go far.'

'Yeah. Fair enough then.'

Callum didn't sound totally convinced, but he did sit back and start looking around at the view as they cruised gently out of the canal into the open water beyond. Across the bay they could see the houses and canals of Cudjoe Key tucked among the lush greenery. Sam turned the boat in a gentle arc to the left and opened the throttles further. The boat surged forward, the prow gently lifting as the power bit. Within seconds, they were skipping across the wavelets at speed leaving a frothing white 'V' behind them as they raced south and east towards the deeper water.

Sam laughed aloud. The exhilaration he felt as he opened the throttles still further was amazing. His father rarely drove the boat this fast, preferring a more sedate pace, and Sam had only ever been allowed to do so once before. The throttles were barely more than half open. How fast could the boat go? What would it feel like at its top speed? It was a question he had often asked his dad, but Matthew Cutler had shown no interest in finding out.

For a moment, Sam considered opening the throttles all the way while they were still in the calm waters of the shallows, but to his intense annoyance he found he couldn't do it. If he had been alone, then maybe, he thought. But Callum was here and while it would be great to show off, if anything was to go wrong . . . Inwardly cursing common sense and the deeply ingrained sensibilities of his father, Sam settled for tweaking up the power one more rebellious notch.

They skimmed across the water with the wind in their hair, laughing as the spray began to kick up from the prow.

'Isn't this great?' Sam yelled above the roar of the engines.

'Fantastic!' Callum agreed.

The swell increased, making the ride bumpier. The boat felt as if it was bouncing from wave to wave, hitting the upslope of each one with a resounding *thump* and sending a huge plume of spray into the air. Sam throttled back until the ride became more comfortable.

'Look,' he called to Callum, pointing at a tiny island to their left. 'I'll bet Mr Jones would like that place.'

'Mr Jones the maths teacher?'

Sam nodded, his lips forming a broad grin.

'Come on then. I can see you're itching to tell me. Why would old Jonesy like that island.'

'It's called Pye Key.'

'I didn't realise Mr Jones liked pie.'

'Oh, come on! He's always had a thing about P.I,' Sam laughed. 'It's his pet subject.'

'Yeah, right! Ha ha. Very funny.'

'OK, so it was pretty lame,' he admitted, giving a shrug.

'Well lame, Sam. I hope your chat-up lines are better than your jokes or you'll never land a hot girlfriend.'

They both laughed.

'Not much further now,' Sam shouted, reaching across and turning on the sonar. 'We should be deep enough in a few more minutes.'

When Sam did close the throttles, the sudden quiet was almost eerie. The fizzing rush of water slowed to a gentle lapping in a matter of seconds and the motion of the boat changed dramatically. Instead of thumping along, climbing and falling in the direction they were travelling, the boat began to climb and fall on the swell, rocking and rolling, dipping and twisting with every little wavelet. Sam was quite comfortable with this new motion, but he could see the colour draining from Callum's cheeks.

'You OK, Cal? Don't worry. We won't be stopped for long. I just want to get you set up with a decent lure and we'll get moving again. Drifting takes a bit of getting used to.'

'I'll be fine,' Callum replied, looking far from it. 'What are you planning to do with any fish we catch?'

'We'll throw them back,' Sam said. 'This is just for fun today. Risking Dad's wrath is one thing, but I don't want to deliberately set up a confrontation.'

'What do you think he'll do if he finds out?'

'I don't know and I don't care,' Sam said defiantly. 'But he's not going to find out, so let's not worry about it. Here – hold this rod a moment. I just want to change the lure for something more flashy.'

Callum watched as Sam pulled out a penknife and cut the silver lure free and dropped it into a plastic drawer under the main console. The multicoloured monstrosity he then lifted out of the same drawer looked nothing like any fish Callum had ever seen.

'I thought a lure was supposed to fool a fish into thinking it was attacking another smaller fish,' he observed.

'That's the basic idea,' Sam agreed. 'But this lure uses bright colours and movement to attract attention. A large predatory fish will attack anything small that moves. Some colours attract attention better than others. I like to cover a good spread.'

'You're not kidding!' Callum said, looking at the bright orange, yellow, blue and white contraption that Sam was expertly tying onto the line.

'There you go. Now let me just cast it out for you and we'll get going again.'

'Great, thanks.'

Sam took the rod from Callum, released the clutch on the reel and flicked the lure a good distance out to the side of the boat.

'Right, now just hold onto this and let the line run out until I call, then flick the clutch lever this way,' Sam instructed, demonstrating how the reel worked. 'Then hold the rod upright, hang on tight and wait.'

'How will I know if a fish is biting?'

'Oh, you'll know!' Sam laughed, turning and taking control of the boat again. He gently throttled up the engines until the boat was moving at a sensible trolling speed. 'And whatever you do, please don't let go of the rod. If we lose it, we really *will* be in big trouble.'

Sam swung the boat gently round to run parallel to the coast before glancing over his shoulder. Callum looked as if Sam had just handed him a lit stick of dynamite. He was holding the rod all wrong, but he seemed to have a good grip on it so Sam decided not to say anything until it mattered. He counted slowly to forty.

'That should do,' Sam called over his shoulder. 'Engage the clutch and lift the rod up until it's vertical. That's it. Great. Now hold on tight and wait for your first fish.'

For the next ten minutes they drove slowly south and west along the coast towards Key West. The bite, when it came, seemed to take his friend completely by surprise. Sam knew from experience that it was all too easy to become used to the steady pull of the lure as it zipped through the water.

'Whoa!' Callum yelled suddenly. Sam throttled back and looked over his shoulder. Callum's rod tip dipped hard towards the back of the boat.

'Keep the rod up and start winding in,' he called. 'You've got to keep the tension on the line or you'll lose it.'

Callum did as he was told.

'Good. That's it. Nice and steady. Don't rush it. As you wind, gradually lower the rod tip while keeping the tension, then you can pull the fish towards you by raising the rod again. Think of it like a pumping action.'

'The line's going slack,' Callum called, his voice sounding panicked.

'Wind faster! The fish is making a run towards us.'

Callum wound frantically for about ten seconds

before the rod tip suddenly lurched down again.

'Excellent! He's still on,' Sam said, unable to keep the excitement from his voice. 'From the bend on the rod, I'd say it's a good size.'

'Feels like it weighs a bloody ton!' Callum exclaimed, the muscles on his arms looking pumped as he strained to pull the rod up again.

'Keep at it. You're doing well.'

It took several minutes before Callum got the fish close enough to the boat for Sam to see it. The long torpedo shape he spied in the water was unmistakable.

'It's a wahoo!' he exclaimed. 'Looks like a good one too.'

'A wahoo! You're havin' a laugh! Conk? Wahoo? You sure it isn't a "hoorah"?'

Sam laughed. 'A wahoo's sort of like a giant barracuda,' he explained. 'They're ugly sods with big teeth, but they taste amazing. Shame we can't take it back. Looks like about a forty pounder to me. Nice fish. Pass me the rod a mo and take a look.'

Callum was more than happy to pass the rod over. He leaned over the side to look at the fish.

'Bloody hell! It's gotta be over a metre long!'

'Yep. Like I said – nice fish. Now all we've got to do is let it go without hurting it. That might be quite tricky. I don't really want to put my hand near that fella's mouth unless he's too knackered to care. We're going to have to let him run himself out.'

No sooner had Sam finished speaking than the fish charged off at speed, stripping line from the reel. Sam held the rod upright and concentrated on keeping the line taut. Once the fish turned, Sam handed the rod back to Callum.

'There you go, matey,' he said. 'It's all yours again.'

'What do I do?'

'Exactly what you did before,' Sam replied. 'Get him back to the boatside. He'll probably run another couple of times before he gives up. When he rolls over and goes limp, then ease him alongside and I'll try to get the hook out of his mouth.'

For the next six or seven minutes, Callum played the fish. Sam offered occasional advice, but for the most part sat back and watched his friend enjoy the thrill of the catch. As they planned to let the fish go eventually, he wasn't too worried if Callum made mistakes. It gave the fish more of a sporting chance to make its own break for freedom. In the end it did just that, making a sudden turn right next to the boat that took Callum by surprise. One sudden powerful kick of the fish's tail and the lure pinged free from its mouth. One more flash of silver and the fish was gone.

Sam laughed.

'Not to worry, Cal,' he said, noting the disappointment on his friend's face. 'I could have gaffed him a couple of times if we'd been looking to keep him. You did fine. Shall we try for another?'

'Can we? That would be great. But can we take a break for a couple of minutes first? My arms feel like jelly after that.'

'What a wimp!' Sam taunted. 'Worn out by a little fish.'

'Yeah, maybe I am,' Callum replied, not rising to the bait. 'Though it didn't look that little to me, and I'd rather not drop the rod, Sam.'

'Good point. OK, we'll just . . .' Sam's voice trailed off as he turned to face the front of the boat. 'What's that?' he asked, a strange note in his voice as he stared ahead.

'What's what?' Callum asked, climbing to his feet and moving to stand beside Sam in the cuddy.

'There, just ahead of us,' Sam said, pointing. 'The sea looks strange . . . wrong somehow.'

'What do you mean? The water's a slightly different shade, but that's not unusual, is it? Don't you get that when the depth changes?'

'Not when you're this deep.' Sam eased the throttles forward, taking the boat slowly closer. 'I've never seen anything like it before. It's weird.' He looked up at the sky, but there were no clouds to cast shadows. He looked back at the sea ahead. 'The water's not just a different colour. It seems to be moving differently. Look. The wave pattern's all screwed up.'

'Oh, yeah! Spooky.'

Callum stood up, fishing rod in hand, and looked round the side of the cuddy to see if it was a trick of the light playing through the perspex screen. No. The sea definitely looked different.

'There's nothing unusual showing on the sonar,' Sam observed, running his top teeth back and forth over his lower lip as he considered the strange phenomenon. He went suddenly still and sniffed the air. 'Do you smell that?'

'Smell what?'

Callum sniffed the air a couple of times, testing it like a dog.

'I don't know,' Sam said warily. 'I thought I caught a whiff of sulphur.'

'I can't smell anything. Are you trying to freak me out or something, Sam? Stop messing around. Let's do some more fishing or go home.'

'Yeah, right. Fishing. Sure thing. But first I just want to . . .'

As the boat crossed into the strange water, Sam suddenly felt as if he was going to pass out. His head spun and for a bizarre moment he could have sworn he heard Niamh's voice screaming his name inside his head. She sounded terrified. Callum staggered backwards and sat down on one of the side seats with a thump. The boat rocked alarmingly and Sam grabbed hold of the steering wheel to keep from falling. The wave of disorientation lasted no more than an instant, but Sam knew from the second they crossed into the dark, churning water that he had made a huge mistake. The boat began to dance on the choppy waves that peaked and fell in a strangely unpredictable fashion.

'Oh, my God!' Callum exclaimed. 'Get us back into the calmer waters, Sam. I think I'm going to puke.'

Sam didn't need asking twice. He swung the boat in a tight arc and opened the throttles slightly to power into the turn. As he spun the wheel, he looked around and a tight knot of icy coldness hardened in the pit of his stomach.

'That might be a problem,' he said.

Impossible though it seemed, the strange boundary on the water had vanished. And so had all sign of the Florida Keys.

CHAPTER FIVE

Niamh couldn't settle. She felt tight with anger at her brother's pig-headedness. Why did he always have to push the boundaries? What was he thinking, taking the boat out without permission?

'Dad's going to do his nut!' she muttered, shaking her head again.

She put her book down on the coffee table. It was no use. The words were just meaningless blurs of ink across the page. She had read the same paragraph at least five times and still couldn't have said what it was about. She needed to do something to release the tension creeping through her shoulders and down her back. A swim was the obvious answer.

She crossed the living area and slid open the glass door to the deck. As she left the pleasant air-conditioned environment, a wall of heavy heat mugged her. For an instant, it felt as though all the air had been stolen from her lungs.

'Phew!' she breathed, closing the door and sweeping her hair back from her forehead. Grabbing a large towel from the wall cabinet on the patio, Niamh stepped quickly across the hot white surface to the nearest sunbed. Seconds later, she had shed her T-shirt, shorts and flip-flops and was standing on the edge of the pool in her white bikini. If anything, she felt hotter for the lack of clothing.

Niamh hesitated on the brink. She dipped the toes of her left foot into the water, trailing them around in a quick arc. The air temperature was so hot that the water was never going to feel warm. Getting in slowly would only prolong the agony. She took a deep breath.

Geroni— she thought as she prepared to jump. Her lips tightened in a hard line as she cut the word off midway in her mind. 'Geronimo!' was what Sam normally yelled as he leapt into the pool. 'Stuff you and your stupidity, Sam!' she muttered aloud.

She stepped off the side, tucking into a tight ball as she hit the water. The shock was not as bad as she had anticipated. The water felt cool, but not unpleasant. Pushing up from the bottom, Niamh stretched out and began to swim.

The pool was not long enough to do any more than a few strokes in each direction, but the physical exertion was enough to warm her and disperse some of the tightness in her back and shoulders. After racing back and forth for several minutes, she stopped. Her heart was pumping fast and she was breathing hard.

Closing her eyes, she laid her head back in the water and tried to imagine her heart and lungs purging the tension from her body. It didn't work. Rather than relaxing, Niamh could feel muscles throughout her body tightening still further. She hadn't felt this sort of nervous anticipation since . . . a shudder rippled through her body . . . since she couldn't remember when. She'd been angry with Sam plenty of times, but her anger had never made her feel like this before.

She opened her eyes and looked around, spinning suddenly in the water to scan the area immediately surrounding the pool. Was she missing something? Was her body instinctively reacting to a danger she wasn't consciously aware of? There were some dangers in the Florida Keys. The worst normally came in human form, though there were a few animals that could pose a threat. Niamh scoured the poolside and nearby bushes and trees. The chance of a dangerous animal threatening her here at the house was remote, but she couldn't imagine much else that would bring her this close to outright panic.

The barest breath of a breeze was playing gently with the palm fronds overhanging the deck at either end of the pool. A gecko skittered across the poolside, head bobbing as it went, and feet moving impossibly fast. The ever-present chirruping of the cicadas was the only obvious sound. Niamh concentrated, listening hard. The distant sound of cars travelling along the Overseas Highway was just audible, but there were no signs or sounds of anything threatening.

'This is crazy!' she exclaimed aloud. 'I'm getting paranoid!'

She checked her watch. How long had the boys been gone? About an hour? If Sam kept his word, it would be roughly another hour before she could expect them to return. She turned, intending to push off and scull the length of the pool on her back when a sudden overwhelming terror enveloped her.

Niamh wanted to scream, but she couldn't. It felt as though her chest was crumpling like a paper bag sucked empty of air. There was a surreal moment as her mind seemed to separate and the part that had become detached looked down at her body in the pool. Then, for the briefest instant, she seemed to be looking at Callum holding a fishing rod. It wasn't a dream. There was too much detail and texture to the vision. And it couldn't be a memory, because she had always declined to go on fishing trips, preferring instead to spend the time sunbathing.

A pulling sensation inside her head suddenly ripped with such terrible violence that it felt as though her brain was being torn in two. Her hands flew to her temples, fingertips spread and pressing hard against her skull as if she could somehow push them through the bone and hold everything in place. It was agony. It was ecstasy. It was an eternity of torture in an instant. Without warning the pain vanished. And with it, the vision – cut off as if someone had hit the power button on the TV. She could breathe again. Her fingers relaxed the pressure against her scalp, but she didn't remove them. She felt empty. As if a part of her was missing.

She screamed something: a single word. All strength deserted her legs and Niamh fell backwards into the water. The surface closed over her and for a moment she lay under the water watching streams of bubbles from her body wriggling up towards the surface in dancing silver columns. Slowly, her natural buoyancy lifted her, and as soon as her face surfaced, she began to gasp in great mouthfuls of air. Tears mingled with the streams of pool water tracking across her cheeks as she panted, her heart thumping with urgent rhythm against her ribcage.

Gone! Gone! Gone! The word repeated over and over in her mind. What was gone? She didn't know. Something. A part of her was missing. The hole gaped in her mind and inside her chest. Emptiness. Void. It felt wrong. That was as much as she could rationalise.

With a supreme effort, she regained enough control of her body to get to the side of the pool and haul herself out of the water. Despite the heat of the Florida sun and the hot surface of the pool deck, she felt cold. Goose pimples raised the skin on her arms and legs. She began to shiver. Intense muscle spasms began to run up and down her body, causing her to moan as one cramp overtook another. She wanted to cover herself, to wrap a towel round her shoulders and feel the comfort of the soft material squeeze her arms and body, but the thought of crossing the deck to where her towel was slung over the back of a sunbed made her feel sick.

Her mind replayed the image of Callum holding the fishing rod. His face had worn an expression of curiosity. Then had come the moment of separation.

The word Niamh had screamed as her strength had deserted her was her brother's name. The feeling of emptiness – of being incomplete – suddenly made horrifying sense. Something had happened to Sam. Was he dead? Was that why she had felt the tearing sensation?

Niamh had always shared a close empathic bond with her twin brother. Even when they were apart, there had been occasions when she had known Sam was experiencing particularly intense emotions. She didn't know how it was possible, but she could predict his moods with uncanny accuracy when she rang him. He had confessed to similar experiences, though from what he had told her, Sam's perception of her was not as strong. The only times he had ever felt her was when her emotions were particularly powerful. Instinctively, she knew that the hole inside her was something to do with the strange link they shared. Panic gripped her tighter. Could Sam feel her now? She had never had such a strong sensation of fear before. She had to tell Dad.

Forcing herself up onto her hands and knees, Niamh crawled to the nearest chair and used it to help get to her feet. Her head was still spinning as she crossed the deck to the glass door. It took every ounce of energy she could muster to slide it open. The telephone was on the breakfast bar, just a few short steps away.

Now she was on her feet and into the air-conditioned living area, her head was clearing fast. Her strength was returning and she crossed to the break-fast bar with relative ease.

What if I'm wrong and the boys are fine? she asked herself as she picked up the handset. She paused. *They'll be livid that I've ratted on them to Dad.*

The hollow feeling of loss and emptiness denied that possibility. She knew she *had* to make the call. Without further thought, she punched in the number and lifted the handset to her ear. It seemed to take an eternity for the line to connect.

'Come on! Come on!' she urged, hugging her spare hand round her body and rubbing at her other arm. Her shivering was getting worse again and her teeth had begun chattering, but this time from genuine cold. The cool air from the nearby overhead air-conditioning unit played across her wet body.

'*We are sorry, but the person you are calling is not available right now. Please leave a message after the tone . . .*'

'NO!'

Beeeep.

'Dad! It's Niamh. Ring me now! It's urgent. *Pleeease* ring. I think something terrible's happened.'

She hung up and instantly dialled the number again. Hopping from one foot to the other as she waited again for the connection, she prayed that he would pick up this time. The ringing tone began.

Again it rang and rang until the automated message began. There seemed little point in leaving a second message. She hung up and tottered across the living room and along the hallway to her bedroom. There was nothing more she could do until she was warm, dressed and thinking more clearly.

Rather than dry off, Niamh elected to have a shower first to rid her body of the smell of the pool chemicals. Moments later, she was standing under the powerful spray of hot water and the stream of warmth cascading over her body ended her shivering. The heat felt almost therapeutic. She closed her eyes and tilted her face upwards to allow the water to beat against her forehead, eyes, cheeks and nose. Turning, she rinsed her hair, feeling her body relax as the heat washed over her.

It was a good five minutes before she left the shower. Once out, she was quick to get dried and dressed. What to do next though? The overwhelming sense that something bad had happened to her brother had not gone away. She returned to the living room and tried ringing her father again. As before, there was no answer. She hung up.

Who could she ring? Instinctively, her fingers began a text to her best friend Beth, but she had barely keyed in a line before she abandoned it. Beth was a good friend, but not renowned for level-headedness.

Niamh needed to make rational decisions. Texts from Beth were likely to be a distraction.

Her right index finger hovered over the number nine. Should she dial 911? Who would she ask for? The coastguard? The Sheriff's Office? And what would she tell them? 'Hi, I'm a fourteen-year-old girl visiting from England. My brother's been an arse and nicked our dad's boat. I've got this feeling that he's in trouble. Please send out your men to find him.' They'd probably think she was some sort of crackpot.

No. Any official agencies would need something more concrete to go on than the intuition of a teenage girl.

Suddenly, Niamh had an idea. Mr Mitchell had a boat. Maybe he would go out and look for the boys. He might even take her with him; though she was not sure she wanted to go. In the back of her mind, she was worried about what they might find. Niamh grabbed her mobile from the breakfast bar, took the house keys from the hook on the wall nearby and started locking up. Although she had not seen the Mitchells for a couple of years, they were good friends of her father and she had often spent time at their house when she was younger.

It was only a two-minute walk to the Mitchells' house, but despite still feeling shaky, her legs suddenly seemed to take on a life of their own and she broke into a run. As she raced around the corner and tore up the Mitchells' driveway at a sprint, she caught a glimpse of someone moving inside. A warm rush of relief welled inside her. The Mitchells were lovely. They would help. She knew it.

Moira Mitchell answered the door. 'Niamh, honey! Look at you! You're all grown up! We missed seeing you last year. Come inside. It's great to see you. What's the big hurry? You're looking kinda flustered. You on yer own?'

'Yes, Mrs Mitchell,' she panted, interlocking her fingers in front of her body as she stepped through the door. She took a deep breath to calm her breathing. 'That's kind of why I'm here.'

'Please call me Moira. Mrs Mitchell makes me feel so old!'

Niamh smiled. It was hard to imagine Moira Mitchell ever being old. She had one of those ageless Hollywood faces: beautiful skin, perfect teeth, immaculately styled auburn hair and not a hint of a wrinkle in sight.

'So the boys have gone out and left you, have they?' Moira continued, ushering her through to the living area. 'That's not very friendly of 'em. Come on through and I'll fix you a drink. Whaddaya fancy?'

'A fruit juice would be nice, thank you, Moira,' Niamh said. The name felt strange on her lips. 'Um. Is Mr Mitchell around today?'

'He was, but he went out fishin' a few hours back. Is there a problem? Did you need a hand with somethin'?'

'No ... that is, yes ... I'm not sure. It's Sam. He and his friend took Dad's boat out without his permission earlier and I've got a dreadful feeling that something bad has happened to him.'

'Were you expecting him back already?'

'No, it's not that ...' How could she explain the experience by the pool to Moira without sounding neurotic? 'It's just that Sam and I have always been close. I know it sounds weird, but I can sometimes sense when he's in trouble.'

'You're twins, ain't you?' Moira said, nodding. 'I've heard stranger things. Come on. If it'll make you feel better, we'll call Sam on the radio. Your dad's boat's got a radio fitted, don't it?'

'Yes.'

'We've got a VHF transmitter in the garage. I got it so I could remind Mitch to come home an' eat occasionally. The range ain't great, but I can usually holler loud enough to get his attention. If they don't answer, Mitch will. Worst comes to worst, Mitch can go look for 'em.'

'Sam was talking about fishing just beyond the reef. He should have his radio on, but I expect he's several miles away. Will your radio reach that far?'

'Who knows, honey? I just press the button 'n' yell. Mitch normally answers pretty quick. He knows his life won't be worth squat if he don't. Let's give it a try, shall we?'

CHAPTER SIX

'Could it be a sort of illusion?' Callum asked.

Sam could hear the note of fear in his friend's voice and his face looked ghostly pale. He hesitated to respond. He wanted to assure Callum everything was fine, but he knew that the moment he spoke, his own voice would betray the panic rising inside him. His chest felt as though an invisible strap was tightening round it, restricting his breathing. Speaking at all was not easy.

He felt hollow inside, as if something was missing. Within a few seconds, he realised that whatever was wrong, it related to Niamh.

'I don't know what's going on,' he admitted, forcing the words out. 'The satnav has lost its lock and the compass is going nuts. Also, I've got a horrible feeling that something bad just happened to Niamh.

Call it intuition. Call it telepathy. I don't know what it is, but we need to get back to shore as fast as we can. The only good news is that the sun hasn't deserted us. I'll set a course north and a touch west. That'll take us back into shallow water.'

'OK,' Callum said, his face shadow-grey. 'The sooner the better, mate.'

'Breathe deep and slow,' Sam advised. 'Clip the rod into the holder and concentrate on looking forward as much as possible. Watch the approaching waves. The more you anticipate the movement of the boat, the better you'll feel.'

Sam turned the boat and focused on following his own advice. The pattern of the waves was confused and irregular, making the boat rock and wallow, lurching and dipping in a most uncomfortable fashion. Although he was eager to open the throttles and power them back towards shallower water, he knew better than to do anything rash. Why couldn't he see the Keys any more? They had to be ahead somewhere, yet he knew instinctively that something had changed. He had a cold, hollow feeling in his belly and knew in his head that this was nothing to do with the movement of the boat.

All the tales his father used to tell him of strange occurrences in this region, including the mystery of his mother's disappearance, began to fill his mind:

Flight 19, the USS *Cyclops*, the *Star Tiger*. Were Callum and he going to become the latest victims of the Bermuda Triangle? There was a strange odour in the air. Something literally didn't smell right.

'Cal, I'm not being funny, but can you smell anything strange now?'

'Yeah,' he replied. 'Sort of like rotten eggs. You farted?'

'No,' Sam replied, glancing back at his friend and giving him a quick grin. 'Not me. But think about it – what gives off a scent of rotten eggs?'

'Stink bombs. Charlie Popkins after he's been eating spicy food. The chem lab . . .'

'And volcanoes,' Sam suggested. 'The smell is sulphur.'

'There's a volcano in the Keys?' Callum asked. 'I had no idea.'

'That's just the point. There's no volcano anywhere near the Keys that I know of. I'm just wondering if there's something happening on the seabed. Maybe there's seismic activity down there that's releasing gas. That might explain the strange wave patterns. Keep your eyes peeled for any signs of large bubbles. There are some people who think boats are lost in the Bermuda Triangle region due to streams of rising gas. I don't want to prove them right.'

They continued for several minutes, both boys

looking ahead for any sign of trouble or land. As they drove on, the waves increased in size, forcing Sam to throttle back still further on the power. A gusting breeze began to rise from the south, and the weather on all sides appeared to be closing in on them. Flashes of lightning behind and to their right preceded the ominous distant growling of thunder. Sam was becoming increasingly worried. He had no desire to be caught out in open water by a passing storm.

His memories of being caught out in a heavy shower with his dad a couple of years ago were awful. The increasingly frequent flashing of lightning gave warning that the approaching weather was far worse than anything he had encountered before.

'That doesn't look good,' Callum commented, pointing back at the approaching wall of dark cloud. He watched as the sun was swallowed. The air was still warm, but the temperature was dropping. 'Do you think we should use the radio and call for help?'

'The radio!' Sam exclaimed. 'Of course! Thanks, Cal. I was so focused on getting us back that I forgot the obvious.'

Picking up the handset, Sam twisted the dial to the distress frequency. He paused for a moment to mentally compose his message. He had sailed and flown many times with his father. The phraseology his dad used when he was talking on the radio was familiar, but he'd not used it. Sam didn't want to press the button and make a fool of himself.

'All stations, all stations, this is *Dream Chaser*, over.' He paused, his heart racing as he waited for a reply. The hiss of static was interrupted by an occasional louder crackle, but there was no immediate response. 'All stations, all stations, this is *Dream Chaser*, I repeat, *Dream Chaser*. Respond, over.'

Nothing.

'All stations, all stations, this is *Dream Chaser*, registration: Foxtrot Lima wun niner fife fife. Two persons on board. We're having navigational difficulties. Bad weather approaching. Please respond, over.'

Static.

Why was no one responding? They couldn't be out of range. The radio Dad had installed in the boat was one of the best on the market. There should be any number of people monitoring the emergency frequency. Aside from the static, the only thing Sam could hear was a faint string of clicks and growling, burping noises that made no sense whatsoever. It wasn't Morse code. He double-checked that he had selected the right setting. He had. He transmitted the distress call again. Nothing but the same.

'Weird!' he muttered.

'Not great,' Callum admitted. He sounded terrified.

Sam glanced back at his friend. Callum was hunched over his mobile, tapping away on the keys.

'What are you doing?'

'Sending a text.'

'Have you got a signal, Cal?' Sam asked, amazed.

'No, but it will automatically send when I do get one.'

'Good idea . . . automatic! That's it!' Sam reached forward to the dashboard and pressed another button. 'I should have thought of the EPIRB straight away.'

'E purb? What's that?'

'E.P.I.R.B.' Sam said, spelling out the initials. 'I think it stands for Emergency Position Indicating Rescue Beacon or something like that. Dad's never skimped on safety kit. Setting it off should kick the coastguard into action pretty sharpish.'

'Great! But what makes you think the signal will get through? No satnav. No radio response. No phone signal. What makes that thing any more likely to succeed?'

Sam didn't respond. The truth of it was, he had no answer. Instead, he sucked in his lower lip and ran his teeth across it, trying hard to keep his own rising panic from overwhelming reason. The waves were piling higher with every passing minute and the wind was strengthening at an alarming rate as storm clouds raced towards them from the southeast. The taste of crystallised salt was strong on his tongue, but even the salt didn't taste right.

The sound of Niamh's voice screaming his name echoed in his mind. Why had he heard her voice at the precise moment they had crossed into the strange water? There was something particularly disturbing about the memory of that cry. It was immediately after it had cut off that the strange hollow feeling had begun. Sam had a vague sense that she was suffering some sort of trauma, but it was as if the sensation was being muffled, or blocked, or happening at a vast distance. There had been many times during his life that he had instinctively known when Niamh was hurting, or in trouble, but it had never felt like this before. This entire experience was bizarre.

Concentrate on getting back to the Keys, he told himself silently. *There'll be time to think about the more difficult questions later*.

It was good advice, but he was rapidly losing confidence in himself. *So much for the fun fishing trip*, he thought.

There was still no sign of land. A particularly bright flash from behind made him look over his shoulder. The dark clouds bearing down on them bubbled and boiled with black-hearted menace. Rolling across the water, the crack of thunder that followed the flash was much louder this time. If anything, the air beneath the cloud looked even darker than the cloud itself. The knot of fear in Sam's belly tightened still further. They should be in shallow water by now. He glanced at the sonar screen, hoping to see they were approaching the shallows. What he saw brought no comfort. Controlling the boat in the roughening sea was becoming progressively more difficult. He didn't want to risk getting distracted by fiddling with the sonar settings.

Callum chose that moment to throw up. Twisting, he retched over the side of the boat.

'You OK?' Sam asked.

'Oh, yeah!' Callum groaned. 'Never felt better.' He retched again.

'Glad to hear it. Hang on in there. I'm taking us home as fast as I can.'

'Great. Don't mind me, Sam. Just thought I'd put out some ground bait for the next fishing trip.'

Sam laughed, but there was little mirth in his voice. He picked up the radio microphone again. 'Mayday, mayday, mayday! This is *Dream Chaser*, *Dream Chaser*. Mayday, acknowledge. Over.'

Nothing but static and clicking. Sam's fear began to transform into the heat of anger.

'MAYDAY, MAYDAY, MAYDAY!' he repeated, shouting into the microphone as if the power of his voice could somehow carry the transmission further. 'ACKNOWLEDGE. OVER.'

'Sam!' Callum gasped.

'What?'

'The sonar! Look! What's that?'

'It's probably just a dense shoal of fish,' Sam said, glancing at the screen. Much as he hated to admit it, the return on the sonar was as unusual as everything else that had happened in the past few minutes. If it was a shoal of fish, then it was a particularly dense one. 'Or it could be a whale,' he said.

'A whale! Are they dangerous?'

'Not normally,' Sam replied, unable to keep the note of uncertainty from his voice. 'At least, that's what Dad says. To be honest, I've never seen one before.'

At any other time the sonar picture would have fascinated Sam, but his attention was fixed on controlling the boat in the growing swell. He could only spare momentary glances at the screen. The sea was piling up in great rolls ahead, white trails of foam frothing from the crests. The danger posed by the growing waves was his immediate priority.

Callum retched over the side of the boat again. Sam heard him, but kept his focus forward.

'You still OK?' he called.

'I've felt better,' Callum groaned. 'But I'm still here. Hey, that thing on the sonar screen is coming closer! You sure a whale won't attack?'

'Short of Moby Dick, I've never heard of a boat being attacked by a whale.'

'Gah! I never did like reading stuff like that! Now I know why.'

Sam laughed and shook his head. That was what he liked most about Callum. No matter what the situation, his friend always seemed to have the ability to make him laugh.

A bright flash from behind was followed very quickly by a monstrous crack of thunder.

'Bloody hell!'

Sam automatically assumed Callum's curse was in response to the thunder and lightning. A huge splash to their left drew his attention, but he was too slow to see the source.

Callum had. His mouth had dropped open with shock and horror as a gigantic head had risen out of the water on a long, black neck. The thing's face was elongated like a crocodile, but smooth and black like the skin of a sea lion. Its enormous mouth was easily big enough to swallow a man whole. Great pointed white teeth gleamed in a terrifying grin. For a brief moment the creature had stared at him from

76

obsidian eyes before plunging back down into the water.

'It looked at me, Sam!' Callum called. His voice was full of awe and disbelief.

'What looked at you? The whale?'

'I don't know what that thing was, but it was no whale. If we weren't in Florida, I would swear I just saw the Loch Ness monster!'

'Stop messing about, Cal! In case you hadn't noticed, this isn't the time for it.'

'I'm not kidding, Sam,' he insisted. 'A bloody great head with a mouthful of teeth the size of kitchen knives came right up out of the water on a long neck. It looked at me for a second and then it dived down through the next wave.'

Normally, Sam would not have hesitated to laugh at his friend's joke, but having realised just how fast the storm was closing on them, he suddenly found himself too scared to appreciate the humour. If they didn't get to land soon, they were unlikely to get there at all.

'Sorry, Cal. I'm too busy to play games.' He glanced at the sonar again. The creature was showing as being ahead of them now. Was that a hint of a long neck at the front of a large body? No, he decided. Callum was hallucinating. He was dehydrated and seasick. There were no sea monsters! The very idea was ridiculous.

'I'm telling you, Sam, I'm not making it up,' Callum insisted. 'There's something out there. Something very big and unlike anything I've seen outside of a book of legends. We need to get the hell off the water as fast as we can. I don't want to be anywhere near the sea when that thing gets hungry!'

Sam didn't answer, but he could not resist glancing at the sonar again. The return was already too far ahead to offer any conclusive evidence. Whatever it was could certainly move at an impressive speed. The boat pitched over the top of another wave, dipping down into the trough beyond. The prow plunged into the wall of water that reared ahead, throwing great clouds of spray into the air as the boat tipped upwards again. Indeed, there was so much spray in the air now that neither of the boys noticed exactly when the rain began.

No sooner had they noticed that not all of the water in the air was spray than the clouds released the full force of their fury in a deluge. Cold rain sheeted down, turning the sea around them into a turbulent, hissing cauldron that steamed and churned. Visibility dropped as the grey curtain enshrouded them.

'MAYDAY, MAYDAY, MAYDAY!' Sam yelled into the radio microphone. 'ANYONE WHO CAN HEAR THIS, PLEASE RESPOND, OVER.'

The boat plunged so deep into the next wave that the tip of the wave came straight over the prow and for a split second, it was all Sam could do to hang onto the wheel as the blast of water hit him. Suddenly, the deck was awash. Water sloshed round his ankles, leaving Sam in no doubt just how easy it would be for the sea to claim his life. Sturdy though *Dream Chaser* was, she had not been built for these conditions.

'Cal! Grab a bailing bucket. Front hatch. Down there,' Sam ordered, sparing a hand to point at the storage locker for a brief moment. 'If we take too many waves like that, we'll go under.'

'Are we going to be OK, Sam?'

'Of course we are,' Sam responded automatically. Inwardly, he was shocked. Callum's voice sounded more despondent than he would ever have believed possible. 'Just hang on tight and trust me. I'll get us back.'

The words sounded as hollow as he felt inside. Was he making empty promises? Another enormous wave reared, lifting the front of the boat to an alarming angle. It crossed Sam's mind that for the first time in his life, he would actually welcome the sound of Niamh's voice telling him, 'I told you so!' He was not looking forward to facing the wrath of his dad, but even that confrontation would be better than staying out in this storm.

Where was the land? By all rights, they should be in shallow water by now.

He gripped the wheel tighter as the rain pounded his head, shoulders and back with increasing fury. The rain felt icy, and the seawater sloshing around the deck, even colder. The combination of salty spray and driving rain stung his eyes, making it hard to see. His T-shirt and shorts were plastered to his body and his muscles were tightening, partly in reaction to the drop in temperature, but more from fear. Out of the corner of his eye, he saw Callum locate the bailing bucket. Within moments, his friend began emptying bucket after bucket of water over the side.

'I will get us back!' Sam swore under his breath. 'I will.'

CHAPTER SEVEN

'*Dream Chaser*, this is Mitchell Home Base, how do you read? Over.' Moira released the transmit button and waited. There was a long pause. She tried again. '*Dream Chaser*, *Dream Chaser*, this is Mitchell Home Base, can you hear me, Sam? Over.'

Nothing.

Suddenly, the radio receiver crackled into life.

'Hi, hon! Is there a problem? Over.'

Moira smiled and gave Niamh an encouraging look. 'Hey, Mitch, yeah! Matt Cutler's boy Sam and his friend have taken Matt's boat out and Niamh's worried about them. We don't seem to be able to raise him from here. Can you try, please? Over.'

'Wilco, hon. Stand by . . . *Dream Chaser*, *Dream Chaser*, this is Mitch. Sam, can you hear me? Over.'

Pause.

'*Dream Chaser, Dream Chaser*, this is Mitch Mitchell. Please respond, Sam. Over.'

Nothing.

'Home Base this is Mitch, no response, hon,' Mitch reported. 'Do you want me to go look for 'em? Over.'

Niamh nodded at Moira. 'Please!' she mouthed.

'That would be great, Mitch. Niamh tells me they were planning to go out just beyond the edge of the reef. Over.'

'No problem. I'll call you back when I get out there. See you later, hon. Out.'

'Thank you so much, Moira,' Niamh said, her heart pounding. 'I can't thank you enough.'

'You're welcome, honey,' she said, giving a broad smile that flashed her perfect white teeth. 'Come on. Let's go back in the house and get comfortable for a bit. It'll take Mitch a little while to get out to the edge of the reef. He doesn't normally head that far out.'

Every thirty minutes for the next two hours they went back out to the garage and called Mitch. Each time, the answer was the same. He had seen and heard nothing of the boys.

Although the sensation was strangely remote, Niamh could feel that Sam was in terrible danger. In her mind's eye she could feel him battling the boat through monstrous waves. He was terrified, but alive. She looked out of the window. The weather was fine outside. Was she imagining it? The feeling was so faint that she was not sure if it was real or her mind was playing tricks on her.

In the past when she had sensed her brother's emotions, they had been much clearer. Often she found herself literally feeling his pain, or experiencing his emotions, as if they were her own. This was different. It was as if a dense veil had descended between them. The sensations were strangely detached and the hollow feeling inside her remained, gnawing at her mind in the same way that hunger sometimes chewed inside her belly.

Niamh felt something of that hunger now, but she couldn't eat. Even the thought of chewing made her stomach churn. Moira had made her a beautiful fish salad for lunch, but as she held the fork in her hand and looked again at the food, Niamh realised that she had done nothing but push it round the plate. How could she eat when the boys were in such danger? She should have tried harder to stop them. As soon as she had realised what Sam was intending to do, she should have taken the keys to the boat and hidden them. Could she have done that? There must have been something she could have done to keep them from going.

Was this what Dad felt like when Mum disappeared? she wondered. She had no solid proof that anything had happened to the boys. They might come back at any minute, but she couldn't help thinking about how her mother had vanished off the Keys in a boat of similar size. Something about today felt horribly familiar.

Suddenly, her mobile phone rang. Its loud, warbling ringtone made Niamh jump. She scrambled to dig the handset from her pocket. It was her father.

'Dad! Thank goodness! Why haven't you been answering my calls?'

'Sorry, darling. I went up for a quick trip in the seaplane with Geoff, so I had to turn my phone off for a while. I should have rung and told you first. Sorry about that. I just got your message. What's the problem?'

'It's Sam and Callum, Dad. They took the boat out.'

'They did WHAT! Where are they? Put Sam on. I want to talk to him right away.'

'That's just it, Dad – I can't. They haven't come back. I was expecting them back by now. I've got a really bad feeling . . .'

'I'll be back in about five minutes. Don't panic, Niamh. I'm . . .'

'Dad, I'm at the Mitchells' house,' she interrupted, sensing he was about to hang up. 'Mr Mitchell's out looking for them.'

'Oh! OK. Don't go anywhere. I'll be right there.'

Niamh looked up at Moira Mitchell who was giving her a sympathetic look.

'Don't worry, honey,' Moira advised, her voice as upbeat as ever. 'I'm sure the boys'll turn up. Boys are kinda irritatin' like that. Believe me, there'll be times when you'll wish they stayed lost for longer. I sometimes think that God must have somethin' in for us womenfolk, inflictin' the likes of them on us.'

It was hard not to smile. Moira's irreverent humour had an infectious quality. Mrs Mitchell put her hand to the side of her mouth and added in a conspiratorial stage whisper, 'Of course, some of 'em do have one or two redeemin' features.'

'Which are?'

'Give it a few years, honey,' she answered with a smile. 'I feel sure that with looks like yours, you'll find one who'll show you. Just you wait an' see if you don't.'

For the next few minutes Niamh sat perched on the edge of the couch, nervously twisting her empty glass round and round in her hands. With Dad on the way, she began to feel sick again. What would he do when he got here? Would he blame her for not stopping the boys? He seemed to expect her to mother her brother despite the fact they were exactly the same age. It wasn't fair. He expected too much.

'I'm just goin' to see if Mitch has any news for us yet,' Moira announced. 'Do you wanna come?'

'Absolutely,' Niamh said without hesitation. Then she glanced out through the front window.

'Don't worry. I'll leave the garage door open. Not that we wouldn't hear him arrive from in there. Come on, honey. Hopefully, we'll be able to put your mind at rest before your pa gets here.'

Why Moira thought this radio call would be any more fruitful than the previous ones, Niamh didn't know. The woman seemed to be an eternal optimist. It had been nearly half an hour since their last communication with Mitch. Maybe Moira was right to be positive, but Niamh knew inside that Moira was chasing false hopes.

Rather than turn on the lights in the garage this time, Moira pressed the button to open the main door. Even as the door began its clanking ascent, she crossed straight to the workbench where the metallic-grey radio box was neatly positioned. Sitting down in the swivel seat, she flicked on the power, checked the settings and picked up the microphone.

'Mitch, this is Home Base. Over.'

There was a slight pause and then the unmistakable sound of Mr Mitchell's voice responded. 'Home Base, this is Mitch, go ahead. Over.'

'Any news of the boys, Mitch? Over.'

'Negative, Home Base and I'm runnin' low on gas. Returning this time. Over.'

'Roger, Mitch. See ya shortly, honey. Out.'

'ETA Home Base in ten minutes. Out.'

Moira replaced the hand microphone in its holder and turned to Niamh with an apologetic shrug. At that moment, Niamh heard a car approaching and turned to see her father swing on to the driveway in the hired SUV. The car skidded very slightly as it stopped too abruptly. Niamh glanced at her watch in surprise. He had not wasted any time in getting here. The car had barely stopped before the door was open and Matthew Cutler was out, his face a picture of worry.

'Glad to see ya made it in one piece, Matt,' Moira drawled. 'Hope you didn't frighten too many locals on the way. They get kinda testy if you screech around like a lunatic.'

'Hi, Moira,' he replied. 'You know I don't normally drive that fast, but needs must when the devil drives.'

'Oh, you don't wanna let him drive,' she said, with a dismissive wave of her hand. 'The devil makes for a lousy driver.'

'Yes, well . . .'

Niamh ran to him and wrapped her arms round him, clasping him tight to her. He looked frantic with worry, and as she hugged him, she could feel the tension throughout his body. Moira was trying to lighten the moment with her humour, but Niamh knew it was unlikely to get through to her father now. The circumstances would be touching all sorts of raw nerves within Matthew Cutler, but she knew that if anyone could work out what was happening, he could. Now he was here, she felt instantly better. He would know what to do and where to look. He knew this area intimately.

'Moira, thanks for looking after Niamh for me,' he said eventually. 'Is there any word from Mitch? Has he found them?'

''Fraid not,' she said with a shake of her head. 'He's on his way back now to pick up gas, but I'm sure he'll head on out again as soon as he can. Would you like a beer while you're waitin'?'

'No thanks, Moira,' he said, his eyes distant. 'Have you rung the coastguard yet?'

'And tell 'em what, Matt? "My neighbour's son and his friend've taken a jaunt in his pa's boat an' not come back yet." The Key West coastguards are busy people. We can't prove the boys are in trouble. They've only been gone a few hours. The weather's still fine. They could be messin' about on Picnic Island for all we know.'

'If they are, then there'll be hell to pay when they get back,' Matthew growled. 'Sam knows the weather's due to turn stormy later.'

'*Something's* happened to them,' Niamh said firmly, locking eyes first with Moira and then with her father. 'I *know* it has. They're in danger. I can feel it.'

Moira caught hold of her hand and gave it a sympathetic squeeze. 'I believe you, honey,' she said. 'But what do you think the coastguard is goin' to make of your feelings? They get a lotta hoax calls.'

'Are you saying you think Niamh is making this up?'

Niamh was surprised to hear the threatening tone in her dad's voice. He rarely got angry, and certainly not with someone as well intentioned as Moira.

'Of course not, Matt!' she said immediately. 'I'm just tryin' to stop you from jumpin' the gun, that's all. No use in irritatin' the good folks before-times. You want 'em on your side, don't you?'

'Of course I do!' Matthew replied. 'But I can't just stand here and do nothing. Niamh has always had an uncanny sense when it comes to her brother.'

'I had a feelin' you might see it that way.' She beckoned to Niamh. 'Come on, honey. Let's leave him to his call.'

Niamh watched as her dad took out his mobile and dialled 911. Moira opened the door from the garage into the house. She waved Niamh to follow her in, and hit the switch to close the garage door, flicking off the light switch at the same time.

'Hello. Yes, coastguard, please. Thanks.'

Niamh hesitated at the threshold. She didn't want to be rude and let all the cool air inside the house escape into the garage, but at the same time she didn't want to miss her father's conversation with the emergency services. The garage door was making its noisy, clattering descent. Her dad had placed a hand over his free ear to better hear the person on the other end of the line. Just as the door completed its descent with a final clash of metallic slats, he looked up and saw her pleading look. With a nod and a weak smile, he followed her into the house.

'Hello? Coastguard? That's great! I'd like to report a missing boat . . . no, my son and his friend took it out from Summerland Key earlier today and they haven't come back . . . yes, they're overdue . . . No, just the two . . . Atlantic.' He placed his hand over the mouthpiece.

'What time did they leave?' he asked Niamh softly.

'About ten,' she replied.

'About ten this morning,' he repeated. 'Well, they should never have taken the boat at all, but I would have expected them back by one at the latest . . . no, no, I don't want to declare the boat stolen. Overdue is fine . . . Yes, it's a thirty-one-foot Pursuit 3070. I'll have to get back to you with the FL number. I can't remember it off the top of my head. The tanks on the engines were only half full so . . . oh, wait a minute.'

Niamh was waving at him frantically and shaking her head. 'Sam topped them up with the spare cans,' she told him. 'He said the tanks were nearly full before they left.'

Her father sighed. 'Apparently, they've got virtually full tanks, which would give them a possible range of at least a couple of hundred miles . . . yes, that's right. EPIRB, Digital Select Calling, six life jackets, two throwables – a ring and a cushion . . . that's right, six day flares, six night flares, a VHF radio . . . thank you. I like to think I keep the boat well equipped . . . Well, that's a relief! But I'd still appreciate . . . yes, I know, but . . . a bulletin? Are you sure that's all you can do? How long overdue will they have to be before you start searching? . . . Yes, you can be sure I'll keep you informed . . . thanks a lot. Goodbye.'

Niamh looked at her dad expectantly.

'They're going to send out a bulletin to their cutter crew telling them to keep an eye open for them,' he said sourly.

'That's it?'

'For the moment,' he said. 'But don't worry, darling. They'll do more. Trust me. On the positive side, they said they've not picked up any EPIRB signals today, so the boys are still afloat somewhere.'

'Dad, I don't know why, but knowing that doesn't make me feel any better.'

'We'll find them, Niamh,' he assured her. His voice sounded comforting, but Niamh could see fear and emptiness in his eyes. It was as if the life was draining from them. Was this how he had looked when Mum disappeared? He often had a haunted look about him when they came here on holiday, but she had never seen him look like this.

'I'm going out to see if I can spot Mitch yet,' he said. 'I'll start getting the fuel cans ready. Don't worry. We'll be out there and looking in no time.'

'Wouldn't it be better to go back to Geoff's and take the seaplane up again? You'll cover a much bigger area in that.'

'Clever girl!' he exclaimed, his eyes lighting up. 'Why didn't I think of that?'

'Can I come too?' she asked eagerly. 'I don't want to be left behind.'

As suddenly as it had brightened, the spark fizzled from Matthew Cutler's expression. 'I could see storms already brewing in the east as we came back from our jaunt earlier,' he said. 'Much as I love your idea, Niamh, I'm not sure Geoff will agree to it.'

'If storms are forecast, then surely there's all the more urgency,' Niamh insisted. 'If you can't use the seaplane, then what about renting a light aircraft from the Summerland airstrip?'

Her dad's expression became thoughtful. 'I'll try,' he agreed reluctantly. 'But it looks like a fairly extensive line of thunderstorms. I doubt they'll be keen to let me take anything up given the forecast. We might actually do better in Mitch's boat.'

'Won't it be rough?'

'Most likely, but Mitch has a good boat. It'll be fine.'

'Plane or boat, I'm coming regardless.'

'Are you sure? I thought you didn't like going out on the boat when it's rough.'

'I'll make an exception today,' Niamh said, putting as much steel into her voice as she could muster. 'I'm not going to be left behind.'

When he nodded his agreement, she felt a warm rush of relief. Moira was lovely, but the way she felt right now, Niamh wanted to be with her dad. As things stood, he was all the family she had left. She listened as Matthew phoned first his friend Geoff, and then the local airstrip. As he had predicted, neither was willing to let him go flying in their aircraft. Even as he hung up from the second phone call, Niamh heard the sound of Mr Mitchell's boat approaching. She ran across to the back window just in time to see it ease alongside the mooring posts.

'Mitch is back,' Moira announced from the kitchen. 'Let's go give him a hand to dock.'

She crossed the living area to the sliding door that opened on to the pool deck and beckoned for Niamh to follow. She glanced at her dad. He nodded and followed on behind. They skirted the pool and watched as Moira responded to her husband's directions.

Moira was very businesslike as she looped the ropes round the bollards, checking the fenders and giving her husband a hand up onto the deck. She was clearly very practised.

'Hi there, Matt! Nice to see you, Niamh.'

'Mitch' Mitchell looked the epitome of a United States Air Force officer: sharp haircut, V-shaped torso, square jaw and bright eyes that shone with intelligence and humour.

'Sorry I don't have any news of your boys,' he added. 'Don't know where they've disappeared to.

There's not many boats out there today, what with the approachin' weather an' all.'

'It's good of you to go looking, Mitch,' Matthew responded, meeting his firm handshake with a strong grip of his own. 'Much appreciated. Are you OK to go back out? I'm pretty anxious to find them.'

'No problem. Top her up with gas, grab some eats to keep us fuelled up and we'll be on our way in no time. Looks like it's gonna get rough out there soon, though. Not sure it's gonna be a good idea to get too far offshore. Any ideas on where the boys might have headed to?'

'Not really,' Matthew said with a shake of his head. 'Niamh says they went out fishing. I suspect they'll have gone pretty much straight out to the drop off, but after that . . . who knows?'

Niamh couldn't voice her feeling that they were looking in vain. Deep inside her she could still feel a strange, hollow space that something of her brother had previously occupied. He felt terribly distant. Dead? No. Reaching into the depths of the void where the sense of her brother had normally been so strong, she could still feel a faint hint of his presence. She had a vague impression of him: scared, cold and tired, but alive and battling to stay that way. The feeling should have been an encouragement, but for some reason, it deepened her sense of panic.

Although her memories were sketchy, Niamh still remembered something of the days immediately after her mum had disappeared. Most of it was vague, but a few clear flashes remained, especially her dad telling her that 'Mummy was lost' and that 'Lots of people are out looking for her'. She could hear the phrases and the intonation in her mind, but not how he had looked as he had said the words. Had his expression been as lost and empty as it was now? Did he already believe the boys to be the latest victims of the Devil's Triangle? The thought sent chills running up and down her spine.

Callum might be absolutely fine of course. It seemed likely that he would still be with Sam. The last clear image she had seen through her link with Sam had been of Callum, but equally they could have become separated by now. Niamh had no way of knowing. Answers were out there somewhere, but her dad had been searching for clues about her mum's disappearance for nine years. If this was any indication of what they were up against, finding her brother was unlikely to prove easy.

CHAPTER EIGHT

'Geoff, you're a star! I can't thank you enough,' Matthew Cutler said, his mouth curving into a broad smile. He gave Niamh an excited 'thumbs up' gesture. 'Yes, I'll be careful. Don't worry. I won't do anything silly. I'll stay below the cloud base and head straight back to the field when the weather starts to close in. Thanks again. I owe you one.'

He ended the call and put the mobile into his pocket.

'Change of plan, Mitch,' he announced. 'Geoff changed his mind. He says I can take up the Cherokee to do an aerial search. The water is going to be too rough for landing his seaplane this afternoon, but he said that I can fly his Cherokee so long as I land ahead of the storms.'

'That's great, Matt,' Mitch replied. 'I'm nearly good to go again. I should be headin' out in about five minutes. We'd better coordinate. No sense in us both covering the same area. Which way shall I head?'

Matthew looked thoughtful for a moment.

'Go out to the edge of the reef and turn south-west. I'll go north-east,' he said.

'Sure thing. I'll stay out as long as I can. Good luck.'

'You too, Mitch. And thanks again. I really appreciate you helping out like this.'

'You're welcome, Matt. And try not to worry too much – the boys'll be fine, OK? Now get goin'. I'll be listenin' out on Channel 16 for any news from the coastguard. If you need to get a message to me, you'll have to relay through them. I don't think the frequencies on my radio are gonna be any use for chattin' directly.'

'That's fine, Mitch. I'll relay if I have to. Niamh, why don't you stay here with Moira? I know you want to come, but . . .'

'I'm coming with you, Dad,' Niamh said quickly, matching her father's quick stride as he made to leave. 'You're not leaving me alone.'

'Honey, I'd love to have you keep me company while the men are out,' Moira offered quickly.

A fire ignited inside Niamh. She wanted to yell at them, but she bit her tongue. What was it with the adults? Did they think she was totally useless?

'No offence, Mrs . . . Moira,' Niamh replied, quick to correct herself. 'But I'd really like to go with Dad and help look for Sam and Callum. If dad is flying the plane, then he won't be able to give his full attention to looking out for them. I know I can't do much, but I can be an extra pair of eyes.'

She looked her dad in the eyes. There was reluctance there for a moment, but it melted away in the face of her determined stare. He stepped towards her and gathered her into a hug. Having his arms round her had never felt better.

'You're right, Niamh,' he said, planting a gentle kiss in her hair. 'But you're so much more than just a pair of eyes. I just want you to be safe, do you understand?'

'And I want you to be safe too,' she countered. 'Which is why I need to come along. You won't be tempted to do anything silly if I'm with you. Without Sam around, you're all I've got, Dad. I don't want to lose you too.'

'She's a feisty one, ain't she, Matt?' Moira observed.

'She is that,' he agreed. 'Come on, Niamh. Let's get going. Moira, you wouldn't happen to have a set of binoculars that Niamh could borrow, would you?'

'You know, I just might at that! You guys just hang fire for a minute and I'll see if I can find 'em.'

'Great! We'll wait in the car, Moira.'

Despite her worries for Sam, Niamh could not help feeling a little excited about the prospect of going flying with her dad. Flying in a little aeroplane was nothing like flying in a 747 across the Atlantic. There was something more real about it. Flying on an airliner didn't feel much different to riding in a train, or a bus, but flying in a light aircraft was unlike anything else she had ever done. Every bump on the runway and every slight shifting air current transmitted through the aircraft. It was like the difference between sailing in a dinghy and taking a trip on a massive cruise liner.

They jumped into the SUV and had barely strapped in before Moira was there with the binoculars.

'Thanks, Moira,' Matthew said, starting the engine. 'We'll see you later. Sorry if I was a bit abrupt earlier.'

'No problem, Matt,' she said. 'Good luck and be careful.'

'Always.'

They reversed off the drive and sped off up the narrow road towards the Overseas Highway. The airstrip was less than five minutes away and before she knew it, Niamh was out of the car again and running after her father towards the hangar.

'Ned! Can you do me a favour?' he called, catching sight of a man in blue overalls on the other side of the building.

'Sure, Matt. Whaddaya want?'

'Ring Miami and file me a VFR flight plan, would you? Sam's gone out in my boat and not come back. I'm going to go and look for him in Geoff's Cherokee.'

'OK. One VFR flight plan coming up. How long are ya plannin' on headin' out for?'

'About two hours should do it,' Matthew said. 'I doubt the weather will let me stay up for that long, but I'd rather overestimate.'

'It'll be in by the time you get her fired up,' Ned promised. 'Do ya know where Geoff keeps the keys?'

'Yes, thanks.'

'Fly safe.'

'Thanks, Ned. See you in an hour or so.'

Niamh found she was almost running to keep up with her father as he made a beeline for a smart-looking aircraft to the right of the hangar, conveniently parked near the main door. It was mainly white, with two mustard-coloured stripes along the length of the fuselage – a thick one with a thinner one above it. Every surface of the machine shone as if it had been freshly polished.

'The door's open,' her father told her as they approached. 'You can take the right-hand seat today, but you'll have to wait until I finish the preliminary checks and the walk round or I'll have to climb over you to get in. I'm just going to pick up the keys.'

'I'm going to sit in the front?' she asked.

'Yep. You're going to be more than just a passenger today, remember?'

Waiting behind the right wing for her father to get the keys, Niamh felt all knotted up inside. She stuffed her hands into her pockets and shifted her weight impatiently from foot to foot as she watched her father run across the hangar and retrieve the keys. The sense that Sam needed help had not abated. She could not help feeling that if they didn't find him soon, it might be too late.

Matthew returned, climbed up onto the wing and into the cockpit. He had barely climbed in before getting out again. He raced round the aircraft, moving control services, checking panels and muttering the whole way round. There was no mistaking the urgency in the way he was moving. At one point, he touched something that set off a buzzer in the cockpit, but after a flash of panic, Niamh remembered this from previous trips. It was supposed to happen.

A minute later and he was back, climbing onto the wing root again and urging her to follow him up.

'Remember to stay on the black area,' he warned as he climbed in through the door and across into the left-hand seat.

Sitting in the front for the first time, she found it tempting to grab the steering yoke and play with it. Rather than annoy her father, however, she stowed the binoculars and strapped herself in. The straps were similar to that of a car, but instead of pushing the shoulder strap fastener into a slot, she found it hooked onto a metal spigot. It was a bit weird, but not difficult.

'All set?' Matthew asked. 'OK. Put the headset on,' he directed, pointing to where it was hanging. 'We'll just be a moment. I've got some checks to do before we can go, but they won't take long. Can you pull the door shut for me?'

Niamh did as she was told, and he leaned across her for a moment and fiddled with the door until he was convinced it was secure.

'It's not that I don't trust you to shut a door,' he said, giving her an encouraging smile. 'But Cherokee doors have a bit of a reputation for coming open in flight. Let's not take any chances.'

She watched with fascinated admiration as her father's hands flashed around the cockpit, setting instruments, flicking switches and manipulating controls. He muttered an incomprehensible stream of jargon the entire time.

'CLEAR PROP!' he yelled suddenly, apparently to no one in particular, and with a cough and a splutter, the propeller chattered into life.

There was another quick flurry of hands and mutterings.

'Temps and pressures in the green,' he said clearly.

As Niamh related 'green' with 'go', that sounded good. It was. With a quick look around to make sure no one was anywhere close, Matthew Cutler released the brakes and began to taxi the aircraft out of the hangar and towards the end of the grass strip. Niamh knew enough to realise that his weaving path was to check the steering and compasses, rather than due to any lack of control.

Craning his neck to make sure no one was approaching the airstrip to land, Matthew drove them out on to the grass runway, lined them up and eased the throttle up to full power. Despite her anxiety about Sam, Niamh felt a thrill of excitement. The aircraft began to accelerate down the runway, bumping and hopping as it went. One final hop and they were airborne, climbing gently away from the ground.

Niamh loved this part: the throbbing roar of the engine and the rapid change from the real world to the surreal, detached view from high in the air. It was the most wonderful feeling.

'Key West radar, this is Cherokee November tree ait fife fouer Echo, VFR out of Summerland, 500 feet, climbing 1000, turning north-east.'

Niamh glanced across at her dad. He sounded so different talking on the radio. It was almost as if he was talking another language. A woman's voice suddenly responded, sounding loud through the headphones.

'*Cherokee fife fouer Echo, good afternoon. Continue VFR to the north-east. Nothing to affect. Contact Miami FSS. Report on recovery.*'

'Cherokee fife fouer Echo, wilco.'

'What was that all about?' she asked.

'I was just telling the local radar station where we're going,' he explained. 'It was a courtesy call. We're flying under something called VFR, which is short for Visual Flight Rules. In most places around the world we wouldn't have to talk to anyone, but the airspace around here is quite sensitive. Once we're checked in with the Flight Service Station, I'll just have to make position reports every ten minutes. They like to keep an eye on light aircraft in these parts, probably because of all the problems they have with drug runners.'

Easing the steering yoke to the left, Matthew tipped the aircraft into a banked turn that carried them across the Key and out over the water. The turquoise water of the shallows sparkled in the sunlight. Beautiful. *Real picture-postcard material*, Niamh thought. But she didn't dwell on it. Even as they rolled wings level, she drew out the binoculars and started scanning the water for boats.

Niamh spotted Mitch's boat quickly. He was well on his way to the edge of the reef. She pointed him out and her father nodded.

'We'll just go and let him know we've seen him,' he said.

Niamh felt her stomach rise as her father pushed forward on the yoke, nosing the aircraft into a shallow dive. The sensation was rather like going over a humpback bridge, but it went on for longer. She could see Mitch's boat clearly now through the binoculars. Mitch was waving.

'He's seen us!' she exclaimed. 'He's waving.'

'Great. Let's wave back then.'

To Niamh's surprise, her father began rocking the wings of the plane left and right in a rapid oscillation.

'Whoa!'

'That should do it.'

'I should say so!' Niamh gasped. 'Can you warn me next time you plan to do something like that, please, Dad? You nearly gave me a heart attack!'

'Sorry!'

He glanced across the cockpit at her and gave an apologetic smile. The haunted look was still there in his eyes and yet, despite the circumstances, she could see he was getting pleasure from flying the plane. Flying was like a drug to him, Nimah realised. It was easy to see the attraction – especially in a location like this.

'Apology accepted,' she said. 'OK, let's see if Sam is where he said he was going. There's a boat over there that's about the right size.'

The next fifty minutes raced by as they checked all the boats close to the reef line for about twenty miles to the north-east. On the first return run, they flew over all the boats they could see up to about three miles further out, though there weren't many. The line of huge black clouds rapidly approaching from the south-east had clearly put off the more cautious boaters from venturing far.

Next they flew up and down over the more immediate shallow waters off Summerland and the nearby Keys. There were many more boats here, some of similar size and design to theirs.

'There!' Matthew announced eventually, pointing with his throttle hand while easing the aircraft into a turn towards the boat he had spotted. 'Eleven o'clock. Approximately one mile. It looks like our boat. Is it them?'

Niamh followed his directions and the line of his finger. The boat did look like theirs. She focused in the binoculars and tried to steady them.

'Turn left a bit more, please,' she said. 'I can't see them well enough.'

It took a moment before she could make out the occupants. The vibration of the aircraft combined with the distance made it difficult. The air was also growing progressively more turbulent as the storms approached.

'Unless either Sam or Callum has suffered dramatic hair loss and doubled his body weight in the past few hours, then I'm fairly certain that's not them,' she said, trying to lighten the mood. She shook her head and looked again. 'There also appear to be two scantily clad women on board,' she added.

As she lowered the binoculars from her eyes, there was a loud *bang* from the front of the aircraft and everything began to vibrate. Niamh hugged the binoculars to her chest.

'What's that?' she asked quickly, not sure she wanted to know the answer.

'Not sure yet,' Matthew replied. 'Give me a moment.'

A stream of smoke started emerging from the engine cowling behind the propeller. Matthew eased the throttle back slightly and tapped at one of the gauges.

'Oil pressure's dropping and the temperature's rising. This doesn't look good,' he muttered.

The engine gave a cough and Niamh screamed. She could not help herself.

Matthew squeezed the throttle forward again, pushing it all the way to maximum, but all it seemed to do was make the vibration worse.

'Sorry, sweetie,' her father said, his voice remarkably unflustered. 'This might be a bit of a rough ride home. Even with the throttle and prop levers at full, we're barely maintaining our height and I'm not sure how long the engine is going to keep going.'

'Are we going to crash?'

'Don't panic, Niamh,' he said, his voice remaining calm. 'Something's gone a bit wrong with the engine. It's probably not too bad, but it's overheating and smoking a bit, that's all. I'm going to put out an emergency call and sort things out. OK?'

The engine coughed again and the vibration got worse. Occasional thicker puffs of black smoke spewed from under the cowling. A suffocating smell of burning oil filled the cockpit and streaks of black fluid began to run up the windscreen. Niamh sat rigid with fear, putting her arm across her mouth and nose in an effort to filter out the smell with the sleeve of her T-shirt. Her father reached across to the radio, clicked on to the emergency frequency and keyed the transmit button.

'Mayday, mayday, mayday. Key West Control, this is Cherokee fife fouer Echo declaring an in-flight emergency.'

'Cherokee fife fouer Echo, Control, your in-flight emergency is acknowledged. Launching Search and Rescue this time. Squawk emergency if able and state the nature of your emergency.'

At that moment, the sky darkened as the sun disappeared behind approaching cloud. Niamh shivered. It was like the sensation she had felt in the pool earlier all over again, except this time the danger was hers. She glanced across at her father. He looked . . . businesslike! There appeared to be no real concern on his face – more lines of concentration than there had been earlier, but no fear.

'Make sure you don't touch the throttle, sweetie,' he warned. 'The engine is still working and I want to keep it that way as long as I can. Any sudden changes in power might kill it.'

'Don't worry, Dad,' she mumbled through her sleeve. 'I won't touch anything.'

A bright flash of lightning streaked between two black clouds to the south and the aircraft simultaneously lurched through a pocket of particularly severe turbulence. Niamh's stomach churned and despite feeling cold with fear, she could feel sweat breaking out on her forehead. She had never been airsick before, but had the distinct feeling she might be about to add that experience to her list of firsts. There were sick bags stowed somewhere in the side pockets. She began fumbling for one, while trying to keep her mouth and nose covered. How could her dad breathe in this?

The engine gave another cough and the propeller momentarily stuttered before resuming its droning pitch. A particularly dense cloud of inky-black smoke filled the windscreen. When it cleared, more streaks of oil plastered the perspex.

'Control, Cherokee fife fouer Echo, fife miles south-east of Summerland Key, 1,200 feet on the altimeter, two niner niner fouer, heading two niner fife. Overheating engine. Suspect mechanical damage. Recovering to Summerland for immediate approach.'

'*Cherokee fife fouer Echo, your heading is good. Report finals.*'

'Are you sure we're not going to crash?' Niamh asked nervously.

'There's nothing to be scared of, Niamh,' Matthew assured her, though this time he didn't sound quite so convincing. 'I'll get us down safely, I promise.'

He pulled out a checklist and turned to the pages edged in red.

'I've already done this from memory, but can you read me that emergency drill aloud as a double-check?' he asked, pointing at a list.

'Sure.'

Another fork of lightning stabbed at the sea with jagged tines. The storm clouds were racing shoreward now and although the approaching weather was still some distance away, the air seemed to tremble and quake at the impending onslaught. They had completed the emergency checks and were directly abeam the airstrip at a distance of about three miles when the engine gave a final spluttering cough and died. So, too, did the vibration. The sudden silence made it feel as if the aircraft's heart had stopped beating, but to Niamh's amazement, her father did not seem perturbed by this development.

'Cherokee fife fouer Echo, engine has failed. Commencing glide approach, finals this time,' he transmitted. His voice sounded unnaturally matter-of-fact to Niamh. Could he really be as calm as he seemed?

'*Cherokee fife fouer Echo, engine failure acknowledged. Summerland have been advised of your in-flight emergency.*'

Niamh could feel the pressure building in her cheek muscles as she instinctively clenched her teeth tighter. Her father eased the nose of the aircraft down and started a gentle turn.

He grabbed the checklist from her and flipped the page.

'That one now,' he ordered.

She read the list quickly, checking to make sure her father responded as the checks required. He did. She was impressed that he was so quick and confident with his answers. They were descending quickly now, but to Niamh's amazement, the approach did not look much steeper than those she had experienced before. After nearly an hour of feeling the droning vibration of the engine through her ears and body, the relative silence of their approach felt both surreal and unnerving. The wind rush outside seemed to whisper to her in a strange, otherworldly language that sent shivers running up and down her back. A grumbling crackle of thunder that would not have been audible if the engine had been running added a dark undertone to the whispering voice. To make matters worse, the further around the turn they went, the steeper their approach became as Matthew continued to lower the nose of the aircraft more and more.

Visibility through the front windscreen was virtually non-existent. Once they lined up with the runway, they would be flying blind. Niamh couldn't help wondering how her father intended to land when he couldn't see anything. She watched as he reached and lowered a lever. There was a pause and for the first time a look of real concern crossed her father's face.

'Come on, gear! Lock down,' he muttered.

'What's the matter, Dad?'

'The undercarriage isn't lowering,' he explained. 'I'm not sure . . . damn! Of course it isn't lowering, Matt, you idiot! Without the engine, you've got no hydraulics! Don't worry, Niamh. There's an emergency free-fall system. If I just pull this lever . . . Come on, baby. Don't let me down now.'

There was a *clunk* from underneath their seats.

'Three greens!' he announced triumphantly, pointing at the undercarriage position lights. He reached to his left and opened the storm window. 'We have wheels. Now for the tricky bit.'

'Do we have to go down so steeply?' Niamh asked, edging as far back in the seat as she could.

'Yes, honey,' Matthew replied, his voice steady and reassuring. 'We have to keep our airspeed up or we'll stall. Can you take your feet off the rudder pedals, please? You're making it hard for me to move them. Thanks.'

From the little Niamh could see out of the side windows and the smeared front screen, the ground

114

was rushing to meet them now. It appeared that her father was wrestling with the controls as the turbulent air bounced them around in the final moments of the approach. The aircraft bucked and rocked like a mad bronco all the way down to the ground. Niamh couldn't really see much, but she had the feeling that the aircraft was sliding to the left and her father flew the entire approach with his head all but stuck out of the little storm window he'd opened on his side of the cockpit.

In the final seconds, just as a crash seemed inevitable, Niamh shut her eyes, tucked her chin against her chest and tensed her body in anticipation of the impact. She couldn't help herself. Her insides churned as the aircraft gave a sudden surge at the last second and twisted like a roller coaster entering a sudden climbing turn to the left. They thumped onto the ground, bouncing twice before they settled. Even then, Niamh could feel the gusting wind pushing at the machine – testing and flexing its invisible muscles as it sought to flip them over.

The familiar rumbling sensation of the wheels on the runway as they rolled to a stop left her feeling weak with relief as she cracked her eyes open. They were on the ground. Safe. Matthew let out a long sigh.

'Well, that was entertaining!' he said, removing his headset. He unclipped his harness and leaned across to give her a quick hug. 'Geoff's not going to be best pleased with the state of his aeroplane, but at least we're down safely. Are you OK? You look a bit green around the gills.'

For a moment, Niamh was lost for words. Even had she not been reeling from the intensity of the experience, 'entertaining' would not have featured in her choice of descriptive words. Alarming. Terrifying. Even heart-stopping, but not 'entertaining'.

'I'm fine, Dad,' she said eventually. 'Or at least I will be when my heart and stomach get round to realising we've landed.'

CHAPTER NINE

'Niamh's in trouble!' Sam yelled over his shoulder.

'And we're not?' Callum called back, wearily heaving another bucket of water over the side of the boat.

'She's terrified. I can feel it,' Sam added, ignoring his sarcasm. 'I think she's with Dad. They're looking for us, but something's gone wrong. They're in danger.'

'Well, unless you've been holding out on me and you're really Superman in disguise, then I don't see there's much we can do about it.'

To Sam's frustration, Callum was right. It was all he could do to keep them alive, and he would not have been able to do that if his friend had not been bailing out the boat continuously for what now seemed to both of them like forever. Callum looked worn out, but they could not swap places. There was no way he was fit enough to control the boat, even if he had known how.

For about the next ten minutes, Sam felt tightness in his chest that was nothing to do with his battle for survival. When the sense of fear turned suddenly to relief, he nearly fell over with the shock of the change.

'She's OK,' he announced. 'They both are. Whatever the danger was, it's gone.'

Callum was busy retching over the side. 'Whoopee!' he replied lamely.

Sam gritted his teeth in a defiant grin as he returned his focus to the mountainous waves ahead. He knew his friend well enough to know that the sarcastic response was automatic. Niamh was safe, and the knowledge of this gave him renewed heart and strength. The boost proved invaluable, as the storm refused to let up and Sam was forced to dig deeper and deeper to find the strength to keep fighting it. Time ceased to have meaning as he negotiated wave after wave. When, finally, he spotted the flickering point of light ahead, he could not help wondering if his mind was playing tricks on him. Was it a miracle or a mirage?

'A light!' he called, a thrill running up through his stomach to his chest. 'I'm sure I just saw a light ahead!'

In normal daylight he would never have seen it, but the clouds overhead were so thick that it felt as though night was falling early. Sam was soaked to the skin, shaking with cold, and his arms were weak from what felt like an age of wrestling to keep the boat from capsizing in the monster swell. Constant pricking needles of salt spray stung his eyes and his lips were sore from repeatedly licking away seawater.

A sudden spark of warmth ignited inside him as hope flared. He glanced back over his shoulder at Callum.

'Did you hear me, Cal?' he asked. 'I said I saw a light.'

'Great!' his friend replied automatically, his voice barely audible above the wind and his tone registering little real interest. Callum appeared lost in a personal world of misery. He looked exhausted and hideously pale. Sam felt for him, but there was nothing he could do. He could not leave the wheel or they would both die. Callum had been sick so many times that he had nothing left to throw up, but his empty stomach had not halted his retching.

'There it is again!'

It was barely more than a flicker – just to the right of their current course. It hadn't been a hallucination. Sam could not tell if the light was coming from a point onshore or from another vessel, but he didn't care. He turned the boat towards the source, watching intently for further telltale flickers.

A glance at the sonar screen told him they were still in relatively deep water, though it was definitely getting shallower. Given the visibility, he would have expected to be on top of the reef if the light was coming from the Keys. The swell alone was bigger than the two metres of depth he would have found there. His heart sank. The light had to be from another boat. There was no other explanation.

Another pulse of particularly intense rain lashed at him, driven on by the wild, gusting wind. It drummed on the boat's surfaces so hard that Sam could feel the vibration of it, distinct from that of the engines. Forward visibility was poor at best, but for a moment, he felt as if he was driving blind.

He had little choice. Following the light was their only hope for survival.

When the change came, it came quickly. Sam glanced at the sonar again. They were entering much shallower water. The rhythm of the waves was changing and he could hear a booming roar ahead that could only be surf. The strange thing was that he wasn't approaching the reef – that would have appeared like a wall on the screen.

'This is all wrong!' he muttered again. He must have thought the same words a thousand times over since they had entered the strange patch of water. 'Hang on, Callum. It's hard to tell for certain, but I think we're getting close to the shore.'

'Thank God!'

'You can thank who you like,' Sam called. 'But we're not out of trouble yet. Give it one last push with the bailing. It might make all the difference.'

Sam knew that even if they were not driving towards a reef, getting through the surf without capsizing would take a miracle. And if they made it to the beach – what then? How could he secure the boat? His dad would kill him if he wrecked it! But given the choice between staying alive and facing the wrath of his father, it was a no-brainer. His dad would want him to be safe rather than keep the boat unscathed. The boat was insured. They could always get another one.

'I can't see the light any more, but I can definitely see the shore now, Cal,' he announced as he began to make out a treeline in the gloom ahead. 'It's not far. Hang on extra tight and be ready to jump over the side as soon as I yell. It's going to get a bit hairy as we run at the beach. If I get it wrong, the boat could easily flip. How's your swimming?'

'Normally, I'd say that I'd beat you to shore any day,' Cal replied. 'Feeling like I do now, I'm not so confident.'

'You'll be fine,' Sam assured him. 'Just do as I say and we'll be back on solid ground in just a few minutes.'

'Great.'

Timing would be everything, Sam realised. He needed to pick a wave and follow it in, staying in the calmer water between waves without getting caught in the back current as they made their final approach. He was glad the boat had such powerful engines. He could see the beach ahead clearly now. It looked sandy, and fairly shallow, which was a relief. It would allow him to hit the shore at speed and drive right up on to the sand without risking too much damage.

'Before we go for it, Cal, can you open that cupboard to your left and pull out the yellow bag inside?'

'I'll try.'

There was a pause as Callum shuffled along the bench seat to the cupboard and fumbled with the latch. Sam did his best to slow the boat's advance towards the shore, but he suddenly realised he had got too close to stop. A massive wave was building behind them, threatening to break earlier than the ones ahead. It was too late to try to turn back and go over it. They would flip for certain.

'Hurry, Cal!' he said, beginning to panic. 'I can only give you a few seconds more.'

He heard the distinctive sound of the cupboard latch snapping open.

'Got it!'

Sam gunned the engine and the boat leapt forward sending Cal reeling back. Instinct made him drop the bag and grab the side of the boat. The yellow satchel hit the deck and slid towards the stern.

'Whoa!'

'Sorry, Cal,' he called. 'It's now or never. Grab the bag and don't lose it. It's a survival kit.'

'I can't reach it!'

'You've got to! We're in the middle of nowhere, Cal. We *need* it.'

Callum looked back at the bag. It was sliding around in several centimetres of water that had surged to the back of the deck. His eyes did not stay on the bag for more than an instant. They were drawn to the gigantic wall of water rearing up behind them. 'My God, Sam! Behind!'

Sam flicked a glance over his shoulder and opened the throttle a little further.

'I've got the wave,' he replied. 'You get the bag.'

The wave was closer than he would have liked and was even bigger than he had anticipated. It reminded him of the monsters that surfers in Hawaii dreamed of riding, except it was not glistening blue, but a dark, ominous grey laced with thick veins of creamy foam.

'Now, Cal! GRAB IT!'

Callum didn't move. He was frozen with fear.

Sam could not see him. His focus was already divided between driving at the beach ahead and keeping his distance from the monster wave behind.

'GRAB IT NOW, CAL!' he yelled again, instinctively sensing his friend had not reacted to his first order.

The urgency and authority in Sam's voice spurred Callum into action. There was so much water still sloshing around that the bag was in serious danger of being swept over the low wall of the stern by the engines. Dropping onto his hands and knees on the deck, Callum began to crawl towards it. A sudden surge as Sam gunned the engines sent him sliding and rolling to the back of the boat. He impacted the back wall hard, momentarily wedging his body under the twin engines. They were hot, searing his left side with burning heat as he wrenched himself free.

'Aaaarrrggghhh!'

The surge of power died and the change in momentum carried Callum forward this time: half rolling, half sliding across the slopping deck. The survival bag was swept with him and with a frantic scrabble, he grabbed it at precisely the moment he collided with the back of Sam's legs, sweeping his friend's feet out from under him.

Sam was taken totally by surprise. He crumpled onto Callum, desperately trying to retain his grip on the wheel. As he fell, he inadvertently dragged it to the right. The boat heeled round in a tight turn through ninety degrees just as the incoming wave broke behind them with a booming roar.

Now side on to the wave, the approaching wall of water sucked at them, a slavering maw of gigantic proportions. Sam scrambled to his knees, rammed the throttle to full with his left hand and spun the wheel to the left with his right. The engines roared and the boat reared in the water, twisting like a marlin trying to spit out a hook. The hungry mouth of water chomped behind, barely missing them with its great line of foaming white teeth. Sam felt Callum slide away from under him again, but could not look back to see if his friend was all right.

At full power, the boat raced forward so fast that they leapt over the wave ahead and literally flew towards the beach, thumping down into the shallow water. Still on his knees and barely able to see where he was going, it was all Sam could do to hang onto the wheel.

'BRACE YOUR—' he began. He didn't get to finish the yell. The boat hit land at precisely that moment and despite having tensed his body against the impact, Sam was not ready for the force of the deceleration. His head smacked into the centre of the wooden wheel hard. For a moment, it felt as if he was floating on air. Bright lights flashed in his eyes. Then the pain began.

Confusion. Pain. Disorientation. Pain. He turned, trying to get to his feet. The world spun and he fell. There was a roaring in his ears that was more than that of the surf. Even through his haze of bewilderment he knew he was not safe. There was danger nearby. He had to move. He had to get out of the boat. Callum was flat on his back on the deck. He wasn't moving, but his hands still gripped the yellow survival bag.

'Cal?' The sound of the word sounded strange to Sam as he said it. It was if his voice was muffled and the noise of it echoed around inside his head. He wanted to shake his head, but he was frightened of making the pain worse. He settled for rubbing at his ears and trying again. 'Callum?'

'Urrrrgggghhh!'

'Come on, Cal. We've got to get out of the boat,' Sam urged.

He looked over the stern at the sea. They had not driven far from the waterline and the surf boiled with the fury of the storm. Lightning split the sky again. Once. Twice. The crashing, crackling reports of thunder followed almost instantly.

'Please, Cal!' he begged, kneeling next to him and shaking his shoulders. 'We need to find shelter and get warm. Come on!'

'Can't,' he groaned. 'Need to sleep.'

'Soon, Cal, soon. I promise,' Sam wept, his desperation getting the better of him. 'Come on. I'll help you. Let's just get to the trees over there. I'm cold. You're cold. We both need to get warm. Look, we'll take the flares with us. See? They're just here. We can light a fire with them. Wouldn't that be good? A lovely, warm fire. Come on, Cal!'

It took a combination of nagging, begging and physically pulling, but Sam eventually persuaded Callum to try. The boat was leaning over on the hull, so climbing out over the side was not difficult. As Sam helped Callum down on to the sand, he noticed his friend's glasses were missing. At first, he thought they were lost in the surf, but then he spied them in the footwell. Stretching back into the boat, he grabbed them and tucked them into the top of the survival pack.

'You'll be wanting those later,' he muttered.

Walking up the beach was hell.

The boys linked arms over each other's shoulders and supported one other as they struggled to stay upright in the raging wind. To begin with, the sand was firm, but as they climbed the beach, the footing became more difficult. Their feet sank into the sand at every step, making forward progress difficult and quickly sapping their waning strength.

On reaching the tree line, Sam wondered for a moment if he was making a big mistake by venturing in. Branches were whipping back and forth in the wind, twice catching him with glancing blows. The underlying foliage was dense, with many tall, broad-leaf plants that gave the impression of a jungle. Once they had entered, they could not see more than a metre or two in any direction and it was incredibly difficult to push through it.

'Let's not go too far in,' Sam suggested. 'If it's all like this, it will be easy to get lost. Here. This will do.'

Callum didn't answer. Sam helped his friend to sit down with his back to a tree trunk and looked at him more closely. Callum's eyes held a glazed expression. Sam could see that his friend was in a bad way. He did not know exactly what was wrong with Callum, but his first guess would be a combination of shock and hypothermia.

Sam had learned about cold injuries during a brief stint in the army cadets. He had only gone along to the unit for a few weeks before deciding that all the marching and polishing of boots was not for him. One of the few things that had stuck with him was the session on cold injuries.

The cadets had all filed into the training room to watch a dated video showing walkers succumbing to the cold and then they had discussed treatments as part of a first-aid training programme. One particular fact Sam had been surprised to discover was that the weather did not need to be particularly cold for someone to become hypothermic. It was not truly cold now, but he knew that sitting still, soaked to the skin, combined with the heat-leeching wind-chill factor, could potentially cause a deadly drop to their core temperatures. Sam felt the effects, but he was more weather-hardened than poor Callum, so it was no wonder he had succumbed first.

'I want to go back to the boat and salvage what I can before the tide takes it,' Sam said. 'I'm going to get the knife from the survival pack and hack a path back through to the beach so I'll be able to find you again easily. Will you be OK for a few minutes?'

Callum didn't respond.

'I'm hoping I can find something I can use to warm you up in one of the cupboards,' Sam added. 'I'm not certain, but I've got a feeling Dad keeps a blanket in there. At the very least there's a towel. I'll see if I can keep it dry somehow on the way back.'

He opened the top of the pack and rummaged through it. Callum's glasses looked vulnerable, so Sam took out a foil blanket, wrapped them inside it and tucked them deep into the pack for safety. He hadn't looked in the survival pack for a couple of years, but he was very pleased with what he found.

'Here, Callum,' he said excitedly as he pulled out a small tin and opened it. 'Have a boiled sweet. The sugar will help.'

He put the sweet into Callum's mouth and was pleased to see his friend begin to suck on it. The response was not great, but at least it was some sort of reaction. Next Sam took out the survival knife. It was a real beauty, he thought, kneeling as he drew it from the protective scabbard. The grip felt secure in his hand despite the wet and he mentally thanked his father for being so obsessive about his equipment. He turned and stood, intending to return the knife to the scabbard and secure the scabbard on his belt.

It took a moment before Sam registered the shape standing no more than two metres away. It was hard to say what caught his eye, but he looked up and for a moment, he could not believe what he was seeing. Then he screamed.

CHAPTER TEN

The creature was manlike, but only in the broadest sense. Sam was tall for his age, but the top of his head barely came up to the chest of the thing facing him. It stood upright on two legs, but Sam could never have envisaged a man of similar proportions.

It was covered in scales, reminiscent of the underside of an alligator, with massive, muscular legs and a solid torso. The seemingly mismatched arms were much shorter and, while muscular, looked almost skeletal by comparison. The combination made the creature look very bottom heavy. Its large hairless head squatted on narrow shoulders, the apparent lack of a neck giving it a menacing, hunched look. Forward-facing black eyes were set wide on either side of a huge rounded lump of a nose that ended with two comma-shaped nostrils. Its mouth was broad and lipless, a curving slash across its face that sported the most terrifying pointed teeth Sam had ever seen, and its hands had a strange combination of finger and claw-like digits.

Sam's scream had barely begun when the creature rushed him. He lashed out instinctively with the knife, but his blow didn't land. Instead he felt a numbing impact on his wrist and he lost his grip on the blade. Before he could take in what was happening, the creature had hoisted him into the air and tucked him under its deceptively strong right arm.

Sam struggled with all his might, expecting to feel sharp teeth sinking into his neck at any moment. All his writhing and kicking were in vain. His arms were pinned to his sides and his position did not allow him to kick at the creature with any strength. He was both terrified and furious. He had a black belt at tae kwon do and had been armed with a knife, yet he had not managed to land a single blow before being disarmed and rendered helpless. The lizard-man had moved so fast that Sam had barely had time to flinch. It was both humiliating and terrifying in equal measure.

Squatting down, the creature gently picked up the now unconscious body of Callum with its other arm.

'PUT US DOWN!' Sam yelled, twisting to look up at his captor's face.

To his surprise, there was calculating intelligence in the black eyes that returned his look. The creature opened its mouth and made a strange sequence of clicking and tick-tocking noises. Some of the sounds were not unlike those made by dolphins, except that the pitch was deeper and the variations more complex. Was it trying to speak to him? If it was, then it did not waste time repeating anything. A moment later, it turned and began carrying the boys back towards the beach.

All Sam could do was tuck his chin against his chest and close his eyes as the creature waded through the foliage at speed. Branches whipped and broad leaves slapped against his head and shoulders. In a matter of seconds, they were out in the open and the stormy winds blasted them with driving rain. The creature paused a moment and roared, seemingly in defiance of the weather. Sam opened his eyes. A second lizard-man appeared from the trees, followed quickly by a third.

'Holy crap, there's more of them!' Sam muttered, blinking several times. He bit his tongue to make sure he was not dreaming. The bite hurt. This was really happening. 'Where the hell *are* we?'

The creatures chattered at each other for a few seconds. Was it a form of language? If so, Sam wondered, what were they talking about? Were he and Callum destined to be their next meal? One look at their teeth and it was hard to imagine any other reason for the creature to capture them.

Suddenly, Sam's captor turned left, its arm round his body squeezed still tighter and it began to run. Sam gasped. Nothing could have prepared him for this experience. Sport had always been one of his favourite things and he was quite a good runner for his age, but the speed of this creature was breathtaking. Despite being encumbered with the two boys, it raced along the beach far faster than any human sprinter could. Its powerful legs drove forward with incredible power, each bounding stride carrying them several metres, and the tempo of its pace was astonishing. All thoughts Sam had about breaking free and running away vaporised. Even if he could bring himself to desert his friend, Sam realised that without a massive head start, he could not hope to get far. How much faster would the thing be able to run when it wasn't carrying them? It didn't bear thinking about.

The wind buffeted them as they raced along the shoreline, but the creature's balance appeared unaffected. Minutes passed and it did not show so much as a hint of tiring. Sam marvelled at its strength even as he dreaded the beast's intentions.

Suddenly, for no apparent reason, Sam found himself dumped onto the soft sand at speed. He rolled and slid to a stop. Callum came to rest nearby, his face and hair caked in wet sand. He looked as if he was unconscious. The lizard-creature took a few more paces forward before stopping abruptly, lifting its nose in the air and tilting its head in a quizzical fashion. Quite what it thought it could smell in the middle of this gale, Sam had no idea. He winced as it opened its jaws wide and let out another heart-stopping, primeval roar.

'What now?' Sam moaned. 'Why here?'

The words had barely passed his lips when the answer came in the form of another beastly roar. This one was deeper, louder and longer, leaving Sam wishing he had not asked the question. The unmistakable thumping drumbeat of gigantic footfalls began, accompanied by a sudden sound of cracking trees to their left. Something was smashing through them in a reckless charge.

Breathless, Sam waited for some enormous monster to burst out from the jungle and charge them. To his surprise, that did not happen. Whatever was marauding through the trees was not running towards them. It was running away. What did that mean?

'Can it get any worse?' Sam breathed. 'OK, Niamh. I promise I'll be happy to hear you say "I told you so" if it means getting home in one piece.'

He reached out and touched his friend's face. It felt stone cold. 'Callum?' he called softly. 'Can you hear me, mate? Don't be dead. Please don't be dead.'

No response.

He felt his friend's neck for a pulse, but there was no sign of life. His heart raced as he tried to keep his panic under control.

'Think!' he urged himself. 'It's not surprising you can't feel anything. Your fingers are too cold. Even if you're pressing on the right spot, you're not going to feel anything.'

The other two lizard-men raced up from behind to join the one that had carried Sam and Callum. The three of them stood for a moment watching the forest at the top of the beach. There was a brief exchange of clicking chatter and Sam's captor turned and bounded back over to where he and Callum were sprawled in the sand. It paused to look at them for a moment before baring its teeth in an obvious warning gesture. The other two continued to watch the tree line. Sam saw no point in resisting as he was picked up again. Any one of these creatures would be more than a match for him.

Seconds later, they were racing along the sand again, presumably with the other two creatures following. Despite the mind-numbing fear that seemed to be preventing Sam from making any sense of his situation, he had noticed a couple of interesting things while they had stopped. Firstly, one of the other two creatures following them was now wearing the yellow survival pack from the boat slung round its neck. Secondly, Sam had gained his first look at the creatures from behind and unless his eyes were playing tricks on him, they seemed to have a bony ridge down their spines from the back of their heads to the middle of their backs. Below this was a short, fat stump that appeared to be either the beginnings of, or the vestigial remains of, a tail.

Mrs Davies, his biology teacher, would no doubt go into raptures over them, he thought. Assuming they were contained in a zoo of course. Were these creatures alien? If not, how had they remained undiscovered? They didn't look like any of the monsters he had seen people supposedly searching for on the *Discovery Channel*. And what had been in the trees? Whatever it was had sounded huge and even scarier than their current captors. Could he and Callum have inadvertently stumbled into a top-secret experimental area? Perhaps the creatures were the result of a bizarre genetic experiment. That made a twisted sort of sense. Scientists were constantly messing with genetics these days. But anybody could see they were dangerous, so why were these creatures being allowed to run loose?

Sam found himself thinking about the film *Jurassic Park*. These creatures looked nothing like the dinosaurs in the film, but the thing that had gone crashing through the trees back there had been massive. Hearing it had reminded him of some of the tyrannosaur scenes. In the film it was the most dangerous dinosaurs that had broken through the park boundaries and overrun the Visitor Centre. Was this place a sort of twisted Jurassic Park?

'Wouldn't that be just my luck?' he growled.

'*Whaaat?*'

The moan was barely audible above the wind.

'Cal! Callum? Are you OK?'

His friend lolled under the creature's other arm like a bundle of wet laundry as they raced along the beach.

'Cal? Can you hear me?'

Nothing. Callum looked in a bad way, but Sam felt a warm flood of relief at the thought that his friend was still alive. Escaping with Callum in his current state would take a miracle, but Sam knew he must not begin to think it impossible. Remaining hopeful was essential if he was to keep his mind working.

They had survived the storm on the ocean, hadn't they? What were the odds of that? Long at best, he decided. Overcoming long odds needed a combination of luck and tenacity. He had done it once. He could do it again.

Think positive, he told himself. *Don't give up.*

A tongue of rocks projected down the beach and into the sea ahead. Sam expected his captor to slow as they approached, but the creature's running rhythm barely stuttered as they powered up and over the rocky outcrop. It leapt from rock to rock with goat-like sure-footedness and with a final gigantic leap, they flew down to land on the soft sand of the beach on the far side. Despite the force of the impact, the creature's massive legs appeared to absorb the shock of landing with ease and it continued running without any sign of effort.

'Bloody hell!' Sam swore under his breath. What would it take to slow this thing down?

Rather than running straight on down the beach, they turned left and raced up through the softer sand towards the jungle. Sam knew from experience how hard it was to run through soft sand, but the extra effort did not appear to have any effect on the lizard-man other than a slight shortening of its stride.

It was quieter here, the rocky outcrop providing a natural barrier against the storm winds. As they approached the trees, Sam could see that the foliage was barely moving. Instinctively closing his eyes, tucking his head down and tensing his shoulders in expectation of the same whipping impacts he had experienced when he had first been carried from the jungle, Sam did not see the path coming. It was not visible until they entered it, cutting into the trees at an oblique angle.

The sound of the creature's footfalls changed as they entered the trees. Sam suddenly felt a weird sensation of enclosure. After a few moments, he tentatively lifted his head and cracked his eyes open. He did so just in time to witness the end of the short path and see their destination, which proved to be a whole new surprise. He had expected a cave, or a nest, or a further group of creatures with hungry grins. Instead, he found himself blinking with amazement as they entered a small clearing and approached a large wooden house with a pitched roof. It seemed to be of human design, tucked in the lee of the low rocky outcrop.

They stopped a few paces short of the front door and the creature let out one of its fearsome roars. Sam felt as though his heart might burst free from his chest as his imagination ran wild. Was he about to be saved or did a new horror lurk within?

A voice called out inside the building – a human voice. What was more, the voice held no note of fear.

'Leah! We've got company.'

There was a short pause and the door of the building opened. A man stepped out on to the threshold. He didn't look particularly old, but his thick mop of hair was white-grey and he had a trimmed beard and moustache of the same colour. Sam had never been so pleased to see anybody in his life.

With an abruptness that took him totally by surprise, Sam was dropped to the ground. Callum landed with a thud next to him. The lizard-man made some clicking noises. They were much slower than when the creatures had chattered at each other earlier. To Sam's amazement, the man in the doorway responded with some throat-bending clicks of his own. There was a further exchange and then the man bowed and waved as the creatures turned and raced away back towards the beach.

Sam found he couldn't move. His relief was so intense that all strength deserted him and tears began to flow down his cheeks.

'Are you OK, boy?' the man asked, kneeling at Sam's side and placing a gentle hand on his shoulder. 'Are you hurt?'

'I'll be fine in a minute,' Sam sniffed. 'I'm not hurt, but I think my friend Callum might be hypothermic.'

'Well, don't worry. We'll get Callum inside and warm him up. With any luck, he'll be right as rain in no time. Are there any others with you?'

'No,' Sam replied. 'It was just us on our boat. We did see a light earlier, but that seemed to be coming from the land.' He paused and then continued in a rush. 'Excuse me, sir, but who are you? And what were those things that brought me here? And *where* is here?'

The man looked him in the eye and gave a wry smile.

'Have you ever see the film *The Wizard of Oz*, lad?' he asked in return.

'Yes. Why?'

'Well, let's just say, "You're not in Kansas any more!"'

CHAPTER ELEVEN

'Yes, that's right. They're *still* missing.' Matthew Cutler's face said it all as he spoke into the phone: frustration, pain and anger.

Niamh finally understood the haunted look in his eyes. She had seen it many times before, normally whenever anyone mentioned her mum, Claire, but she had never truly understood it until now. She had felt strangely hollow since Sam's disappearance, but at least she could sense he was still alive. How must it be for her dad? He had never had such assurance with Mum, nor would he have it now with Sam. It was no wonder he looked the way he did.

Niamh had few memories of her mother and those she did have were vague. Blonde hair. Warmth. Feelings of love and security. She had looked at pictures many times of course. Whenever she looked at them, she felt sadness and a sense of loss – not the loss of something tangible, but for something she'd never really had. All the other girls at school had grown up with mothers to care for them and love them and talk girly stuff with them. What would that have been like? Niamh could only imagine. She felt cheated and sometimes confused. Dad had been great at caring for her, but Niamh had often felt jealous when she saw the way her friends acted around their mothers. She could not help feeling that she had missed out on the most special relationship of her childhood.

More recently, looking at the pictures had also created confusion as to which were true memories and which were false, created from the paper and digital images. When she had last looked at the photos, Niamh had finally realised just how beautiful her mother had been. Looking in the mirror, Niamh had appreciated that she had inherited some of her mother's features. It seemed the older she got, the more the likeness grew ever more apparent.

Niamh had noticed an odd look appear in her dad's eyes when he was looking at her sometimes. It had made her feel strangely uncomfortable, and she knew that in those moments it was not her he was seeing.

'As I told you earlier, they left about ten this morning,' Matthew said, impatience rising in his tone. He rarely displayed anger openly, but Niamh could see her dad was building towards an explosion.

'Calm,' she mouthed, making a slow downward gesture with the palms of her hands. 'Deep breath.' She inhaled deeply through her nose, inflating her chest to its full capacity. Matthew gave a wry smile and an almost imperceptible nod. The venom melted from his voice.

'Yes, I can give you the details of the boat again . . .'

Niamh moved away into the kitchen. The pizzas they had ordered should be arriving any time and she couldn't stand eating it straight from the box with her fingers the way the boys normally did. Pulling a large wooden breadboard from the cupboard under the microwave, Niamh set to work laying the dining table.

First she set out the place mats, coasters, knives and forks before putting two plates in a bowl of hot water to warm. After all the trauma and excitement, it felt good to do something so routine, even if it did feel wrong to only set two place settings. As she carefully poured out two tall glasses of fruit juice, Niamh realised that she was still a bit shaky.

With all that had happened today, she could not imagine for one second how she was ever going to sleep again. 'What if' questions rattled round and round inside her head with little hope of any answers. What if the boys were gone forever? What if the coastguards found wreckage, but no bodies? What if the weather was stormy again tomorrow? What if, what if, what if!

There was a knock at the door. Niamh moved instantly to answer it. A pizza delivery boy was standing inside the porch with two boxes balanced on the fingertips of his left hand. His dark hair was plastered to his head and his shirt was soaking wet. Behind him the rain sheeted down in torrents. It was dark enough to be mistaken for evening outside, yet it was barely past four in the afternoon. Where were the boys? Even the thought of being out on the sea in this weather made Niamh shudder. At the moment she could not sense what was happening to Sam, but his presence had not disappeared altogether. She felt confident he was still alive.

'Twenty-three ninety, please,' the boy said, giving Niamh a warm smile. He gave a sideways flick of his head. 'Another fine day in paradise.'

As if to ratify his sarcasm, there was a flash of lightning followed almost instantly by a loud crash of thunder. He visibly flinched, but quickly grinned again in an effort to look as if he was dismissive of the storm.

'Just a sec,' she answered, leaving the door ajar and running silently through to the living area where her dad was still on the phone. She waved to get his attention and signalled that she needed some money. He fished in his pocket and pulled out his wallet, throwing it across to her and continuing his conversation with the coastguard.

Niamh caught the wallet, opened it and riffled through the notes. As she walked back to the door she drew out a twenty, a five and three one-dollar bills.

'There you go,' she said, passing the money over and taking the boxes. She could feel the heat of the pizza through the cardboard and the smell of it was heavenly.

'Thanks,' he replied, noting the tip. 'Enjoy your food.'

'Thank you. We will.'

She closed the door and took the boxes to the table.

'. . . and if there's any news . . . any news at all, you'll ring me. Good. I appreciate that, thanks.' Matthew hung up.

'Perfect timing, Dad,' Niamh said. 'Come and get some while it's hot.'

'I just want to ring the Sheriff's Office . . .' he began, picking up the handset again.

'Please, have some food first,' she begged. 'It'll get cold. Don't make me eat alone. The Sheriff's Office will still be there in ten minutes. You know how I can normally feel when Sam's in trouble? Well, I'm not getting any sense of danger at the moment. He's OK. I've no idea where he is, but I think we can spare a few minutes to eat. Come and sit down.'

Matthew hesitated a moment, then he put the phone down and joined her at the table. Despite feeling hungry, Niamh found that for all her brave words, now the food was in front of her she could hardly eat anything. The aroma from the pizza was wonderful, but from the first bite she found herself struggling to swallow. Hawaiian pizza was her favourite, and this one was a beauty. The thin base was perfectly cooked, and the blend of the meat with the sweet pineapple was just right, but her stomach rebelled. It churned continually with tangled emotions.

Her father ate quickly and in silence. Niamh watched him, jealous of his appetite. He appeared to be viewing the pizza rather like a refuelling exercise. His face remained expressionless and flat as he demolished one slice after another.

'So after the Sheriff's Office, what then?' Niamh asked.

'I'll give my friend Mike a ring. He works with the Florida Wildlife people up in Marathon,' he replied, meeting her eyes for the first time since he had sat down. 'They have several boats – more than the Sheriff's Office, I think. They did a lot of searching for . . . for your mum when she disappeared.'

Niamh had to look away. She couldn't bear to look at him. The pain in her father's eyes tore at her, yet strangely, she did not feel the pain for herself. Was she cold-hearted? It felt as if she was just going through the motions, rather than really believing that the search around the Keys would lead them to Sam and Callum. An empty space yawned inside her like the black mouth of a mineshaft, yet Sam's presence was still there, like a distant echo. She felt no tears welling at the thought of him not coming back because, deep down, she knew that he was alive, just out of reach. But why could she not look her father in the eye? He needed her now, more than ever. Everything was mixed up.

'When are you going to ring Callum's parents?' she asked.

'I don't know,' he admitted, shaking his head. 'I keep thinking about that. I mean, what am I to tell them?'

'The truth?'

'Yes, but how?' He paused, a slice of pizza drooping from between his fingers. 'Oh, God! Can you imagine it?' His voice changed as he began to play-act. 'Hello, Mrs Barnes – Matthew Cutler here. Sorry to disturb you in the middle of the night, but I just wanted to let you know that your son has gone missing in my boat. It'll be dark here soon. There's a storm raging outside and the waters around here have a nasty reputation for being treacherous, but don't worry. I'm sure he'll be just fine. The coast-guards are out searching for him. They're very good at their job.'

He tore a vicious bite out of his pizza slice. Niamh thought quietly for a moment.

'I know there's no easy way of telling them,' she agreed. 'But put yourself in their position: would you rather find out sooner or later that something bad had happened to one of us?'

The little colour that had remained in Matthew's face drained away, leaving his skin the colour of pale margarine.

'You are your mother's daughter, Niamh,' he said softly. 'That's exactly the sort of thing she would have said.'

'Except Mum would have said it with an American accent,' she replied, trying to lighten the moment. 'I'd try, but I don't do accents.'

'Please, don't! You get more like her every day as it is.'

151

'And is that such a bad thing?' Niamh asked tentatively.

'No,' her father said. 'It's actually rather wonderful, but when I look at you now, I keep seeing her. I can't help it. It makes the pain of having lost her seem sharper than ever. Your mother was a very special lady, Niamh, and you are growing up to be just like her. I know I should be counting my lucky stars, but . . .'

Niamh got to her feet and stepped round the table. Turning, she sat down on his lap and hugged him. It felt good to hold him close. Good, but just a little awkward. How long had it been since she had last sat like this? Not since starting secondary school. Sitting on her father's lap made her feel like a little girl again. Since she had left primary school, she had shed so much of the innocent, affectionate behaviour she had shown her father when she was younger. It hadn't seemed appropriate any more. But now, feeling the affectionate squeeze of his arms around her, she began to appreciate what she had given up.

The time of her little-girl innocence had ended, yet her time as an adult had not yet arrived. She was neither one nor the other, but stuck in between. Suddenly, it felt a horrible place to be.

'You will always be my little girl,' he said, seemingly reading her mind. Another bright flicker of light outside cast eerie shadows round the room. The thunder boomed, carrying a crackling edge to it that bore witness to the violence of the burning bolts of lightning. 'Come on. Up you get. I need to be doing something towards finding your brother. I can't stand thinking about him and Callum being out in this.'

'Ring Callum's parents first,' Niamh said. 'They need to know, Dad. You can't keep it from them.'

'All right,' he agreed reluctantly. 'I'll ring them. What time is it?'

'Back home it'll be about 9.30 p.m.'

He picked up his wallet from where Niamh had put it on the corner of the table and pulled out a scrap of paper from behind a credit card. He stared at the number and then at the phone. Niamh could only imagine how he was feeling as he reached for the handset. Anyone looking at him at that moment could have been forgiven for thinking he was preparing himself to pick up a poisonous snake or stick his hand inside a hornets' nest.

The rapid *bee bee bee bop boo bee bee bop* of the numbers keying through were just audible to Niamh. She watched her father wait nervously for the line to connect.

'Hello? Mr Barnes? Sorry to ring at this hour. It's Matthew Cutler here . . . yes, that's right . . . yes, I'm

153

afraid there has been an incident . . . well, that's just it – I don't know. There's no easy way to say this, David, but . . . well . . . Callum and Sam have gone missing . . . They took my boat out without permission and haven't returned . . . About seven hours now . . . Yes, the coast-guard and all the relevant authorities . . . We went out looking . . . Oh! All right. You have my number here? Goodbye.' He put the phone down slowly.

'What did he say, Dad?'

Matthew Cutler's brow furrowed in a deep frown. 'It was really strange,' he said. 'Have I missed some-thing, somewhere? Callum's father turned frosty the instant I told him the boys had gone missing. He only asked a couple of questions and then cut off the conversation. What was that all about? His son is missing for goodness' sake!'

'Beats me,' said Niamh, giving a shrug. 'He seemed friendly enough when he dropped Callum off at our house. Perhaps he's just had one of those nightmare days when nothing goes right. Still you've phoned him now. Duty done.'

'Yes,' he sighed. He picked up the phone, steeled his expression and dialled another number. 'Hello? Sheriff's Office, please . . .'

David Barnes stared at the telephone for several long moments after replacing the handset. He took a deep breath and his eyes flicked across to the nearby coffee table where Callum's postcard was still resting on top of the rest of the day's post. His only child had always been one for playing practical jokes and when he had first read the card, David had laughed, assuming this was another. But the moment Matthew Cutler had told him Callum was missing, he could not help thinking that this time his son might have been at least half serious. It would be just like him to make a joke out of something like that. That was the problem with Callum – even when he was serious, he insisted on being the comedian. He leaned across and picked up the card again. The picture was an aerial photo of the Lower Keys. He flipped it over and read his son's scrawled message again:

Dear Mum and Dad,

Weather is fantastic. Been snorkelling, water-skiing, fishing and generally having a great time. Turns out Mr Cutler is a mad axe murderer, but am keeping my head down and trying not to annoy him too much! Love you lots.

Callum

'Who was that on the phone, darling?' Natalie Barnes asked as she entered the room, a cup of coffee in each hand.

David was not sure how to answer. He knew his wife. She was likely to become hysterical when she realised something had happened to Callum, but he could not keep it from her.

'Come and sit down, love,' he began. 'I think you're going to need something stronger than coffee.'

CHAPTER TWELVE

'You're not doing the old *Wizard of Oz* line again are you, Brad? I'll bet you've not even asked their names yet, have you? Come on. Help me get them inside. They're soaked through and they look frozen!'

'OK, Leah,' Brad mumbled. 'Sorry,' he added, giving Sam an apologetic shrug and stepping out from the sheltered porch into the rain.

Sam grabbed Brad's extended hand and struggled to his feet.

'I'm Sam Cutler,' he said. 'And my friend is Callum Barnes. Thanks for helping us. I was convinced we were about to be eaten.'

'With good reason, Sam,' Leah replied, her voice deadly serious. 'Let's get you and Callum inside and we'll explain what we can.'

Sam found he could barely stand, but with a determined effort, he staggered across to the doorway. He waited while Leah and Brad lifted Callum between them. They looked rather unbalanced, as Leah was so petite and slim next to Brad's fuller, taller frame, that despite being in no fit state to help, Sam felt guilty for allowing her to do the lifting. Leah had a kind face, framed with long brown hair, heavily streaked with grey and tied back in a ponytail that reached halfway down her back. When she smiled at him, her features lit up. To Sam it was like being welcomed by a long-lost friend. She flicked her hair out of the way as she draped one of Callum's arms round her shoulders. The couple half-carried and half-dragged him inside. He showed no sign of consciousness. Sam followed, closing the door behind him and hooking the simple wooden latch in place. The sudden quiet as the sound of the wind was abruptly muffled made Sam's head swim.

Callum was placed gently on a sofa that had been roughly fashioned from wood and adorned with what looked like waterproof boat cushions for padding. Leah leaned over him, checking his throat for a pulse and hovering her cheek across his nose and mouth to see if she could feel him breathing. When she straightened up, she turned to Sam and smiled.

'I think he'll be fine,' she said. 'We just need to get him out of these wet clothes and wrap him up nice and warm. Brad and I can do that. Please, sit down. Here. Come and sit near the fire. You'll feel a lot better too once you've warmed up.'

There were several other chairs in the room, all clearly hand-made from wood. Some had cushions. Others were just bare wood. The one Leah indicated looked to be the most comfortable. Sam did not need any more encouragement. He crossed the room to the chair and gently collapsed into it. The warmth of the fire and sudden overwhelming feelings of relief and security combined to create a powerful soporific effect. Sam's mind was swimming with questions, but no sooner had he leaned back than he began to feel very sleepy. He had a vague awareness of someone removing his shoes and T-shirt. In a semi-dream he felt a blanket draped over his body and legs and then sleep claimed him totally.

Sam awoke in a panic, heart pounding and a scream hovering in the back of his throat. The nightmare had been more intense than any he could remember. The after-image of a horrible creature with terrifying teeth and overwhelming strength haunted the corners of his vision as he sat bolt upright. He took a deep breath and tried to relax. It had been years since he had last had a nightmare that felt so vivid.

'Must have dozed off in front of the box,' he mumbled.

The room was dark, but warm. *What on earth had he been watching to trigger that response?* he wondered. It was only as he sat up and looked to where he expected to see the TV that he realised he was not in the Key-side house. The day's events came flooding back. The nightmare had not been a reaction to something he had been watching. He had been reliving reality.

Sam groaned.

The only light in the room came from the glowing embers of the fire. They were still giving off quite a lot of heat, but only the faintest amount of light. The distant sound of wind in the treetops and of heavy rain pounding the outside of the house told him that the wild weather was not over yet. If anything, it sounded worse than ever.

He shifted his weight and the blanket slipped from his shoulders. He was still wearing his shorts, but at least they felt dry now. How long had he been sitting here? What time was it? He remembered Brad and Leah bringing them in. Where were they now? And Callum? He had been nearby. Was he still there? Sam couldn't see well enough in the dark to tell.

'Cal?' he whispered. 'Callum?'

'Sam? Is that you?' came a sleepy reply.

'Cal!' he exclaimed, keeping his voice low. 'Thank God you're OK! You had me so worried.'

'Where are we?'

'I've got no idea, but I think we're safe for now,' he said. 'Try to get some more sleep and we'll worry about getting answers in the morning, OK?'

'Sure . . . and Sam . . .'

'Yes?'

'Thanks for keeping us alive.'

'I wouldn't be too quick to thank me,' Sam said. 'You don't know how much trouble we're in yet.'

'What do you mean?'

'Call it intuition,' he said. 'Try to get some more sleep. We'll talk tomorrow.'

Sam leaned back and closed his eyes again. It was easy to say, 'We'll worry about it in the morning,' but sleep felt a million miles away. His mind was fully alert now and he could not imagine getting back to sleep again. He played back the events of the day again and again, trying to make sense of what had happened. The sound of Callum's breathing settled quickly to the slow, steady pattern of sleep. How long he sat awake, Sam would not have liked to guess. He did not feel as if he had dropped off at all, but when he opened his eyes on hearing someone moving across the room behind him, he was surprised to see daylight filtering through cracks in the wooden shutters.

'Good morning,' he said, getting to his feet.

It was Leah. 'Good morning, Sam,' she replied, giving him a warm smile. 'Did you sleep well?'

'Not really, if I'm honest,' he said. 'I couldn't help thinking about . . . well, everything, I suppose.'

'Coming through is traumatic for everyone,' she observed.

'Coming through? Coming through what? The storm? Leah, please tell me – where exactly are we?'

'Exactly?' she replied. 'I wouldn't like to say *exactly*. But as far as we've been able to work out, we're where the Florida mainland should be.'

'You're talking in riddles! Surely we're either on the mainland or we're not. Aside from the Keys, there's no other land around.'

'That's just it, Sam,' she said, taking something that looked like a melon down from a shelf and putting it on a wooden board. 'We're sort of in Florida, but we're not. The moon and the stars in the sky look the same, but we're not in the same world we grew up in. Miami doesn't exist here. None of our cities do. In fact, the only humans here are those like you and us who have come from our world.'

'That's impossible!' Sam exclaimed. 'Callum and I were only a couple of miles off Summerland Key. We weren't abducted by aliens or anything.'

'Summerland Key, did you say?' Brad was standing in the doorway. He let out a long whistle of amazement. 'Jeez! You boys did well to get that far. How big was your boat?'

'Just under ten metres.'

'Metres?' Brad frowned as he thought for a few seconds. 'So that would be about thirty feet?'

'That's right.'

'Impressive! I don't think I've ever heard of anyone making it to shore from so far out before. When Leah and I crossed, we were out of Key Largo and heading towards Miami. There are no Keys here. The sea levels and the topography seem to be different. Our short spell in the storm we came in on was hair-raising enough. Let me guess: the water looked strange and then all your navigation equipment failed. Without warning you found yourself surrounded by storm clouds.'

'Yes, but . . .'

'That was when you crossed.' Brad stated it confidently, as if it was a proven fact. 'Do you ever watch any sci-fi? *Star Trek*, that sort of thing?'

'I do,' Callum said suddenly, sitting up. Sam jumped. He had not noticed his friend wake up. 'Are you saying we're in a sort of parallel world?' Callum asked.

'Precisely!' Brad said. 'This place is *like* Earth, but it's not the Earth we know. It seems to occupy the same piece of space as the world we all come from, but in another dimension or something.'

'Those lizard-men . . .' Sam began.

'Lizard-men?' Callum asked, confused. 'What are you talking about? Sam, I'm blind as a bat without my glasses. Do you know what happened to them?'

'You dropped them in that frantic charge at the beach. I found them and put them into the survival pack, but I've not seen that since last night,' Sam admitted.

'Is this it?' Leah asked, dropping the bright yellow pack on Sam's lap.

'That's brilliant, Leah!' he exclaimed. 'Thanks you have no idea how happy I am to see this again.'

Sam unclipped the top. To his astonishment, he found the survival knife that he had thought lost forever in the trees was there in its scabbard right at the top. He removed it and tucked it under his leg while he rummaged deeper. His stomach tightened as his hands sifted through the survival gear searching for the foil-wrapped glasses. Where had they gone? He gave a deep sigh of relief as his fingers found the blanket. He drew it out and carefully unwrapped the glasses. They appeared undamaged. He passed them to Callum.

'Thanks,' Callum said. 'That's much better.' He looked first at Leah, then at Brad and then back at Sam. 'Now what was that you were saying about lizard-men?'

'The creatures who brought you to our house are the dominant species here,' Leah answered. 'I'm no biologist, but everything we've seen here in the Reserve seems to point at them having evolved from raptors.'

'As in *dinosaurs?*' Sam could feel the blood draining from his face. 'But they didn't look much like any pictures of raptors I've ever seen.'

'That's right,' Leah said, carefully cutting the huge piece of fruit into thick slices. 'Like I said, they've evolved – probably over millions of years. They're nothing like the fossil records in our world showed them. For one thing, they're warm-blooded, and for another, they are highly intelligent.'

'Evolved or not, why would you let raptors into your Reserve?' Callum asked, his voice thick with amazement. 'They're carnivorous. Deadly killers.'

'That they are,' Leah agreed, smiling. 'But you've got the wrong idea totally, Callum. We don't get to decide who lives here. The raptors do. *We're* the protected species in the Reserve.'

165

'What!'

Sam and Callum looked at one another in horror.

'Nipper and his friends saved you last night, didn't they? The raptors find us fascinating. They've been studying us for years now and tend to look out for new arrivals after storms.'

'Nipper?' Sam prompted.

'Well, that's what we call him,' Brad explained. 'Most humans can't pronounce his real name and I nicknamed him Nipper because of his age. He's the youngest of his group, yet he's become their leader.'

'You spoke with him,' Sam said, pointing at Brad with wide eyes as he started to piece everything together. 'All that clicking and stuff. That's how they talk, isn't it?'

'That's right. I can only communicate at a very elementary level, but I have picked up some of the basics.'

'Brad has always been good at picking up other languages,' Leah said, handing out bowls of sliced fruit. 'He's tried to teach me, but I'm useless at it.'

'Languages have never been my thing either,' Sam admitted. 'I prefer the sciences. I guess I take after my . . .' His eyes went wide. Suddenly, he began speaking urgently. 'There are others here – other humans in the Reserve, right?'

'About thirty at the last count,' Brad replied.

'And some of them have been here a long time?' Sam asked.

'Yes.' Brad and Leah glanced at one another. An unspoken question passed between them.

'Is there anyone here called Claire? Claire Cutler. She would be about forty years old. She would have come here about nine years ago.'

Sam felt Callum's eyes on him, but his focus was totally on the reactions of Brad and Leah. The couple looked at one another again. Both wore frowns. Sam's heart sank. He did not need to hear the answer to know what it would be. Leah was first to reply.

'I'm sorry, Sam,' she said. 'There's no one in the Reserve called Claire. If she came here, she's not here now.'

'That's not to say that she isn't here somewhere in this world,' Brad added quickly. 'The raptors have recognised that human knowledge of some areas of science is superior to theirs. I've heard there are a few humans who now work alongside raptors in some areas of scientific development.'

'She was a marine biologist,' Sam said, unable to keep the bitter disappointment from his voice.

'Then maybe she is one of those the raptors were interested in,' Leah suggested.

Sam recognised the false brightness in Leah's tone instantly. From the way she spoke, he could tell she felt it far more likely that his mother never made it to shore. For a brief moment he had felt there might be a silver lining to this nightmare, but the flash of hope died as quickly as it had ignited. It would have been amazing to find his mother after all this time, but he was very much a realist.

'No,' he replied, shaking his head. 'Don't worry. It was a ridiculous idea! My mother is dead. I've lived with that for the past nine years. It's just I thought . . . I hoped . . .'

He couldn't finish. Instead, he picked up a piece of fruit from his bowl and took a tentative bite. It was succulent and sweet, but unlike anything he had ever tasted before. It had the texture of a watermelon, but it had a far stronger, more distinct flavour. He wanted to say it was like mango, but it wasn't. Neither was it like a kiwi fruit, yet the flavour reminded him of that as well.

'Mmm! Delicious. What is this?' he asked, deflecting the subject towards less painful territory.

'Some of us call it a KFC fruit,' Brad said with a grin.

'KFC?' asked Sam. 'As in Kentucky Fried? But it doesn't taste anything like chicken.'

'No, we don't call it KFC fruit for the flavour,' he explained. 'It's because they're everywhere and nobody gives a damn if they're healthy or not 'cos they're finger-lickin' good.'

'This is all really hard to believe,' Callum said, changing the subject again. His expression was thoughtful as he remembered the strange creature that had looked at him from the sea. It seemed like a dream now, the product of his imagination and sickness. 'It all sounds so far-fetched. How far have you explored? Are you sure we're not in the middle of a secret genetic experiment? Or an elaborate hoax?'

'Oh, we're sure all right. It's real,' Leah insisted. 'I've visited some of the raptors' housing and seen how they live. Everything here is unlike anything I've ever seen before. Some of their technology is several steps beyond ours, yet some looks positively archaic.'

'Yes,' Brad agreed. 'Their nuclear technology, for example, is way beyond anything our scientists have developed.'

'The raptors use nuclear power?' Sam gasped. 'But the ones I saw seemed like savage beasts. They didn't even wear clothes!'

'Don't let their appearance fool you,' Leah said, shaking her head slowly. 'The raptors around here have no practical need for clothing so they don't wear it. Apparently, those who live in colder regions wear garments made of excellent insulating materials. Clothing is a poor indicator of intelligence though. According to Nipper, the raptors developed nuclear power centuries ago – long before humans had even started playing seriously with electricity.'

'Right!' Callum said, clearly unconvinced. 'You'll be telling me that the local tyrannosaurs have PlayStations next.'

'Thankfully, I don't think you need worry about meeting a T-rex,' Brad said seriously. 'I've not travelled extensively here, so I could be wrong, but as far as I can tell, tyrannosaurs were wiped out by the raptors several million years ago. They were probably considered too dangerous a rival. But trust me, Callum, even without the T-rex, this world has more than its share of dangers.'

CHAPTER THIRTEEN

Niamh sat up on the sunbed as she heard the sound of tyres crunching to a slow stop on the gravel drive. After a terrible night of tossing and turning, unable to sleep, she had come out to the pool early for a swim to clear her head. A glance at her watch confirmed it was just past eight. The warm caress of the morning sun was enough to make drying out a pleasure, though it was hard to imagine anyone calling at this time unless they had news of the boys.

Hidden from the arriving car by the hedge round the pool, Niamh was poised to get to her feet when she froze as she overheard the low voices.

'Got yer cuffs ready?'

'Yeah, I'm all set.'

'Let's go get him then.'

'D'ya think he'll come easy? The boss says he's up for multiple homicide.'

'I ain't gotta clue, Bud. Just be ready for anything, OK.'

Homicide? A shock ran through Niamh as she realised what was happening. The police were here to arrest her father. She wanted to stand up and tell them her father was no murderer, but instinct stopped her. Why should the police listen to her? They wouldn't.

What should she do? They were already approaching the front door. Staying low, she nipped round the pool and over to the furthest patio door. Praying that the door would not make a noise, she slid it open just far enough to slip inside. Amazingly, she made it without being seen just as the men thumped on the front door. Although Niamh knew they were going to knock, the heavy thumping sound still made her jump.

On silent feet she raced across the living area to her father's bedroom door. It opened as she approached and Matthew Cutler emerged, drawing a dressing gown round his body. Niamh put a finger to her lips as she approached and, grabbing him round the waist, pulled him back through the door into his room.

'What's . . .'

'Shhh!' she hushed, clamping a hand over his mouth. 'It's the police. They've come to arrest you. We've got to get out of here. They think you murdered the boys.'

'What?' her father exclaimed in a low voice, the colour draining from his face. 'Have they found bodies?'

'They didn't say,' she said, her voice urgent. 'But they can't have found Sam's. He's alive. I know it.'

'Well, they've probably just come to get more information. Talk of murder is just nonsense! What made you think that?'

'I overheard them talking as they got out of the car, Dad,' she insisted. 'If you answer the door, they will take you away. Don't go. Please, Dad!'

'Don't be so silly, Niamh,' he sighed. There was a second set of loud knocks. They sounded more insistent this time. 'You don't think I've done anything to the boys, do you?'

'No! Of course not! I know you haven't.'

'Then I'm going to answer the door. You must have misheard them. And even if you didn't, I've got nothing to hide. You know that.'

'But how can we search for the boys if you're locked up in jail?' she asked, desperate now. 'Please, Dad. I'm begging you. Don't go.'

Her father removed her hands from his arms and placed them gently by her sides. Giving her a final warning look, he reopened the door and left the bedroom.

'One moment,' he called out. 'I'm coming.'

'Damn it!' Niamh muttered under her breath. 'What am I supposed to do now?' Her legs felt suddenly weak. She sunk down onto the edge of the bed, her mind racing. The police would take her father, but what then? Would they take her too? They would have to, she realised. She was a minor. She would not be allowed to stay here alone. But then all hope of finding the boys would die.

The coastguard wouldn't find the boys. Niamh didn't know how she knew this, but she *knew*. Could she find them? She wasn't sure. But, given her strange bond with him, she felt she had a better chance of finding Sam than anyone else.

Run! she told herself. *It's your only option.*

Her decision was spontaneous, but she could hardly run away wearing nothing more than a bikini. Without further thought, Niamh slipped back out of her father's bedroom and into her own. She heard him open the front door even as she began to pull on the first pair of shorts that came to hand.

'Matthew Cutler?'

'That's right, officer. What can I do for you?'

Niamh rifled through her bedside drawer and grabbed her purse.

'Sir, you are under arrest. Please keep your hands where I can see them. My partner here's gonna cuff you and take you out to the car where he'll read you your rights.'

'This is ridiculous! What am I being arrested for? I haven't done anything wrong.'

'Thank you for your cooperation, sir. Now if you'll come with us and get into the car, I'll secure the house and we can get to the station.'

'But I'm not even dressed! Can I just put some clothes on? It'll only take a minute. I also need to tell my daughter what's happening.'

Niamh grabbed a T-shirt and her sunglasses. She was out of time.

'Daughter? Is your daughter here in the house?' she heard. That was it. She sprinted out of her room and across the living area towards the slightly open door to the pool area.

'We'd better take her along too. Bud, you go get the girl and some clothes for Mr Cutler. Sir, you come with me . . .'

Niamh didn't wait to hear any more. She squeezed out through the door.

'Hey, you girl! Stop!' The policeman's voice held a note of surprise tinged with anger as he spotted her making her escape.

She was out and running. There was a curse. She

heard the faint rumble of the door as it was yanked open, but she was already around the end of the building and sprinting across the lawn to the front fence. In an instant, she was up and over it, dropping down on to the road behind. She landed awkwardly and fell.

'Stop! Police!' the man yelled again.

Niamh did not hesitate. She scrambled to her feet, turned left along the road away from the driveway and set off again, sprinting as fast as her legs would carry her. Praying that the short cut over the fence would give her a good lead, she angled right, racing across the road and along a path into the trees on the far side. The houses here were spaced at irregular intervals. No two residences looked the same along this part of Summerland Key and she could not run far without running out of land. She turned left along the path that ran behind the houses. What she needed was a place to hide. With only one person chasing, she wouldn't need to evade him for long to make him give up. He would return with others of course, but if she acted quickly, there was a chance she could slip away before the police could organise a proper search party.

The path was narrow. As long as she stayed on it, she was making it easy for the man to follow. Her breath rasped loud in her ears, as she pushed herself to keep running as fast as she could. Another garden appeared ahead and to the left. In a split-second decision, Niamh changed direction and cut through a gap in the bushes. As she approached the wooden fence surrounding the garden, Niamh tried to imagine it as a high hurdle like the ones on the sports track at her school. Too late, she realised that the fence was a bit higher than the training hurdles she was used to. Committed by her momentum, Niamh focused all her energy into her final bounding paces and launched herself over the fence with a mighty leap.

Heart racing, the world seemed to momentarily drop into slow motion as her front foot cleared the top of the fence and she sailed into the air. A burning sensation ignited along her right shin in mid flight. As she landed and the world exploded back into normal speed, she realised that her trailing leg must have scraped the fence top. It tingled as she landed, but she didn't look down.

Her panting breath tore at her throat as she reached the corner of the house and rounded it. Pressing herself flat against the wall, she paused. The metallic tang of blood at the back of her mouth was unmistakable as she fought to regain control of her lungs. A tickling trickle tracked, stop-start, down her right leg. She glanced down. A long graze was speckled with welling spots of red and a single scarlet line of blood ran down her shin. It didn't look bad, but the gently burning heat she had felt when hurdling the fence was now resolving into a line of fiery pain.

Niamh closed her eyes and leaned her head back against the wooden wall of the house for a second. She couldn't stay here. It was too open. It would be better to double back across the road. If she could turn left again and loop back to the Mitchells', Moira might hide her. Could she trust Moira that much? No. Moira might see it as her duty to hand Niamh over to the police. But there was their garden shed . . .

'There you are!' the policeman exclaimed from the other side of the fence at the end of the garden.

Fear erupted inside her again.

'No! Don't run! I don't want to hurt you.'

But Niamh did not hesitate. She turned and ran again, along the side of the house and out into the front garden area. The policeman cursed and began struggling over the fence. A dog began to bark as Niamh entered the front garden. She registered the large white shape emerging from its kennel on an intercept course and swerved to avoid it. The dog reached the end of its chain and stopped abruptly, but continued protesting her presence loudly as she sprinted across the street and into the garden opposite.

Ducking and weaving through the shrubs and trees, Niamh looped around the house, through the back garden and out on to the path along the edge of the canal, turning left again towards home. Stretching out her strides, she accelerated still further in an effort to maximise her advantage. A gap in the trees yawned to her left and she ducked through it into yet another garden.

There were still two more houses before the Mitchells'. Would it be better to hide now or to keep running? She didn't know how much of a lead she had. No more than a few seconds at best. A fire raged in her lungs, and her throat felt hot and dry. She looked around frantically and then inspiration struck.

Seconds later, the policeman came running along the path. His footfalls sounded heavy and his breathing laboured. As he approached, he slowed. Niamh lay absolutely still, holding her breath as the man came closer and closer.

Keep going! Don't stop! she prayed silently. She closed her eyes, not daring to look.

His footsteps stuttered to a stop and Niamh could tell that he was looking and listening for clues as to which way she had turned.

'Damn you, girl!' he panted. 'It's too early for this! Where've you gone now?'

Niamh cracked her eyes open and it felt as though someone had reached into her chest, grabbed her heart in his hand and squeezed it hard. The man was right below her. There hadn't been time to climb very high into the tree, so she had concentrated on getting above a runner's natural line of sight and staying as still as possible to avoid attracting attention. Runners naturally spend much of their time looking at the ground ahead to avoid tripping. He had no reason to look up.

Please don't look up! There's nothing here! Move on, she thought, willing the man away with every fibre of her body.

He didn't look up, but neither did he move. He just stood there looking first one way and then the other.

'GIRL!' he called in a loud voice, the sudden increase in volume causing her to tense up. 'If you can hear me, please listen. I just wanna take you to the Sheriff's Office to keep you safe. We're gonna ask your pa some questions, but you're not in any trouble, I promise you. Please, come on in with me now, and stop messin' around, OK?'

Niamh could feel sweat trickling down the middle of her back. Beads were also beginning to track down her forehead and she felt one slip between her eyebrows and make a run down her nose. It reached the end and began to form a drip. Her eyes crossed as she tried to focus on the end of her nose. The droplet dangled. The sensation as it grew was agonising. She desperately wanted to jut her lower lip out and blow it clear, but feared to make even the faintest of whisper sounds. The man was directly below. He would hear for sure.

More drips were forming on her hands, but she did not dare move. Her chest ached with the agony of controlling her breathing. The man turned this way and that as he dithered over which way to go, but still he didn't move away.

Please go. Please! she thought.

The droplet at the end of her nose extended and fell. Her eyes widened as she watched it go. By some miraculous chance, the man chose that moment to take a half-step, shifting just far enough for the drop to miss his head and hit a fold on the back of his shirt. For a moment Niamh thought he must surely have felt it, but he didn't. Everything blurred as a wave of relief left her feeling faint. Another drip was already forming at the end of her nose and he had shifted his weight back again.

'Hey, Bud?' The distant shout of the policeman's partner drifted through the trees. 'You got her yet?'

'NOPE,' he yelled back. 'I THINK SHE'S GONE TO GROUND.'

'Well, leave her. She won't go far. Let's take the father in and we'll come back for the girl later.'

'OK, I'LL BE RIGHT THERE.'

Don't look up! Please, don't look up! Niamh prayed fervently. *Go! Go on. Listen to your partner . . . go! What are you waiting for?*

The man didn't move. He appeared to be listening and thinking. The second drop at the end of her nose began to stretch, preparing to fall.

For Pete's sake, GO! she willed.

With a final tickling wobble, the droplet of sweat detached and Niamh knew instantly that this one would not miss.

CHAPTER FOURTEEN

With a final blast of ferocious rain at about midday, the storm clouds relented, giving way to washed blue skies and puffy, white fair-weather cloud. A stiff breeze continued to blow, but the bright sun's determined glare was so fierce that the boys welcomed the presence of the wind as they set out to see what had become of the boat.

'You sure you don't want me to come?' Brad asked from the doorway.

'You're sure the raptors won't hurt us if we go without you?' Sam asked.

'You're unlikely to see any, but if you do, they'll leave you well alone as long as you stay within the boundaries of the Reserve.'

'What about other dangerous creatures? Are there any we should know about?' Sam asked, starting to think that going out alone might not be the best idea.

Brad thought for a moment. 'Nothing that should trouble you at this time of day, so long as you stick to the beach,' he said. 'The raptors keep the jungle around here pretty clear of predators, but every now and then one finds its way in, so it's best to be on the safe side and stay in the open.'

'In that case we should be fine, thanks,' Sam told him. 'We're just going to walk along the beach and back to see if the boat survived the storm and take a look around. I'm not sure exactly how far Nipper carried us last night, but it can't have been more than a couple of miles at the most.'

'Well, OK then. If you're sure,' Brad said. 'I don't know what you think you're going to do with the boat if you find it, but if you wanna go try, then I'm not goin' to stop you. It might be further than you think, remember. The raptors can run seriously fast. Make sure you're back by nightfall. Even in the Reserve it's not a good idea to wander around after dark. Oh, and if you come across a man on the beach fishing, that will be Bill. If you see him, say hello and give him my regards.'

'We will,' Sam assured him, still finding it bizarre that a small group of humans had made this world their home.

'Happy hunting then.'

Sam led the way through the trees to the beach. He had the distinct impression that Brad and Leah thought the trip was a waste of time, but with luck, the boat would be salvageable, and he and Callum could use it to find a way home. Besides, even if the boat was no longer seaworthy, there were lots of things around Brad and Leah's house that had clearly been salvaged from various wrecks. Just recovering the fishing tackle would make it a worthwhile trip. Having a way of catching food in this strange world had to be a good thing.

Sam was on edge as they followed the path to the beach. He kept one hand on the hilt of the knife he now wore on his left hip until they were out on the open sand. The rocky outcrop that Nipper had scaled while carrying them the previous night proved a tricky climb. Although the sun was rapidly drying the surfaces, many rocks were still slick with slippery green weed and treacherous footing was not the only danger. Molluscs with razor-sharp shells waited patiently on open rock surfaces, poised to slice exposed skin at the slightest contact, and rubbery curtains of seaweed hid thousands more. Every crevice appeared to hold a pool, many teeming with creatures both familiar and strange.

Where Sam might have spent hours nosing through the pools collecting shrimp, crabs and little fish in a bucket when he was younger, this was nothing like his visits to the rock pools of Amroth and Saundersfoot in Wales. His curiosity was tinged with wariness. If Brad and Leah were telling the truth, this was not his world and there was no telling what dangers these pools might harbour. Callum showed no such caution as he scrambled up the rocks to the top. He was a surprisingly agile climber.

'Hey! Wait up, Cal!' Sam called, as his friend vanished from his view over the top lip. 'Don't get too far ahead.'

'What's the matter, Sam? Can't hack the pace?' Callum taunted, looking down from above.

Sam had to smile as Callum enjoyed his rare moment of triumph.

'It's not a race, Cal,' he said casually. 'If it was, trust me, I'd have whupped you.'

'Oh, yeah? And my Aunt Aggie drives a McLaren F1!'

'Did you never wonder why she has her hair cut short?'

'What?' Callum asked, reaching down and giving Sam a hand up to the final tier of rock.

'Your Aunt Aggie – has her hair cut short, doesn't she?'

'Well, yes actually. But you haven't met my . . .'

'It's cut short to make the racing helmet more comfortable,' Sam interrupted, keeping his face straight.

Callum looked at him for a moment and then they both erupted into fits of laughter.

'The only racing my Aunt Aggie's likely to do is on a broomstick,' Callum said, shaking his head. 'Harry Potter has nothing on her!'

They stood on the top of the promontory for a moment, gazing along the broad crescent of sand that stretched ahead. The tide was further out than it had been last night, but there was no sign of the boat.

'We must have beached it in the next cove,' Sam observed, though looking at how far it was to the headland at the far end of the beach, he was not so sure. 'Come on. Let's climb down and get going.'

Getting down was more treacherous than climbing up, but both boys managed the descent without injury and within a few minutes they were hiking along the sand at a fast pace. The surf was still pounding the beach with a constant booming roar that filled their ears and quelled their conversation. Where the waves had been an ominous grey the previous evening, now they were an idyllic blue-green, tipped with pure white foam that fizzed as it rushed towards the sand.

Sam scanned the sand for any sign of footprints, but the tide had clearly been in and washed all evidence of the raptors' presence away overnight. The sand was smooth and soft underfoot. To begin with, this was pleasant, but the boys soon felt their legs aching as the extra effort required to walk began to take its toll. They stayed well away from the tree line, but even above the constant roar of the surf, strange cries could sometimes be heard coming from the jungle. Sam kept a nervous eye on the trees for any signs of the huge creature that had made its charging run the previous evening, but there were none.

'Hey, look at that!' Callum exclaimed as they reached the very heart of the bay. He pointed at the surf and ran off at a sprint towards the water.

Sam followed. It took a few seconds for him to realise what Callum was so excited about. The shallows were literally boiling with fish: not small fry, but a mass of medium- and large-sized fish thrashing around, apparently throwing themselves at the beach. Sam had never seen anything like it before.

'Come on! There's so many, we should be able to grab them with our hands,' Callum yelled. 'I'm sure Brad and Leah would appreciate an easy meal.'

'I'm not sure, Cal,' Sam replied, stopping short of the water. 'I've never seen fish behave like that before.'

Callum ran on into the shallows, heedless of the spray he was kicking up. Suddenly, he turned back towards Sam, plunged his hands into the water and attempted to scoop a fish into the air. His first effort failed as the fish he tried to lift slipped from his fingers and barely broke the surface, but on his second attempt Callum succeeded in sending a good-sized fish sailing through the air towards Sam. It landed with a wet slap and instantly began to flap and flip around on the sand.

Drawing his knife, Sam reversed the blade and crouched down with the intention of clubbing the fish on the head with the handle. As he did so, a shadow in the surf caught his eye and his heart leapt. A dark shape was racing along the wave and into the shallows faster than Sam would have believed possible.

'CALLUM! LOOK OUT!'

Callum looked up and then around at the sea. For an instant, he couldn't see what Sam was yelling for, but then a monstrous head erupted through the waves and he screamed in terror. It was a thing of nightmares and it was coming straight for him at speed. His first fleeting impression before he ran was of a huge gaping maw filled with a mass of teeth, bulging green eyes and a long, sinuous black body. Then he was flying from the water, bounding through the shallows with long, high steps.

'Holy crap!' he shouted as he reached Sam's side, breathless and eyes wide with shock. He turned and looked in horror as the enormous eel-like creature thrashed and writhed through the shallows eating fish after fish. 'What the hell is that?'

'Who knows?' Sam replied. 'But I've gone right off the idea of an afternoon swim.'

'It's got to be at least ten metres long!' Callum panted.

'And it's not alone,' Sam observed.

Three more of the monsters appeared, angling through the surf at high speed. They also ploughed into the stranded shoal of fish and began to feed.

'I'm glad I didn't know about those things when we were on the boat yesterday. They're even scarier than that Nessie creature that came and took a look at us. I'd have been bricking myself if I'd realised there were a whole bunch of monsters hiding beneath the waves.'

'Um, Cal,' Sam said, backing slowly away from the sea.

'Yes?'

'Have you ever seen a conger eel move on sand?'

190

'No, why?'

'Trust me, they move pretty quick and I think that big fella over there fancies more than just fish for lunch. RUN!'

Callum did not need telling twice. The creature's body hissed through the shallows and across the sand as it began to chase them up the beach. Sam ran as fast as he could, a surge of adrenalin racing through him as he tore up the beach. He could hear Callum just behind him. His friend was not a natural runner, but it appeared that he could run faster than most when motivated.

Sam glanced over his shoulder. The beast had not given up. Its green eyes held a deadly focus and it was slithering across the sand at frightening speed. By chance, in that instant of looking back, Sam's right foot landed in a particularly soft patch of sand. Before he could react his ankle turned and he was down. He cursed as he hit the sand and rolled to a stop. Sam flinched as Callum hurdled him and kept running.

The creature was closing fast, its mouth opening wide in preparation to strike. In a flash, Sam had scrambled to his feet. He suddenly became aware of the survival knife that he was gripping hard in his right hand, but one more look at the creature was enough to dispel any thought of heroics. There was no hope of stopping something that size with a knife.

He turned and ran again with the creature literally snapping at his heels. His right ankle felt as though it was on fire as he ran, but Sam closed his mind to the pain and he concentrated on trying to catch up with Callum.

He dared not look back again until he was nearly at the trees. Callum had stopped there. He was red-faced, panting and speechless, but the fact that he had stopped told Sam what he needed to know. The creature had given up the chase. Putting his hands on his knees, he turned and spat, raising his eyes to look at the retreating monster. The horror from the sea had turned back only when it reached the flotsam line where the sand turned from wet and relatively hard to the dry, fine and soft stuff at the top of the beach.

'That's one ... for the blog,' Callum gasped. 'Shame I didn't have ... my camera with me. That beastie had ... a wicked smile.'

Sam nearly choked as he laughed and panted simultaneously. He put a hand on his friend's shoulder and shook his head, unable to speak.

They both watched as the monster snaked its way back down to the water and slipped into the surf. By the time it finally disappeared, Sam had recovered his breath.

'Come on,' he urged. 'Let's get away from here. I don't think it will come back, but I'd rather not wait around to find out. I can't help thinking that I know now why we haven't seen any sign of the guy Brad mentioned.'

'You think he's been . . .'

'Either that or he read the signs and made himself scarce,' Sam suggested. 'Who knows?'

The two boys set out along the beach again, this time staying just below the high tide line. Callum was very quiet. Sam got the impression his friend had not really believed all the stuff about evolved dinosaurs and parallel worlds, but then he hadn't seen the raptors and heard the roar of whatever had been in the trees last night. Given the number of nervous looks he was affording the nearby jungle, Sam could see he believed it now.

The sand was softer here than it was near the water, but they laboured on in unspoken agreement. This line kept them a comfortable distance from the monsters in the surf, while also affording a margin from the jungle, which suddenly looked all the more menacing.

It took about another half-hour to reach the headland, by which time it had become obvious that the tide was on its way in. As they rounded the end of the bay and looked along the next, Sam was disappointed to see no obvious sign of the boat.

'Look, Sam!' Callum exclaimed suddenly, pointing. 'Up there by the trees. Is that the boat? I think it is!'

The two boys began to run, the soft sand making it difficult to get up any speed. As they approached, they slowed further as they realised the prow of the boat had been dragged under the trees. It was way up above the flotsam line and a trail through the sand showed clearly where it had been dragged up the final part of the beach to the edge of the trees. It would take a dozen strong men, or more, to drag a ten-metre boat that far up the beach. Whoever, or *whatever*, had done this would have to be immensely strong.

'The engines have gone,' Sam noted, stopping a dozen paces short of the boat.

'Maybe whoever dragged it up here took them off to reduce the weight,' Callum suggested.

'I don't know,' Sam said softly as he began to circle the back of the boat in a wide arc, taking care to keep his distance. 'I don't see them anywhere on the beach. No. Something tells me that's not it.'

With muscles tensed, ready to run at the first sign of danger, step by careful step Sam moved in closer. Callum held back, watching with breathless anticipation. The boat was resting at an angle, the deck tipped away from them. Closer and closer he crept to the stern. He reached it and looked in from where the engines should have been.

'What the . . .?'

There was a loud scream from above his head and Sam dived away from the boat, rolling like an acrobat across the sand and up onto his feet. Heart racing and poised to run again, Sam was embarrassed to witness a whirr of wings and a flash of colour through the trees as a startled parakeet beat a hasty retreat.

Callum laughed, though he looked as nervous as Sam felt. 'Oh, my blog entry for today just keeps getting better and better,' he said. 'First the sea monsters and now seeing Sam Cutler scared by a parrot! All I need is a computer to write it on.'

'Well, you're not going to find one in the boat,' Sam said, his shoulders relaxing as he recovered from the fright. His voice was serious now – serious laced with a touch of anger. 'In fact, you're not going to find anything at all in it. It's been gutted.'

'Gutted?'

'Absolutely stripped clean. Look's like there's nothing left but a fibreglass shell. This boat isn't going to get us home any time soon.'

CHAPTER FIFTEEN

Even as Niamh watched the droplet of sweat plummet towards the policeman, his weight shifted forward again. Although he did not move quickly enough for the drop to miss, instead of impacting his head square on, it struck the hair at the back of his head and ran straight down to end as a tiny trickle at the back of his neck. The man's right hand automatically rose and reached around to smooth the back of his hair.

It's over, Niamh thought, closing her eyes again and waiting for the order to climb down. To her amazement, it didn't come. She opened her eyes again. The man had failed to look up and was moving away, stepping lightly in an obvious effort to conceal his movement. It looked as though he was hoping to catch Niamh out with his stealth. Perhaps he was thinking that if he moved more slowly than she expected, Niamh would make another move and betray herself.

A warm feeling of relief flooded through her body as she realised she was not going to get caught, but the sense of reprieve was short-lived. To her dismay, the initial rush of warmth did not disperse as she expected. Instead, it lingered, focusing into a burning sensation in her bladder as she continued to stay as still as she could. Her relief at evading the policeman, combined with the physical pressure from the branch against her belly, made the urge grow with unnatural speed into an intense need. She could not stay here long.

Every second stretched as Niamh's discomfort intensified over the following few minutes. Ideally, she would have waited much longer before moving, but once she had started thinking about needing to go to the toilet, it became impossible to think about anything else. She couldn't hear the policeman any more, but neither had she heard the car leaving. Would she hear it from here? Probably not, she decided. Had she waited long enough? It was impossible to tell, but she didn't feel she could stay even a moment longer.

Tipping her body off the branch, she hung for a moment by her fingertips before dropping lightly to the ground. For a moment, she remained in a crouched position, one knee on the floor and senses alert for any sign that she might have been detected. The change of position had relieved the immediate pressure, but the desire had not gone away. Did she dare go home? There was a spare key hidden at the back of the house. The drive to the Sheriff's Office building at Key West would take at least fifteen to twenty minutes. By the time they got there, booked in her father, gathered a search party and returned, Niamh estimated it would be at least an hour before they came in force to search for her. Even so, going to the house seemed risky.

'I need a way to get off Summerland Key – and fast,' she breathed. *But I'm not going anywhere until I've been to the loo*, she added in her mind.

Moving silently, she flitted from bush to tree to bush along the line of the canal until she approached the Mitchells' house. There was no sign of the policeman anywhere. From her concealed vantage point near the Mitchell's mooring, Niamh could see Moira moving around her kitchen, presumably making breakfast. On seeing her, thoughts of hiding in the shed vanished. With one final look around, Niamh raced up to the window and tapped urgently on it with her fingernails.

Moira looked around in surprise, but her expression turned immediately to a smile as she recognised Niamh. First she waved and then crossed the living area to the patio door to unlock it.

'Mornin', honey,' she said. 'Any news of the boys?'

Niamh shook her head. 'No news yet,' she said.

'Really?' Moira said, sounding genuinely worried for the first time. 'I'd have thought they'd turn up by now. You been walkin' the canal? Come in, come in! Don't stand out there like a stranger.'

'Had to stretch my legs.'

Moira nodded. 'Well, I'm just heatin' up some waffles for breakfast. Mitch is just gettin' dressed. He'll be right through. Would you like to join us?'

'That would be wonderful, Moira. Thanks,' Niamh replied. 'But can I pay a quick visit to your rest room first?'

'Sure. Go right ahead. You know where it is. Oh, that's a nasty scrape! How did you get that?'

Niamh looked down at her leg to where Moira was pointing. She had been so focused on getting away from the policeman that she had completely forgotten the graze she had got from hurdling the fence earlier.

'I tripped and scraped it down on the path,' she said quickly. 'Don't worry. It doesn't hurt much. I'll clean it up.'

'You do that, honey,' Moira agreed. 'And I'll have some antiseptic cream ready for you when you come back out.'

Niamh nipped across the living area to the far door and out into the hallway.

'So has Matt gone out and left you alone already?' Moira called after her.

'Pretty much,' she called back. 'I don't think he's going to be back for a while. He's gone to the Sheriff's Office in Key West.' Niamh hated lying, but this was close enough to the truth that she did not feel too uncomfortable.

'So are they searchin' in force yet?'

'Oh, yes!' Niamh called back, thinking of the charges that had been made against her father. 'I'm pretty certain everyone is out looking for the boys now.'

'Well, that's somethin' then. Don't worry. They'll turn up, honey. You'll see.'

By the time Niamh returned to the kitchen, an idea had begun to form in her mind. Could she fool Mitch and Moira for long enough to make it work? Her heart began to race just thinking about it.

'What do you like on your waffles, honey? I've got strawberry jelly, maple syrup, peanut butter . . .'

'Maple syrup would be lovely, thanks,' Niamh said quickly. 'Good morning, sir,' she added as Mitch entered through the far door.

'Mornin' Niamh,' he replied. 'And please – I'm no "sir" these days. I get all twitchy if folk call me anythin' but Mitch. Gets me thinkin' I forgot to retire.'

Niamh laughed nervously. 'I can see how that might be disturbing,' she said. 'Um, Mitch, would you be able to go out and search for the boys again today? My dad and I would really appreciate it.'

'So they didn't come back last night then,' he said, looking worried. 'Of course, I'll be happy to go out again. Did Matt say where he'd like me to go lookin'?'

'No, he shot off to the Sheriff's Office in a bit of a hurry this morning, so I was hoping that I might be able to come with you today. I told Dad that I'd be coming over here to ask.'

Mitch looked across at his wife, who nodded.

'I don't see why not. The forecast is pretty good. We should be able to cover a lot of water. Did you bring the glasses with you?'

Niamh's heart dropped into her stomach and she knew her face must be reflecting her internal reaction as she struggled for an excuse not to go back to the house. 'I think I left the binoculars you gave me in Dad's car,' she groaned.

'Don't worry, Niamh,' Mitch assured her quickly, holding up a hand to stop any attempt at an apology.

'I've got another set on the boat. We'll just grab a bite and then we'll get right on out there.'

'Thanks.'

Breakfast with the Mitchells proved a severe test of nerves. Moira insisted on smothering her graze in antiseptic and made a big fuss over her as she did so. The cream stung, but not too badly. Niamh then struggled to eat her waffles, spending the entire time fighting an inner battle to keep from looking at her watch every thirty seconds. The maple syrup tasted sickly sweet, but she forced it down. Once she got away from Summerland there was no telling when she might get hot food again.

As she ate, she tried to second-guess what the police might do next. Would they radio ahead and call for a search team to come out? If so, there could be patrol cars arriving within just a few minutes.

'All right then, Niamh,' Mitch announced suddenly, making her jump. 'I can see you're itchin' to get goin', so let's go down and fire her up, shall we?'

'Great!' she replied, leaping to her feet. 'Sorry for all the trouble.'

'It's no trouble,' he assured her. 'I'd have only been out fishin' or playin' golf. I'm sure the fish'll wait, and the real golfers'll probably thank you for keepin' me away. I don't play well and I think I irritate 'em with my attempts at hackin' round the course.'

'If you hold fire for two minutes, honey, I'll put together a pack up, so you've got some food with you,' Moira offered.

'That'd be great, dear,' Mitch said, giving his wife a peck on the lips as he headed for the door. 'I'll just go and get the boat ready. I'll be back for it in a couple of minutes.'

Niamh could not help taking a good look round as they left the house. To her relief, there was no one else about and Mitch didn't seem to notice her furtive glances.

The Mitchells' boat was a beauty. It was slightly bigger than her dad's and it boasted a proper cabin below the deck, complete with a bed, a tiny fridge and some storage space. The name emblazoned along the stern read *Aloan Again*. She smiled. It was very in keeping with Mitch's sense of humour.

'Hop on in,' he said, extending a hand to help her down.

Niamh did as she was told and watched intently as Mitch went round the boat, checking the engines, the cupboards, the fenders and the stowage bins. He worked methodically, appearing to check that every last thing was where it should be. *It must be his military training*, she thought. *Dad never checked half the things that Mitch is looking at.*

Her chance came sooner than she expected.

Mitch started the twin engines, switched on the radio, did a couple of further checks and then leapt up onto the bank, leaving the boat running at idle.

'Back in a sec,' he said. 'Just goin' to get our lunch from Moira and we'll head on out.'

'No problem!' Niamh replied, heart pounding hard again. Could she do this? Was there enough time?

She stood up and watched Mitch cross the patio to the door. As he entered, she leapt up on the bank and ran to the front mooring rope. It was looped loosely over the concrete mooring post. She unhooked it, threw the rope onto the front of the boat and ran to the one at the stern. This one was similarly secured.

'Hey! What are you doin', Niamh?' Mitch called from the doorway. 'Don't release the ropes, honey!'

Even at idle, the boat was pulling against the final mooring rope. Niamh hauled on the rope, pulling the boat back to gain the slack she needed and then, carrying the end of the rope with her, she leapt down into the boat.

'NIAMH!'

Mitch's voice had turned angry now as he realised that she knew exactly what she was doing. She grabbed the wheel with her right hand and the throttle with her left. A single glance was enough to realise that Mitch was sprinting towards her, face like thunder. There was no decision left to make. She was committed.

'NO, NIAMH, DON'T!'

He was too late. Niamh pushed the throttle straight to half open and turned the wheel to the right. The boat responded instantly, surging away from the mooring with a guttural roar of power. Having pulled far enough from the bank to ensure there was no way Mitch could jump aboard, Niamh cut the throttle to idle again and looked over her shoulder to where he had skidded to a halt at the water's edge.

'Sorry, Mr Mitchell,' she called. 'I need to borrow your boat for a while. I haven't got time to stop and explain, but I'll bring it back as soon as I can, I promise.'

'Don't be a fool, Niamh,' he shouted back, clearly trying hard to control his anger. 'This is stealin'. Think what you're doin'. You don't want to be gettin' lost like your brother. Don't make me call the Sheriff's Office. Get back over here and we'll go out lookin' for the boys together like I promised.'

'It's not that easy, sir,' she replied. 'There have been . . . complications. Sorry, but I've got to go now. Please don't think too badly of me.'

Turning away, she pushed the throttle forward as far as she dared. The engine roared, the prow rising as the boat surged forward. There was no time to worry about speed limits. She wanted to get as far from Summerland Key as she could before the police returned. Niamh had never driven a boat before, though she had seen her father and brother do it on lots of occasions. It did not seem hard.

Moira added her voice to Mitch's, but Niamh closed her mind to both of them and concentrated instead on the waterway ahead. She could see the end of the canal and the open water beyond. She had never really paid much attention to what the boys had been doing when she had gone out with them on her dad's boat. Where should she look first? Where *could* she go that the police would not find her?

As she sped from the canal into the shallow open water beyond, the realisation of what she had done began to sink in. A cold shiver ran down her spine. She had stolen a boat – and not just some little rowing boat, but an expensive cabin cruiser! There was no escaping the scale of it. Stealing something like this was a serious crime.

Niamh was awash with feelings of guilt, yet she was also inexplicably excited. She had stolen the Mitchells' boat! The more times she said it to herself, the less real it seemed. She tried to imagine what Beth would say when she heard.

'I haven't stolen the boat,' she corrected herself aloud. 'I've just borrowed it. I'll take it back just as soon as I find the boys.'

She closed her eyes and tried to picture her brother. It was not as easy as it had been before he and Callum had disappeared. Although she still felt the gaping hole inside her where a part of her brother had apparently resided, the vague wisp of him still haunted the darkness. It was not much, but Niamh felt sure Sam was still alive. Could she use that wisp like a compass to find him? She didn't see how, but given time she might be able to figure it out.

Time. It was all about having enough time. How much did she have? It was hard to tell. The search effort for the boys would be increased this morning. Now it would be extended to include her. Had she done the right thing by running? If she had gone with the police, she could have explained how going out on the boat had been the boys' idea and nothing to do with her father. Maybe they would have released him and they could have continued the search together. But her dad had said he'd been out flying in the seaplane with Geoff that morning, so he would be able to provide a credible alibi and clear his name easily without her help. Had running made things worse? Perhaps she should turn back now and apologise to Mitch . . .

Explaining. Apologising. The police. All would eat precious time. No. Her mind was made up. She would follow her instinct and try to use the faint link she could feel with her brother. She might be Sam's only hope. Opening the throttle even more, Niamh turned the boat in a gentle arc until she was driving directly out to sea.

There was no time for regrets now. Her focus had to be on finding the boys. If she could do that, then everything could return to normal. They were out there somewhere. She was certain of that much. Narrowing her eyes against the spray, Niamh set her mind to the task ahead.

CHAPTER SIXTEEN

'Damn it!' Sam exclaimed, as he clambered over the remains of his father's boat. 'What the hell are we going to do now?'

'Well, I'm not going to try to swim out into the ocean, that's for sure,' Callum said, throwing another nervous glance at the approaching tide.

'I think it's safe to say that's not an option,' Sam agreed, thinking hard. He scratched at his chin for a moment. 'Dad will have everyone looking for us by now, but unless they stumble through into this world the same way we did, then there's no way they're going to find us. I think it's going to be down to us to get back.'

'Leah and Brad said that the raptors were technologically advanced,' Callum recalled. 'Maybe they've got their own type of boats as well. It's got to be worth asking.'

'You're right,' Sam said, brightening slightly. 'And if they won't take us out in one, or let us go alone, then we'll just have to work out a way of stealing one.'

Callum nodded and looked up at him with a serious expression. 'Yeah, we'll find a way home somehow. We have to. My dad's booked me a quad-biking day for just after we're due back in England. I'm not going to miss that!'

Sam smiled. His friend was irrepressible. 'Perish the thought!' he said. 'Come on. I think we'd better head back. Oh, by the way I did find one thing. Here, catch!' He tossed his one find down to his friend. It was the conch shell Callum had bought for his mother.

'Thanks! Not sure what I'm going to do with this now.'

'Keep it,' Sam said. 'You can give it to your mum before you go quad biking.'

Sam jumped back down from the stern and let out a heavy sigh.

'Don't worry, mate,' Callum said, patting Sam on the shoulder. 'If there's a way back, we'll find it. Brad and Leah will help. Come on. Let's go and tell them what we found. Maybe they'll be able to tell us where we can find another boat, or at least who has stripped this one so thoroughly and why.'

Sam nodded, but didn't answer.

The two boys trudged through the soft sand as they made their way around the headland. Sam was aware of Callum's vigilance at watching the sea for signs of the eel-like monsters. He appeared paranoid that they were lurking in the surf and watching for a chance to strike again. Sam stared at the sand in front of his feet, lost in thought. Everything about this place felt wrong.

Questions whirled through his mind. Why had they crossed between worlds and how? Was it possible to go back or were they stuck here forever? Brad and Leah seemed content to live under the protection of Nipper and his friends, but why? Why weren't *they* trying to get home? They said others lived here too, but where? How big was this so-called 'Reserve' and what was the world like beyond its borders?

A sudden trumpeting cry cut through his thoughts and he froze. Both boys turned as one to focus on the nearby trees. Whatever was making the noise sounded close. There was a brief pause and then something began to move. Sam was immediately reminded of the previous evening. *Thump, thump, thump.* The earth-shaking footsteps were accompanied by the sounds of cracking wood and the swish of branches being brushed aside and released.

Whatever it was, the creature was coming towards them.

Sam's ankle was still sore from twisting it during his flight from the sea creature earlier. He did not fancy running on it again, but he gritted his teeth in readiness. *Thump, thump, thump.* It was getting closer. Suddenly, a familiar roar sounded from among the nearby trees, causing Sam's heart to leap in his chest. It was Nipper or one of his kind. The approaching creature's gargantuan footsteps faltered. It trumpeted again. This time the sound was one of confusion.

'Look! There!' Callum said, pointing.

Sam looked and could just make out the head of the enormous creature between the trees. It looked bigger than a fully-grown elephant but it had the same grey-coloured skin. Rather than a trunk, however, the elongated face sported a single large horn protruding from the top of its nose. A crescent of five further horns sprouted from what looked to be a wide collar of bone that reinforced the creature's skull.

'It looks like a fancy sort of triceratops,' Sam whispered. 'But it's huge! Bigger than any animal I've ever seen. Look. There are raptors moving through the trees too.'

Although they were much closer, the raptors were far harder to see among the trees and undergrowth.

'They look almost human!' Callum exclaimed softly as he got a better look at one. 'Are they hunting it?'

'I wouldn't be surprised.'

'But they don't have any weapons,' he protested.

'They *are* weapons,' Sam said softly. 'Look at the fear and confusion in that monster's eyes. It knows they're there. It knows to be afraid. They're spreading out. Look at them go!'

Sam and Callum watched with horrified fascination as three raptors sprang into motion, executing a simultaneous attack from multiple directions. The larger creature reared, trumpeting in alarm as it sensed them closing in. It tried to pivot on its back feet and turn, but its legs and horns tangled in the branches of the trees around it. Before it could use its weight to tear itself free, the raptors struck.

Sam felt a cold chill run through him as he witnessed the devastating tactics of the comparatively tiny raptors. Two struck the creature's hind legs, using their razor-sharp centre claws to slice through its thick skin and sever its hamstrings. The third zipped underneath the beast and leapt up high into the air to plunge the point of its right centre claw into the grey belly. Using momentum and muscle in a single mighty heave, this third raptor tore an enormous hole in the beast's belly.

'Holy crap!' Callum breathed. 'Did you see how high that thing jumped?'

The mortally injured beast let out a piteous scream of pain and crumpled, crashing to earth amid the *crack-crunch-snap* of breaking branches. By the time it hit the ground the raptors were long gone.

Sam became aware that his jaw had dropped. 'Now that's what you call hit-and-run tactics!' he muttered.

A raptor appeared, exploding out from between the trees and racing up towards the two boys. Callum flinched, but there was no time to run. The raptor moved far too quickly. Although Sam could not be certain, he sensed this was the same raptor that had rescued him the previous evening. Brad had called it Nipper. Would it understand that name if Sam used it?

The raptor stopped a few short paces away from the two boys.

'Ack,' it said, the vowel sounding forced. It pointed along the beach in the direction of Brad and Leah's house. 'Ack!' it said again.

'Back?' Sam asked. 'Is that what you're trying to say? We're going back now.'

Nipper nodded. 'Ssss! Ack.' It turned and bounded away into the trees again.

'Fast!' Callum breathed. 'So fast!'

'Yeah, I wouldn't want to try to outrun one of those guys,' Sam agreed. 'Come on. I think that was Nipper. We'd better do as he suggested.'

Callum needed no further encouragement. The two boys struck out along the beach again. Sam's legs felt like jelly and the pain in his ankle continued to increase as they went. He found climbing over the rocks at the far end of the beach more difficult than he had on the outbound walk, but he took his time and made it over without incident. Leah was at the top of the beach on the other side. She was carrying a basket. As they approached her, they could see she had been collecting fruit.

'What happened, Sam?' she asked. 'You're limping.'

'Just a twisted ankle,' he replied. 'Nothing bad.'

'It did nearly get him eaten though!' Callum added quickly.

Leah's eyebrows shot up. 'Eaten? Unlikely. The raptors have cleared the forests around here of most dangerous animals.'

'I believe you,' he said, warming to his story. 'We saw three of them kill a huge creature in the trees not half an hour ago, but the thing that tried to eat us wasn't in the trees. It came from the water. You could have warned us! Did you know there're monsters in the surf, Leah? They look sort of like eels, but much, much bigger. One of 'em decided it fancied more than fish for lunch and chased us up the beach.'

'Really? Sounds like the creatures we call sea serpents – of course, who knows what they actually are. How many did you see?'

'Four or five, but only one came out of the water.'

'Interesting. As far as I know, they've not been seen around here for a couple of years now. I'll make sure to spread the word that everyone should stay out of the water for a couple of days in case they're hanging around.'

'You swim here!' Callum exclaimed. 'Are you crazy?'

'Yes, I swim,' Leah said, giving a shrug of indifference. 'Quite a few of us do. Why not? There are many animals that could hurt you in the waters off Florida, Callum. Did that stop you swimming there?'

'No, but that's different,' he replied.

'Really? How so? If I spent my time here worrying about every last thing that could hurt me, I'd never leave the house. What sort of life would that be?' She paused for a moment. 'Changing the subject,' she continued. 'We should get back to the house. There is someone there who I think you'll both be interested to meet. Especially you, Sam.'

Sam's heart skipped a beat. Could they have found his mother? He refrained from asking Leah outright. Something in her voice told him she was looking forward to introducing him in person to the mystery visitor.

The trio entered the narrow path through the trees with Leah leading the way. When they emerged in the clearing and saw the house again, Sam felt relieved to be back. After the excitement on the beach, he wanted nothing more than to sit down and rest his ankle.

'Brad! The boys are back,' Leah called as she approached the door. Before they reached the threshold, the door opened and Brad looked out, a broad grin on his face.

'Successful trip, boys?' he asked.

'Not really,' Sam replied. 'We were nearly eaten by sea serpents before we'd gone more than about half a mile and when we did manage to escape up the beach and find the boat, it had been totally stripped down to the fibreglass hull. Everything had gone . . . and I mean everything! Engines, instrumentation, dashboard, throttle assembly, every last bit of trim, metal, wood . . . everything. If the name had not been painted on the hull, I'd never have believed it was the same boat.'

'Ah! Yes, perhaps I should have warned you that was likely,' Brad said, wincing and looking distinctly guilty.

'You knew!' Callum accused. 'You knew and you let us go anyway?'

'Yes,' he admitted. 'I knew it was likely that the raptors would have stripped the boat, but I thought it was probably better for you to see it for yourselves. What's this about sea serpents though? I promise I didn't expect you to be in any danger.'

'They were shoaling fish into the shallows and then eating them,' Sam explained. 'You might want to check on your fisherman friend, just in case.'

'I don't understand,' Callum interrupted. 'Why would the raptors strip the boat? Have they got their own boats that they want the stuff for?'

'Well, the raptor scientists like to study everything from our world in minute detail,' Brad explained. 'They're particularly interested in our technology, even the low-tech stuff. But as for the raptors having boats – no, at least not exactly. Raptors hate the water. They're not swimmers. They do travel the oceans, but the vessels they use are more like nuclear-powered islands than boats.'

'Not much chance of stealing one of those then,' Sam muttered, glancing at Callum. 'How the heck would you drive an island?'

Callum looked confused.

'Scientists?' he asked, a note of amazement in his voice. 'Are we talking about the same creatures?'

'We've told you, the raptors are more advanced than you think,' Leah said firmly. 'The raptors may look like little more than savage beasts, but they are incredibly clever.'

'But the trim?' Sam persisted. 'What could they possibly want with that?'

'I don't know,' Brad admitted. 'Maybe they wanted to analyse the material to see if they can find applications for it that we've not considered. Look, I'm sorry about your boat, Sam, but we can talk more about that later. Please, come inside. There's someone I'd like you to meet.'

Sam nodded and followed Brad inside with Callum hard on his heels. A man was sitting in the living area. He rose to greet them. The first thing that struck Sam about the man was an ageless quality about his features. Sam would not like to have guessed if he was in his late twenties, mid-thirties or early forties. There were hints of grey at his temples, but with his athletic frame and smooth facial features the colour did not seem to fit with the rest of his appearance.

'Steve, these are the boys I was telling you about,' Brad said, his lips curving into a broad smile. 'Sam. Callum. This is Steve Nawarinski. He was a pilot in the US military.'

'Hiya, guys,' the man began, stepping towards

them and extending his right hand. 'I guess you'd be Claire's boy then, Sam. You have her eyes.'

Sam froze.

'You know my mother?' he asked, his heart suddenly thumping painfully in his chest.

'Yes, I've met her,' Steve replied. 'She's a very special lady.'

'She's alive! Can I see her? Where is she?'

Steve glanced at Brad, and Sam sensed an unspoken request for approval pass between them. The slightest of nods from Brad was enough.

'I can't be a hundred per cent sure,' Steve said carefully. 'It's been some time since I last saw her, but yes, Claire Cutler was very much alive when we last met about three years ago.'

'Where? Is it far? Can I go there?'

Sam couldn't believe it. His mum – alive! Before coming here he had long since stopped dreaming about that possibility. To think that his dad had been right not to give up all these years! It was like something out of a crazy dream. Was it possible that he could find her? His mind whirled as he waited for Steve's response.

'It was a long way from here,' he said carefully. 'I last saw her in the City of the Imperium. And three years is a long time in this world, Sam. I don't want to get your hopes up too much. She could be anywhere by now.'

Sam did not miss the unspoken 'or dead' that was implicit in Steve's answer.

'The City of the Imperium?' he asked. 'Where's that?'

'The City of the Imperium could be described as the raptors' capital city,' Brad explained. 'The Imperium is their governing body. It's about a thousand miles north of here.'

'A thousand miles!' Sam gasped, a cold, sinking feeling in his stomach. 'How did you get there and back in one piece?'

'Oh, getting there and back was the easy bit,' Steve laughed. 'The raptors don't run everywhere, you know. I just took the train.'

CHAPTER SEVENTEEN

As Niamh crossed the edge of the reef into deeper water, she got the distinct sense that Sam was in danger again. Although the feeling was vague, she felt her pulse quicken. He was running. He was on a beach. Something was chasing him. A ghostly pain spiked through her right ankle.

'Where the hell are you, Sam?' she muttered. But now that their link felt stronger again, Niamh suddenly had an idea. Taking a quick look around to make sure the area around the boat was clear, she eased the throttle right back, closed her eyes and deliberately put the boat into a gentle turn to the left. She held her breath as the boat tracked round in a circle.

The motion of the boat was far less predictable in the turn. Niamh nearly lost her balance several times, but refused to open her eyes. Instead, she clung tighter to the wheel and concentrated on trying to establish which direction she could sense Sam most strongly from.

The sensation of distant danger remained for a minute or two before melting away. Turning the boat with her eyes closed had only served to upset her stomach with the strange motion across the waves. On opening her eyes, Niamh turned the wheel until the boat was running straight and took another good look around. The nearest boat looked to be about half a mile away.

'It's no good. This isn't working,' she muttered, drumming her fingers on the wheel. 'So much for the mental compass idea, Niamh! What now?'

When she had sensed the danger, she had felt sure that she would be able to get a fix on Sam. Her failure left her feeling lost and small again. Driving aimlessly up and down the coast was unlikely to achieve anything. From what she had sensed, Sam had obviously landed somewhere and there appeared no point in staying out on the water. It made little sense that Sam was on dry land, yet still in danger. Where could he possibly be? She needed to find somewhere out of immediate sight where she could hide and think. Out on the ocean she was too exposed and vulnerable. If the police or the coastguard caught her, the boys would be completely on their own. Of course, they might reach a phone at any moment and ring home to say they were safe. But it was weird: she just knew that Sam was not going to make that call – *couldn't* make that call. Where could he be?

It was a puzzling conundrum. Was it somehow connected with the Devil's Triangle after all?

Hide first. Then think, Niamh told herself. But where could she go that the authorities wouldn't find her? The boat wasn't going to be easy to hide.

'Of course!' she exclaimed aloud. 'Monkey Island!'

What was it that Dad had said about Monkey Island? It was deserted, having once belonged to one of the big pharmaceutical companies who had used the island as a breeding ground for monkeys to use as test subjects. The monkeys had stripped the island so bare of plant life that the company had been forced to round them all up and find somewhere else to raise them. But from her memories of seeing it from the Overseas Highway, the island had made a full recovery from the ravages of the monkeys, and hopefully there would be enough foliage to hide the boat. Would the satnav on the boat know where it was? Was Monkey Island even its real name?

She tried typing in the name. It was no surprise to her that the database did not recognise it, but the island was not far away – a few miles at most. Niamh had seen it lots of times from the highway and she should remember enough to find it without using the navigation equipment. Surely there would be some sort of mooring there, she reasoned. The people from the pharmaceutical company would have had to moor up when they visited to collect animals for testing. It was certainly worth a try.

Niamh turned the boat parallel to the coast and opened the throttle. The sensation of acceleration was exhilarating as the two enormous outboard motors poured their power through the propellers with a mighty roar. Within seconds, a rhythmic *thump, thump, thump* of the hull against the wave tops began. The boat skimmed from one to the next, giving Niamh the feeling that the boat wanted to leap into the air and fly. A fizzing hiss rose and fell in a softer counterpoint rhythm, as cloud after cloud of dense spray kicked outwards with each thumping impact.

Shaking her hair out in the wind, Niamh was surprised to realise that driving the boat was actually quite fun. If it wasn't for her anxiety over Sam and her father, and the fact that she was now a fugitive, this would have been a fantastic experience. It was no wonder Sam had nagged Dad about driving so much.

Finding Monkey Island proved a little more difficult than Niamh anticipated, but after a few false attempts, she found it. The approach channel was mercifully obvious and Niamh drove the boat along it without difficulty. Unfortunately, the mooring point at the island offered nothing in the way of concealment for the boat. Although it would be shielded from the view of cars travelling along the Overseas Highway, anyone passing nearby in another boat would see it immediately.

Niamh struggled for a minute or two as she tried to manoeuvre the boat into position near the mooring posts. It was not as easy as her dad had made it look. The bump as the boat smacked against the docking jetty nearly threw her from her feet. Recovering quickly, she grabbed the rear mooring rope and leapt ashore. Once she had one rope looped over a mooring post, securing the other end of the boat proved easy.

The silence as Niamh turned off the engines set her pulse racing again. First running away from a policeman, then theft – now trespass. *How many more laws am I going to break before I get caught?* she wondered.

Taking the keys and tucking them into the pocket of her shorts, Niamh decided to take a walk around the island to find a place to conceal the boat. The island was not huge, but it might have an inlet or a

226

second mooring point tucked away out of sight that would suit her purpose.

Before leaving the boat, she ducked down into the cabin to see what the Mitchells kept there. To her delight, she found a half full plastic container of orange juice sitting in an ice bucket. The water in the bucket was cool rather than cold and there was no sign of any ice.

Mitch must have taken this with him yesterday, she thought, taking a sip. 'Nice!' she added aloud, taking several large swigs to quench her immediate thirst. The sweet orange juice quickly washed the taste of salt from her lips.

There were a few packets of nuts and some food bars in one of the little cupboards in the cabin. Niamh tucked a Nutri-Grain bar into one pocket and opened another. It was gone in a few bites, washed down with another mouthful of orange. The waffle she had eaten at the Mitchells' seemed like an age ago even though it had actually been less than three hours.

'Who would have thought becoming a criminal was such hungry work?' she muttered and then laughed. 'Talking to yourself as well, Niamh! Not a good sign.'

She knew food would become a problem if she remained on the run for any length of time, but she had taken the edge off her immediate hunger. Shutting the door of the cabin behind her, Niamh climbed out of the boat and looked around. *Do I go left or right?* she wondered.

'Eeny meeny miney mo . . . right it is.'

Away from the mooring jetty, her progress slowed markedly. Tangled mangrove trees dominated, growing right down to the water's edge. The heat among the trees was stifling and the further she went from the boat, the stronger the stench of rotting vegetation became. The whine of mosquitoes was becoming more frequent too. Niamh slapped at her neck and legs several times, but whether the tickling she felt was from the light touch of insect life, or from trickling rivulets of sweat, it was hard to tell.

A sudden pattering of running feet made her gasp. It was a lizard – a big one. It had to be at least a metre and a half long with a striking black-and-white tail. There was a splash as it hit the water at speed and disappeared.

'Wow!' she exclaimed under her breath. 'If the animals around here get much bigger, I'll have to add monsters to my list of problems!'

Another sound caught her attention. She paused, listening hard. Laughter. Voices – at least two of them. Someone else was on the island. The sound was coming from ahead and away from the water's edge. Although they were too far away for Niamh to be sure, the relative pitch of the voices suggested that at least one was male. Who were they? And what were they doing here? The island was supposed to be uninhabited. For a moment, Niamh hesitated. Should she go back to the boat and leave or should she take a closer look?

Curiosity won the day. Niamh crept forward, slipping between the trees as silently as she could. There was more than enough cover for her to be able to sneak up and get a look at them. As she got closer, Niamh caught a whiff of something other than the stench of the mangroves. She stopped for a moment and sniffed the air. There was no mistaking it this time. Someone was cooking fish.

Laughter rang through the trees much closer this time and Niamh smiled. She couldn't help herself. There was an infectious quality about it. Drawn by the voices, she moved closer until she could see the source of the noise and the delicious smell.

A boy was standing next to a small campfire and feeding it with sticks. Sitting next to the fire, a girl was patiently barbecuing fish over the flames on metal skewers. The boy looked like he was a year or two older than Niamh. He had his back to her, so she couldn't see his face. He looked slim to the point of being skinny, but fit, with a bleach-blond mop of unruly hair and was wearing brightly coloured, knee-length swimming shorts. The girl looked to be about Niamh's age: dark-haired and pretty with the sort of curvaceous body that Niamh craved.

Judging from their deep tans, Niamh felt it safe to assume they were locals.

She pulled back behind a tree. What should she do now? Would it be safe to introduce herself? She peered round the trunk again, but ducked out of sight again when, by chance, the boy standing by the fire turned and locked eyes with her.

'Who's that?' he called out, tensing as if ready to run. 'Who's out there?'

The girl scrambled to her feet. 'What is it?' she asked. 'Don't mess with me, Tony!'

'I'm not messin' with you, Tessa. There's someone out there watchin' us.'

'Carrie? Is that you?' Tessa called.

'What's the matter, Tess?' a girl's voice answered from somewhere to the boy's right. 'You two missin' me already?'

Niamh sat tucked down with her back to the tree trunk, thinking fast. The boy had seen her. From his reaction, she felt sure this group were not supposed to be here any more than she was. Would they be friendly? Her stomach began to rumble. It sounded so loud that she felt sure they must be able to hear it. The smell of cooking fish was so enticing that she decided to risk introducing herself in the hope they might share some.

'I saw someone,' Tony was saying. 'Over there. Couldn't have been Carrie. There's no way she could move that fast.'

Niamh stood up and moved out from behind the tree.

'Hello,' she said, putting on her best British accent. 'I'm terribly sorry to have surprised you like that. I heard you laughing and thought I'd come and see who was making all the noise.'

'See! I told ya, Tessa,' the boy said in a low voice.

Tessa was irritatingly gorgeous, Niamh noted, now she could see her better. Huge dark-brown eyes stared out from under perfectly shaped brows. Classic high cheekbones, a cute, slightly upturned nose and full, pouting lips gave her a sultry look. Niamh felt sure boys would line up to take her out.

To her alarm, Niamh saw that both Tessa and Tony had armed themselves with vicious-looking spears. Both held them poised, but looked more ready to run than throw their weapons.

'What're you doin' here?' Tessa snapped, ignoring Tony and directing her question at Niamh. 'This place is private property.'

'I could ask you the same question,' Niamh

replied, stepping forward slowly and trying hard not to let her envy of the girl's figure colour her voice. 'I'm guessing you're trespassing every bit as much as I am. Would you mind lowering the spears, please? You're making me nervous.'

'Yeah, sure, sorry,' Tony said, glancing at the spear in his hand as if noticing it for the first time. He gave a chuckle and lowered it. Tessa was slower to lower hers. She looked less than pleased by the intrusion. Another girl appeared out of the trees. She was wearing a one-piece, mid-blue swimsuit with aquamarine panels down each side. 'Hey, sis. We've got company,' Tony called out to her.

Niamh could see the sibling likeness immediately. Carrie's hair was the same white-blonde as her brother's, and she had the same striking blue eyes. Niamh felt another swift pang of jealousy. Her own blonde hair and blue eyes felt plain by comparison. Why did she have to be such a plain Jane?

'Niamh Cutler,' Niamh said, stepping clear of the trees into the tiny clearing where the trio had built their fire. She extended her hand to Tony first and her heart gave a flutter as he took it in his. 'Nice to meet you, Tony.'

'That's a neat accent. English, right?' he asked.

'Right,' Niamh confirmed. She turned to Tessa

and offered her hand again. The girl took it reluctantly. She had the sort of grip that her father would have called a limp fish. That thought put a genuine smile on Niamh's lips. Turning to Tony's sister she completed her greeting. 'And you're Carrie? Nice to meet you.'

'Howdy,' she said, flashing a bright smile. 'Carrie Dale – Tony's my big brother.'

'A pleasure,' Niamh said. 'Nice fire,' she added. 'And the fish smells fantastic. Any going spare?'

The three American teenagers glanced at one another. An unspoken agreement passed between Tony and Carrie. Tess looked sullen.

'Sure,' Tony answered. 'If you'll tell us how you got here, and if there's any adults with you.'

'Well, my dad was accused of murdering my brother and his friend. The police arrested him and wanted to take me in too, so I stole a neighbour's boat and came here to hide from them,' Niamh said casually. 'Don't worry. There's no one else with me . . . and I'm not expecting anyone, unless the police find a way of tracking me.'

Tony laughed as the girls' jaws dropped. 'Nice one,' he said, shaking his head and pointing at his sister. 'You girls are just too easy to mess with. It's OK, Niamh. If you don't wanna tell us why you're here, that's cool. So long as you're not gonna rat us out to the cops, I don't really care. We come here 'cos it's a great place for spear fishin' and there's no tourists to bother us. Come on, share some fish and tell us about England. Do the girls there all have cute accents like yours?'

Tessa flashed him a glance of pure poison. Niamh blinked. Had she imagined it? Tony appeared oblivious. Was he flirting with her? Could Tessa be jealous?

Niamh nearly laughed aloud. She was being ridiculous. In what universe would a girl like Tessa ever need to be jealous of her? The pause was beginning to extend uncomfortably. Tony's question hung in the air and she needed to answer, preferably without alienating Tessa.

'Probably,' she replied, smiling nervously at him. 'I guess that after handing out the perfect bodies to the American girls, it was all God had left to give us Brits.'

CHAPTER EIGHTEEN

'Good news, Sam,' Brad announced excitedly as he burst in through the front door. 'I've spoken with Nipper and he's agreed to come with us.'

Sam looked around, surprised. 'Us?' he replied. 'You're planning to come as well?'

'Yeah, well . . .' Brad paused and shrugged. 'You boys'll need someone responsible along if you're gonna stay out of trouble. Besides, you'll stand a better chance of finding your ma if you go with someone who can speak the language.'

A warm rush of gratitude flushed through Sam. He glanced across at Callum who looked as relieved as Sam felt. 'That's brilliant news, Brad!' Sam replied with genuine enthusiasm. 'I don't know how to thank you.'

'Then don't,' he said. 'Just make sure you do as

you're told. Before we go, there are some things you should know about the raptor Imperium.'

'What sort of things?'

'Well for one, the leaders of raptor society don't take kindly to any form of disrespect.'

'I can understand that,' Sam said. 'My head teacher has a similar mentality.'

'No,' Brad said firmly. 'I doubt he has. The Imperium won't give you lines or detention if you misbehave. You're more likely to find yourself being impaled on a huge spike in the equivalent of the local town square.'

'Ouch!'

'I guess you could say that the raptors live in a form of communism,' he continued. 'The majority of their society embraces the most attractive elements of the ideals that communism supposedly encourages. In many rural areas they work together, supporting one another and sharing resources more completely than I've ever heard of in human societies. Unfortunately, as with most forms of society and government, those who sit in the highest positions of responsibility are prone to corruption. The eight raptors who form the High Council of the Imperium are the worst. They control the media, the scientists, the raptor equivalent of law enforcement . . . everything.'

'And we're going into their home turf,' Sam said.

'That's right.'

'And Leah? Is she coming as well?'

'Am I coming where?' Leah asked, entering the living area from the couple's bedroom.

'Ah! Um, yes, dear. I was just gonna talk to you about that,' Brad spluttered. 'I'm . . . er . . . gonna take a trip with the boys for a few days. You'll be OK here, won't you?'

'Sounds like I'm gonna have to be,' she said reproachfully. 'Where're you goin'?'

'The City of the Imperium.'

'The Imperium! Are you crazy?'

'Not at all, honey,' Brad said quickly. 'We're gonna try to find Sam's mom. Don't worry. Nipper's comin' with us to play escort. I wouldn't consider it otherwise.'

'Well . . .' Leah replied slowly. 'If Nipper's agreed to go, I suppose it should be OK. So long as you promise to stick close by him. Just remember that Nipper can't keep you safe if you wander off. There's a lot of raptors out there who would gut you as soon as look at you. You know the superstitions, Brad.'

'Yes and they're total trash.'

'Of course they are,' Leah agreed. 'But some raptors don't see it that way.'

'What superstitions, Leah?' Sam asked.

Leah looked him in the eyes. 'There's some raptors as believe that humans bring bad luck,' she said, her eyes deadly serious. 'They blame us for most of the problems in this world. Normally, I'd be quick to believe human meddlin' had upset the natural balance of a place. As a race, we don't exactly have a great track record, but this time I'm not so sure. It seems that the raptors' problems are more likely of their own making.'

'What sort of problems?' Callum asked.

Leah looked at Brad, who nodded.

'Well, the weather for a start,' she said.

'The weather?' Sam exclaimed. He let out a laugh. 'You're kidding, right?'

'Not at all,' Brad confirmed. 'Humans started arriving about the same time as the first severe magnetic storms began. Seems their weather systems here have undergone changes over the past couple of centuries that make El Niño look like a storm in a teacup.'

'Could the storms be something to do with the global warming in our world?' Callum asked.

'I don't see how,' Leah replied, shaking her head. 'But then I'm no meteorologist. Who knows what's possible?'

'So we get the blame for some bad weather. Is that it?'

'No, there's more. Lots more.'

'Like what?' Callum asked.

'Volcanoes, an increase in raptor mutation rates, unusual behaviour in farm stock, brittle claws, lost teeth . . . just about anythin' and everythin' bad really,' Brad answered. 'You could equate it to the witch-hunts around Europe in the Middle Ages. It's all nonsense, but a surprisin'ly large number of the raptor population believe in the superstitions. Seems strange to me for such an advanced species to believe in such nonsense.'

'And unfortunately, a raptor's imagination is no laughing matter when it turns to paranoia,' Leah added. 'That's why most of us choose to live in the Reserve. Here we're protected by raptors who don't believe the ridiculous superstitions that surround us.'

'There is another theory though,' Brad said, furtively looking over his shoulder and lowering his voice. 'It's been circulating around the human population here for some years, but the raptors refuse to accept it.'

'What sort of theory?' Sam prompted.

'Well, like we told you before, the raptors have been using nuclear power for a very long time – about 800 years or more, if the information we've been given is accurate. In that time they have created billions of tons of nuclear waste.'

'You learned this from Nipper?'

'No. We heard it from humans who've worked alongside raptor scientists,' Brad explained.

'OK, even assuming for a moment that was true, radioactive materials wouldn't cause all the things you mentioned,' Callum said quickly. 'We learned about radioactive isotopes in physics and chemistry. They can't affect the weather.'

'You're right, Callum,' Brad replied, nodding, 'but it's not the nuclear waste itself, it's what they've done with it all that we think is causing all the problems. According to the rumours, some centuries ago a particularly clever raptor scientist devised a way of both disposing of the waste while simultaneously creating a cleaner source of energy that would benefit future generations into the foreseeable future. He initiated a programme of pumping the radioactive materials into the Earth's core.'

'Nice home for it,' Sam said, nodding. 'But how did that create a new source of energy?'

'Over time they pumped enormous quantities into the magma to be burned up,' Brad continued. 'The Earth works a bit like a dynamo with the friction of the magma against the iron core creating the Earth's magnetic field. The burning process heated the magma, causing it to liquefy more and flow faster around the Earth's iron core. Gradually, this made the field stronger. The raptor scientist invented methods of harnessing the increased magnetic field and converting the inherent energy there into electricity. They've been refining the techniques and technology ever since.'

'Blimey!' Callum exclaimed. 'That's genius!'

'Yes,' Brad agreed. 'But there are those of us here who believe that it's the side-effects of what they've done that's causing all the problems. Think about it: heat the magma and it expands. Suddenly, you have increased volcanic activity all over the world.'

'The smell of sulphur!' Sam exclaimed. 'Remember, Callum. I could smell it even before we crossed.'

Brad nodded. 'The combination of the changing magnetic field and the increased vulcanism could be messing with the global weather patterns. And one of the side-effects of the strongest magnetic storms seems to be the rifts between this world and ours. When they are really powerful, the eye of the storm creates a crossing point between dimensions. From what we've learned from careful questioning, this region, and another off the coast of what would be Japan in our world, get the worst of the storms, and these areas correspond with the Bermuda and Dragon's Triangles. What's more, the storms have been getting steadily more frequent, particularly during the last century. The effect is accelerating out of control. Mention this to a raptor though, and you're likely to make him angry. Making raptors angry is not a good idea.'

'I can see that,' Sam observed. 'So when people cross into this world through the rifts created by the storms, they end up here in the Reserve? What about people who don't want to stay?'

'Some try to ignore the prejudices and work with the raptors on scientific projects. But there are others who attempt to get home; most die trying,' Brad said, his voice flat and emotionless.

'How can you be so sure that they die?' Callum asked, his voice rising. 'I'm sorry, but I refuse to accept there is no way back. Cool though this place is, with the dinosaurs and everything, I'm not spending the rest of my life here. Surely, if we can get to the eye of one of those storms, we could cross back the other way.'

'You think we wanted to stay, kiddo?' Brad snapped. 'Believe me, if I thought there was a gen-u-ine shot at getting home, then I'd be first in line to try it. Despite the bucket load of obvious dangers, some have travelled this world their entire lives searchin' for a gateway home. Eventually, one way or another, they all fall foul of somethin'. One of the main problems is that the effect only seems to happen over water – don't ask me why. There's just no boats here that'll stay afloat long enough to get to the eye of a storm.'

'What about one of the floating islands you told us about?' Sam asked.

'Ha! The raptors don't bring those anywhere near the Triangle. They only take them across the ocean along routes where the weather is less severe.'

Sam glanced at his friend. Callum looked thoughtful. Sam could almost see the cogs in Callum's brain whirring. He would think about what he had been told, gather evidence from as many sources as he could and then he would work on the problem alone. Once he set his mind to solving something, Callum was the sort of person who examined every angle until he found a way to the answer he wanted.

I ought to be siding with him, Sam thought. *He's my best friend and he deserves my support. He's also right – we should be looking for ways to get back. But if there's a chance I can find Mum first . . .*

He did not dare to finish the thought. If Sam could find his mother and take her home, then his family would be complete again. A thrill ran through him at the thought of it. Life could finally move forward again, rather than remaining forever anchored to that terrible day nine years ago when his mum had vanished without trace. Now that he knew she had been seen here, if he returned home without trying to find her, he would never forgive himself.

Later that afternoon Sam followed Brad outside, eager to get their journey under way. Nipper and a second raptor were waiting for them.

'They're wearing clothes!' Callum whispered to Sam.

'Perhaps it's the convention at the Imperium,' Sam replied softly, noting the drab brown garments that now covered the raptors' loins and upper body. There was nothing stylish about them. The cloth hung round their bodies looking both out of place and uncomfortable.

'Ssss'amm,' Nipper said, pointing a wickedly curved middle claw.

Sam's eyes went wide. 'Yes,' he said. 'That's my name.'

'K'umm,' Nipper continued, moving the claw to point at Callum.

'Close enough,' Callum acknowledged. He adjusted his glasses up his nose before glancing first at Sam and then nodding at Nipper. The raptor repeated the nod before pointing at the second raptor and making an explosive, rolling huff noise in the depths of his throat.

'Just call him Grunt, boys,' Brad chuckled. 'It'll save you gettin' sore throats.'

Nipper gestured for the boys to follow him. They exchanged a final look of amazement and then stepped out after him. Brad followed close behind, with Grunt bringing up the rear. Leah followed the group to the edge of the trees. The boys turned to say goodbye.

'Good luck, boys,' she said, wiping a tear from her cheek. 'Stay with Nipper and keep safe.'

'Bye, Leah!' the boys chorused back.

'Thanks for everything,' Callum added.

Brad drew Leah into a tight hug and kissed her, first on the top of her head and then on the lips. Their embrace lasted some time, but at last he pulled away.

'Gotta go,' he said.

'Be careful, love,' Leah told him, blinking hard as she tried to stop more tears from welling. There was no mistaking her worried look.

'I will,' he assured her. 'I'll be back as soon as I can.'

Nipper pushed into the dense greenery underneath the trees and the boys followed. A few steps and the dense jungle closed around them. Leah and the house disappeared. Sam looked back at Brad and the older man gave him an encouraging smile. Sam envied him his relaxed attitude. It was hard to imagine ever being able to relax in this environment. There were too many unknowns: too many dangers.

Nipper pushed through the undergrowth with ease. But following him was not so easy for the humans. To Sam, the forest was more reminiscent of the African or Amazonian equatorial jungles he'd seen featured on the *Discovery Channel* wildlife programmes than anything he would have expected to find in Florida. Huge broad-leaf plants and enormous shiny-leaved ferns limited forward visibility between the trees to no more than a metre or two.

Looking up, the dense canopy was many metres above, capping long, relatively spindly tree trunks that stretched up like so many gigantic spears. All around him the air was alive with birdsong and the whining of insects, but if any of the cacophony of sounds were being made by other animals, Sam could not tell them apart. If he had been alone, he would have trodden carefully, wary of the possibility of snakes. Following Nipper, however, all he could do was blindly push forward and hope.

Unlike the stink of rotting vegetation in the mangrove swamps of Florida, the air in this jungle smelt green with life. Sam breathed it in through his nose, trying to separate out the scents, but it was an impossibly complex blend that changed with almost every step. The only constant he could identify was the background hint of sulphur, which seemed to permeate everything in this world.

Branches of bushes and trees whipped back at Sam as the raptor moved forward with no apparent regard for his immediate follower. Sam had no doubt that the raptor could move much faster if he had a mind to, but as the fourth and fifth branches swished back at him in quick succession, he realised this journey was going to be anything but easy. Twisting, ducking and constantly tense, he gritted his teeth and did his best to keep up.

It was hard to tell exactly how long they walked. When they emerged from the trees, Sam was scratched, sweating and sore in several places from having sustained particularly fierce whipping impacts. He guessed they had spent about two hours trekking through the jungle. He had learned quickly to keep his head and eyes down and it took a few moments after entering the clearing before he could bring himself to look around.

'Wow!' he breathed when he lifted his eyes.

He turned to his friend. Callum's jaw was hanging slack with amazement. The gigantic structure in front of them was like nothing Sam had ever seen before. Its many-faceted exterior reflected light in all directions rather like a gigantic distorted version of the mirror ball that had been hung for their school disco. It was impossible to imagine a human architect ever designing such a seemingly unnatural, amorphous-looking shape, but what left Sam's mind reeling was not the shape of the strange structure. It was the dazzling effect of the myriad reflective surfaces.

'Welcome to the local train station, boys,' Brad laughed. 'Impressive, isn't it?'

'You could say that,' Sam choked, barely able to speak.

'Wait until you see inside. Grunt tells me there should be a train arriving any time now.'

Nipper turned and uttered a slow sequence of clicks, grumbles and guttural *tocks* to Brad before firing a much faster sequence of clicking, growling noises at Grunt, who in turn raised his head and gave a strangely restrained roar by way of response.

'What was that all about, I wonder?' muttered Callum. 'That noise Grunt made reminded me of Chewbacca from *Star Wars*.'

'I don't know,' Sam replied softly. 'And I have the distinct feeling that it would be better if we didn't ask.'

Nipper led the way again, stepping out with such long strides that the boys and Brad had to jog to keep up. The raptor did not look back to check on them. He seemed preoccupied with getting into the building. They went left along the outside wall, but the boys could see no obvious point of entry. The irregular-shaped panel Nipper led them to looked no different from any of the others around the building, save for a wide network of well-trodden paths across the ground that all converged towards it. There was no sign of an entry mechanism that Sam could see, but as Nipper approached the panel, it slid diagonally up and left into a hidden sheath within the skin of the building. He moved forward until he was standing in the opening, then he turned and beckoned the rest of the party through.

'Cool!' Callum muttered. 'I wonder what sort of sensors it uses. What do you think, Sam? Movement? Weight?'

'They're DNA scanners,' Brad explained, picking up on their conversation. 'Raptors don't want unwanted species entering the station. That's why Nipper is standing in the doorway. If we were to try to enter without him standing there, the door would slam shut instantly.'

'And I bet that you wouldn't want to be underneath that door if it came down,' Callum added.

'Not a good idea,' Brad confirmed. 'It wouldn't make your day.'

Sam moved quickly through the doorway, looking up nervously as he crossed the threshold. No sooner was he inside, however, than the potentially lethal door was forgotten as his eyes were drawn towards new wonders. The entire interior of the building appeared to be a single chamber.

The first thing that drew his attention was the lighting. Aside from a few transparent panels in the roof that allowed shafts of natural light in like great golden spears, the space was lit by huge glowing globes that appeared to be floating in the air at regular intervals across the main inner chamber. Sam could see no telltale signs of any hidden support structure. At first, he thought it must be some sort of visual illusion, but the globes occasionally appeared to bob, giving an even stronger indication that they were indeed free-floating.

The flooring appeared initially to be bare earth, but there was something about the way it felt underfoot that raised Sam's suspicions. Putting his fingers to the ground, he discovered the surface had the texture of dense plastic, though there was a thin layer of dusty earth on top that had doubtless been brought in from outside by countless raptor travellers over the years.

Everywhere Sam looked there was something amazing to see, but the building was filled with strange contradictions. It was as if someone had been designing a film set for a science fiction film and then decided to build an Iron Age market in the middle of it. Nearby, there were holographic image generators projecting remarkable miniature scenes of raptors hunting not three paces from a huge stack of what looked like home-made wooden cages filled with an entire menagerie of creatures. Even as Sam watched, the constant squawking and screaming of the animals suddenly increased in volume to a terrified frenzy. A raptor was approaching the pile of cages. It stopped and pointed at a specific animal. Sam's stomach churned as he suddenly realised that what he was looking at was the equivalent of a café.

He looked away, turning his attention to an enormous central holographic screen displaying a gigantic raptor face, whose voice was being broadcast above the general hubbub of the station. Brad was also looking at the screen and his face was a study of concentration.

'It's the latest news,' Brad explained as he met Sam's inquisitive gaze.

'So what's happening?' Sam asked.

'Nothin' good,' Brad mumbled. 'Since when does anyone broadcast good news?'

Sam raised a hand to his chest. There was something else here. He couldn't see or hear it, but he could feel it. Underlying everything in the station

251

was a deep thrumming of energy unlike anything Sam had ever experienced before. It vibrated deep in his chest; an unsettling sensation, made suddenly worse by the realisation that every set of raptor eyes in the immediate vicinity had now turned and were focused on the three humans.

A nearby raptor peeled back the lipless flesh round his mouth to reveal rows of razor-sharp teeth, and gave a low warning growl. Sam took an involuntary step backwards and stepped on Callum's toes.

'Ow!' Callum breathed, grabbing Sam by the arms from behind and manhandling him to his right.

Another raptor bared his teeth and then another. Sam could feel his heart accelerating. If the nearby raptors attacked, they would be dead in seconds. The image of the three raptors killing the much bigger dinosaur the previous day was still fresh in his mind.

Brad made several clicking noises, and a rolling guttural sound in the back of his throat. The eyes of some of the nearest raptors widened and then narrowed.

'What did you say?' Sam asked him without looking.

'Well, I think I said, "It's great to meet y'all," but somethin' tells me my grasp of the language might not be as good as I thought,' Brad replied.

The eyes of the raptors shifted as Nipper and his friend prowled around to position themselves in front of Brad and the boys. They radiated confidence with every tiny movement they made. *It's like watching a tiger walking*, Sam thought – majestic and mesmerising, saying, 'I'm the top predator around here and there's nothing you can do that will ever worry me.'

Nipper opened his mouth and roared. The sound was both reassuring and terrifying at the same time. Sam's heart started to thump. A stab of pain in his chest accompanied each beat, as if his heart was bruising itself against his ribcage. The defiance in Nipper's roar caused a ripple of surprised clicking responses through the station, but it had the desired effect. Sam felt the shift. Within a matter of seconds, he, Callum and Brad went from being the centre of attention to being deliberately ignored.

'Nipper and Grunt have declared us their wards,' Brad explained. 'We shouldn't have any problems in the station now.'

By chance, the train arrived at that precise moment and the sight of it took the boys' breath away. Awestruck, and all fear momentarily forgotten, they moved forward to get a better look at the amazing vehicle. Distracted, none of the group noticed a particularly large raptor slide into a convenient shadow nearby. From the concealed vantage point, a single staring pair of eyes followed their every move.

CHAPTER NINETEEN

Niamh woke with a start from a strange dream and it took her a few moments to realise where she was. The confinement of the tiny cabin and the gentle rocking movement of the boat brought it all back in a flash. No one had bothered her during the night, so the camouflage that she and her newfound friends had applied the day before had done its job.

'Thanks, guys,' she breathed as she relived flashes of the previous afternoon.

The three American teenagers had been amazed when she had led them to her boat. Until they saw it, she felt sure they were expecting her to show them a little dinghy. Their reaction when they saw the ten-metre cabin cruiser had been most gratifying. It had taken them a while to believe that there were no adults around and that she was serious about trying to hide the boat somewhere, but eventually, Tony had made the suggestion that had led her to this old disused mooring on the far side of the island.

Getting to it had been tricky. The channel through the reef was very narrow, and if Niamh had faced the task alone, she was sure she would have damaged the boat or worse. Tony, however, was a skilful driver. He drove them through the narrow channel and into the mooring bay with apparent ease, adding only a couple of gentle scrapes against the coral along the way. The tiny inlet itself was so overgrown that they didn't have to add much to the natural concealment of the mangrove trees to make the boat all but invisible from the sea. It would still be partially visible from the air, but Niamh had done what she could to reduce the chances of it being spotted.

Once the boat had been hidden, her new friends had taken her spear fishing. She had proved useless at it, but had enjoyed the experience, laughing along with the others at her awkward attempts. Tony had eventually taken pity and helped her, standing close behind her with his hand over hers on the spear for what had seemed like forever before guiding her to her first successful catch. She shivered at the memory. His body close behind her and his hand squeezing on hers had felt both amazing and intensely embarrassing at the same time. Tessa had not looked happy about the focus of Tony's attention, but she did not intervene.

It had been late afternoon when they had finally left her. They had promised to return today, but had not set a time. Niamh looked at her watch: 09:02. Bliss. It was the longest she had slept in since arriving in Florida. What was the time back home now? Two in the afternoon? Instant feelings of guilt assaulted her. She was not going to find the boys by lazing around. Flashes of her recent dreams caused her to flush. Tony had featured strongly. This was not good. She could not afford to let herself become distracted. She needed to get moving again; start searching the coastline . . .

'Niamh?'

Niamh sat up. It was Tony's voice. A fresh flood of embarrassment washed through her as she considered her recent thoughts about him. She felt the boat tip slightly as someone boarded.

'Tony? You're here early?' she called out. 'Is everything all right? Are the others here?'

She sat up and looked across the boat at her reflection in the mirror. *God, I look like some kind of wild woman!* she thought, attacking her hair with her fingers and trying to tame it. *I can't let him see me looking like this. I'll die of shame!*

'No, nothin's right,' he answered, his voice anxious. 'Listen! Niamh, you've gotta get outta here. Now!'

The urgency in his voice had Niamh bounding out of bed like a spooked deer. She had slept in her shorts and T-shirt, so she had no worries about modesty as she whipped the double doors open to see his bronzed legs, topped with a fresh pair of trendy Bermudas and a snug plain white T-shirt.

Cute! she thought, trying not to be too obvious about looking him up and down as she clambered up out of the low-level cabin onto the deck.

'What's the panic? Are the cops coming?'

'If they're not, then they will be soon,' Tony said, looking around as if he expected to see a SWAT team arriving at any second. She couldn't see his eyes behind his dark Ray-Bans. 'I'm pretty certain Tessa's ratted on you,' he explained. 'An' if she hasn't, then she will soon.'

'Really?' Niamh asked, a sick feeling rising in the pit of her stomach. 'Why? She seemed friendly enough yesterday.'

It was a lie. Tessa had been cold from the moment they had met, but she did not want to appear hostile towards a friend of Tony's.

Tony handed her a plastic bag. Niamh was grateful for the diversion. Opening the bag she found a fresh, neatly folded T-shirt, a pair of sunglasses, some factor 30 suntan lotion and a newspaper: the *Key West Citizen*.

'Look at page nine,' he instructed. 'Tess called and handed me this earlier this morning. I know her. She loves being centre stage. If she hasn't called the cops yet, then it's only a matter of time.'

Niamh pulled out the newspaper and checked the date. It was today's. Flicking through, she quickly found the page. There it was – the story she had told them in a single throwaway line the day before. So Tony knew the truth, yet he was here and helping her. Why? Her heart began to beat harder. Could it be because he liked her? Suddenly, it was difficult to concentrate on the article, but she forced herself to focus. A picture of her dad with her and the boys by the pool was alongside a separate one of Callum. The headline was: 'Mystery or Murder?' They must have got the pictures from her dad's phone, she realised. Both had been taken by the pool earlier in the week.

'I assumed you were joking yesterday when you told us what you were doing here. We all did. It's true though, isn't it?' Tony stated more than asked.

'Well, they've got most of the facts right,' Niamh admitted, skimming through the article to the end. 'It says here that Dad's being held on suspicion of murder. Dad didn't do anything to the boys. I *know* he didn't. In fact, I can't understand why the police have arrested him. Surely the similarity between Mum's disappearance nine years ago and the boys going missing can't be considered evidence. That's rubbish!'

'So why did you run? Why steal the boat?'

'Because the police would have taken me in and sent me home to England,' she explained. He was testing her, she realised. 'The coastguard never found any sign of Mum when she disappeared nine years ago and I'm pretty certain that they're not going to find the boys either. With the police holding Dad, I consider myself the only real chance Sam and Callum have.'

'Do you have some idea where they are then?' Tony asked.

'Honestly?' Niamh said. 'No. But you may have noticed in the article that Sam and I are twins.'

He nodded.

'I know it sounds crazy, but I *know* he's still alive. I can feel him,' she said, tapping her chest. 'In here, I can feel him. I have this . . . invisible bond with my brother. Sometimes, when he's in trouble, I can sense his feelings, but something's changed. It's like he's nearby and yet a very long way away too. I keep thinking it might have something to do with the Devil's Triangle . . .'

Niamh trailed off and she looked away, staring into the distance.

'The Devil's Triangle? What's that?' asked Tony, looking confused.

'The Devil's Triangle is an old name for the Bermuda Triangle. Dad became something of an expert on the Triangle after Mum disappeared. Sorry, I've just got used to calling it by the old name.'

'Oh. That triangle. Right.'

The silence between them stretched into awkwardness until Tony finally spoke again.

'Look, Niamh, I believe you,' he said finally. 'And I wanna help. I sort of know what you mean about a bond. Carrie and me have always been pretty close. We're not twins, but I swear I can sometimes tell what she's thinkin'. Listen, we've got to go 'cos this boat is too hot. You're gonna have to leave it.'

'But if you help me won't that make you an accessory?' Niamh asked. 'I don't want to drag you into this.'

'That depends,' he said. 'To be an accessory I'd need to know you're a criminal.' He grinned as he held out his hands. 'I don't know squat.'

She raised one eyebrow quizzically.

'Besides,' Tony added. 'The cops'll have to catch me first. Come on.'

'Where are we going?'

'To my kayak,' he replied. 'Then I'll take you home to Carrie. Between us, we'll come up with somethin' to throw the cops off your trail. Change your shirt and put on the glasses. It's bright out on the water. I'll wait up on the bank.'

'Thanks,' she said.

It felt such an inadequate response, but Niamh couldn't think of anything better to say. *He must think I'm a total dork,* she thought, mentally kicking herself. *Please, God, don't let me make a fool of myself. He's gorgeous.*

She climbed back down into the cabin, peeled off her shirt and stuffed it underneath the bunk out of sight. The fresh one felt great against her skin. It had to be one of Carrie's, she realised, looking down at the swirling motif on the front.

She slapped a healthy dollop of suntan lotion on each arm and more around her neck and over her face. Having rubbed it in as best she could, she reached into the fridge, grabbed the half empty carton of orange juice and downed the last of it in one long draft. The cool sweetness refreshed her mouth and went some way to filling her rumbling belly.

'OK,' she breathed. 'Now stop acting like some dippy, mooning year seven and concentrate! Focus, Niamh, focus!'

Climbing out onto the deck again, she put on the sunglasses and leapt up onto the bank.

'Better,' Tony said, giving her an appraising look. 'But you still look too much like you. Have you got anything to tie your hair back with?'

'Not really,' Niamh said, 'But give me a minute and I'll improvise.'

There was nothing of any use on the deck, so she descended back into the cabin and rummaged around. Nothing seemed to leap out and say 'hairband' at her and she was about to give up when she had a thought. Reaching under the bunk, she recovered her discarded T-shirt. She had been about to abandon it anyway, so without a second thought, she began to tug and rip at the fabric until she had a usable strip of material. It was a bit frayed along the edges, but it would do the job.

Gathering her hair back into a single high ponytail, she tied a bow round it with the strip of material. Once back outside, Tony flashed her another smile and a shiver went right through her.

'Perfect!' he announced. 'Right, let's go.'

He led the way quickly to where he had tied his two-seat kayak to a mangrove tree that was overhanging the much shallower water just around the corner from the inlet. He drew out the paddles from the seat holes and laid them sideways across the canoe.

'Have you been in one of these before?' he asked.

'Never,' Niamh said, eyeing the narrow craft nervously.

'No problem. Climb in the front. Don't worry, I'll keep it steady for you.'

Niamh had seen people climbing into canoes before. They had made it look so easy, slipping their legs inside the body as if they were sliding into a sleeping bag. The reality of trying to do it for the first time was anything but easy.

'Ow!' she exclaimed, as she found her knees pinned to her chest and her grazed shin pressed up against the fibreglass rim of the cockpit.

'No, don't try to sit down and then straighten your legs,' Tony explained, gently helping her back up. 'Are you OK?'

'Yes, I'm fine,' she assured him, desperately blinking back tears. She didn't want him to think she was a pathetic crybaby. 'It just stings a bit.'

'OK then. Try again, but this time try sitting on the top of the canoe behind the cockpit first and sliding your feet as far forward inside as you can before you ease your bottom forward and lower it into the seat.'

Flushing with embarrassment at her first-time failure, Niamh tried again. This time she succeeded.

The bucket seat was comfortable enough under her bottom, but it felt very strange to be sitting so upright with her legs out straight in front of her. The rim of the cockpit was hard against the middle of her back and the idea of sitting inside for any length of time filled her with dread.

'OK, you're in,' Tony announced, as if it was a major achievement. 'Here you go. This is your paddle.'

'My paddle? But I don't know how to row.'

'You don't row in a kayak!' he laughed. 'Don't worry. It's easy. Just rest the paddle across in front of you for now and sit as still as you can while I get in. I'll show you what to do once we get going.'

The kayak wobbled slightly as Tony climbed in and Niamh was very glad that he couldn't see her face, which she felt sure was turning a bright shade of crimson as she felt his feet slide around her and come to rest against her outer thighs. It felt so intimate. Then they were moving. Out of the corner of her eye, Niamh could see Tony's paddle dipping into the water, first one side and then the other. The blades made virtually no splash as they slipped in and out of the water, but Niamh was amazed at the way the boat accelerated as he powered them away from the shore. Sitting this close to the surface made it seem as though they were fizzing through the water.

'Wow! This is amazing!' she said. 'I had no idea these things went so fast.'

Tony laughed. 'You should try surfing in one,' he said. 'That's a total rush!'

'I'll pass on that for now, thanks.'

'No surf today anyway,' he told her, sounding mildly disappointed. 'So I guess we'll just have to settle for teaching you the basics. OK, lift up your paddle in both hands. Try to make sure your hands are about shoulder-width apart . . .'

Over the next few minutes, Tony talked Niamh through the basics of paddling. First he had her making the motions above the water, progressing her quickly through to dipping the blades without trying to apply power and then on to actually putting some effort into moving them forward. To Niamh's delight, she picked up the rhythm quickly and before long the kayak was hissing through the water even faster.

They rounded the end of Monkey Island quite quickly and set out across the water towards the next island.

'How long is it going to take to paddle to your house?'

'Well, it took me about forty minutes to get to you this mornin',' he replied. 'But I was pushin' it.

My arms are pretty tired. I'd guess about forty-five, maybe fifty minutes. An' it looks like it was a good job I did.'

'Why? What do you mean?'

'We've got company on the way: behind and to our left. Looks like an FWC boat.'

'FWC?'

'Florida Fish and Wildlife Conservation Commission: they're the real cops of these waters,' Tony explained. 'I wouldn't be surprised if the Sheriff's Office hasn't got 'em out lookin' for you. When they come alongside, just wave 'n' smile. Let me do all the talkin', OK? A couple of seconds of your accent and we'll be at the bottom of the ninth, two strikes down, having hit a pop-up to midfield.'

'Whatever that means!' Niamh said, a nervous flutter unsettling her stomach. 'Are you talking American football language or something?'

'Baseball,' he replied. 'Football's OK, but here in the Keys, baseball is the only sport that matters. What I meant was, we'd need a miracle.'

'I understand. Don't worry, if they take me in, I'll tell them I fooled you into helping me.'

Niamh could hear the drone of the motor closing on them now. A glance over her left shoulder revealed a grey dinghy skimming across the water towards them at high speed. The driver was wearing

267

a creamy-coloured, short-sleeved shirt, dark glasses and a baseball cap with a tan-coloured peak. There was nowhere to hide. All she could do was place her trust in Tony and pray he was a good liar.

CHAPTER TWENTY

For all that Brad had told Sam that the raptors were technologically advanced, until the train pulled into the station it had been difficult to believe. Even the construction of the building had not prepared him for this.

'Wow!' Sam exclaimed, echoed a fraction of a second later by Callum.

'That looks like our train, boys,' Brad announced. 'Stick close to Nipper. There'll be raptors on board who may need reminding that we're not the buffet.'

The boys stumbled forward, their focus more on the amazing vehicle than looking where they were going. The train was bullet-like, with a sleek, tapered front end and an almost tubular construction along to an aerofoil-shaped tail end. Unlike the *clickety-clacking* of trains that Sam had ridden on in the UK, this silver beast glided into the station like a shimmering ghost, glossy and silent. Its diameter was closer to that of the aircraft they had flown across the Atlantic in than to any train Sam had seen before.

'How can something that size move so silently?' Callum asked. 'It doesn't seem possible.'

'My understanding is that it works on a blend of nuclear and electromagnetic technology,' Brad explained. 'I know it's hard to credit, but the train floats on a cushion of air . . .'

'A hover-train, but it's huge!' Sam exclaimed. 'And surely there'd be a draught and noise from the fans.'

'No, not a hover-train precisely,' Brad said, shaking his head. 'There are no fans. The train is being held in the air by an incredibly strong magnetic repulsion force. You must have played with magnets in your science lessons at school. Try to push two like poles together and it's tricky, right?'

The boys nodded.

'Well, that's the principle, except the magnetic forces between the train and rail are thousands of times stronger. Electromagnetic forces also drive the train, though I don't understand exactly how it works. The results are spectacular. This thing cruises at over 300 miles per hour.'

'Woah! Cool!' Callum breathed.

The subtle, subsonic *thrum* that vibrated through his body increased in intensity as they neared the train. Sam put his hand on his chest. The vibration ran deep inside.

'Do you feel that?' he asked Callum.

'Yes. What do you think it is?'

'I don't know. Must be something to do with the electromagnetic generators, I guess. Whatever it is, it's not helping my nerves.'

'I know what you mean.'

There was no obvious door into the train, but Nipper led them confidently forward and as if by magic, a large rectangular door shape appeared directly in front of him, sinking first inwards and then sliding sideways to reveal the strange interior of the gigantic silver vehicle.

'Don't we need tickets?' Sam asked.

'No,' Brad said, stepping up and in through the door. 'The raptors don't use currency. They work together in a complex cooperative. Humans could learn a lot from their mentality.'

A narrow aisle ran down either side of the train and another along the very centre. There were no seats, but instead, there were rows and rows of half-cylinders made of something that looked like semi-transparent plastic. They ran floor to ceiling and were all angled back at about twenty degrees from vertical towards the back of the train. Each formed a mini-alcove big enough for a single raptor or person.

'Well, would you look at that!' Callum exclaimed softly. 'They remind me of tilted Borg alcoves from *Star Trek* without all the flashing lights and stuff.'

'I was never a *Star Trek* fan,' Brad admitted. 'But I doubt the Enterprise ever had anything quite like these.'

Nipper led the way along the central aisle until he found a row that was totally empty and then he directed the boys into the alcoves to their right.

'Pick an alcove, step inside and lean back,' Brad told them. 'Quickly! Raptors don't react well to being delayed. That's it. Enjoy the ride, boys. It's probably best if you don't leave your alcove until the train stops. You'll be safe while you stay inside.'

Sam frowned, but moved along the row until he reached the alcove closest to the window. Callum took the one next to him. Leaning against a plastic wall for hours was not exactly his idea of fun. How long would it take to reach their destination? Brad had said it was about a thousand miles away, so it would take at least three hours. With a sigh of resignation, he stepped into the alcove, put his hands against the walls and leaned back.

'WOAH!'

Rather than the cold, solid plastic Sam had been expecting to feel, the surface gave as he leaned back, causing him to lose his balance and fall back harder. He experienced a fleeting moment of panic as he felt his body and the back of his head sinking into the semi-liquid surface. Thoughts of suffocation and drowning flitted through his mind, to be replaced almost instantly by yet another sense of wonder as the strangely elastic quality of the material kept him from sinking too far into it.

He heard Callum's yell from the neighbouring tube and then Brad's calming voice telling them not to panic. The older man's reassuring tones helped him relax. There was a sort of tickling sensation as the substance settled round him and began to harden. Brad stuck his head around the side of the alcove and gave him a grin.

'Interesting, isn't it?' he said.

'Incredible!' Sam replied.

'Try standing up and doing it again, both of you. This time sit back into it, rather than lean. It's more comfortable for a journey like this.'

Sam did as he was told. As he pushed away from the surface, he instinctively brushed at his clothes and ran his fingers through the back of his hair to see if any of the substance was still attached. It wasn't. No sooner had he stood up than the surface of the tube returned to its former shape, looking perfectly rounded and solid. He tried again, more confidently this time, and discovered that Brad was right. It was like sitting into a shallow, reclining chair that had been made specifically for his body.

'It feels sort of like a high-tech beanbag,' he observed.

'That's a pretty good analogy,' Brad agreed. 'Once the surface has settled and hardened sufficiently, you'll find the entertainment begins automatically.' Brad looked first into Sam's alcove and then Callum's, but directed his comments into both. 'My personal favourite is channel three, as you don't need to understand the raptor language to appreciate it. To change the channel, reach out and touch the symbol at the bottom right. The off symbol is top centre.'

'Bottom right of what?' Sam heard Callum ask. 'I don't see anything.'

'You'll understand when it kicks off,' Brad replied. 'The normal default is the news channel that was playing in the station. I'd better go get into my alcove now. We're about to start moving. Have fun.'

Sam settled and sat back, allowing the strange substance to mould and harden around him. As it reached a solid state, he noticed that the edges of the alcove began to grow out and around to enclose him in a complete tube. Brad hadn't said anything about this, but Sam was determined not to panic.

'It's a good job I'm not claustrophobic,' he muttered, as the walls met and sealed.

No sooner was he totally enclosed than a raptor's head appeared right in front of him and its voice filled the tube. Despite expecting something like this, Sam still jumped. The proximity of the creature's pointed teeth was unnerving and for a moment he imagined he could smell its meaty breath.

Several three-dimensional icons appeared around the central image. Bottom right to change the channel Brad had said. Sam reached out with his right hand and extended a finger towards the diamond shape there. There was a momentary snowstorm of static and then he was in a forest, apparently looking through another's eyes. He looked around. It felt incredibly real.

He was moving at a walking pace between the trees. Distant birdsong and more immediate insect noises filled the air. The forest was nothing like the jungle he had walked through earlier. This looked more like the sort of woodland he would have expected to find in Canada or North America: huge trees, minimal undergrowth and an airy, cathedral-like atmosphere. Sam drew in a deep breath through his nose, half expecting to smell the pine scent on the air. His imagination added a hint of it, just as it had with the raptor's breath, and he felt a smile tilt up the corners of his mouth.

A movement ahead and to the right caught his attention. Something was there. His viewpoint paused in its forward motion as if waiting, or listening. Sam found himself holding his breath, not wanting to make a sound. With breathtaking suddenness, he exploded forward, accelerating between the trees with a bounding rhythm that revealed the nature of what he was experiencing. This was a hunt through the eyes of a raptor. Fascinating though it was, Sam knew it was only likely to end one way and although he was not squeamish, he reached for the channel button again.

The brief snowstorm this time was replaced by something totally mind-blowing. It was no wonder that Brad liked this channel, he thought. What he guessed he was seeing was a live feed from the top of the front of the train. Although Sam had not felt any movement since climbing aboard, there was no sign of the station and the trees were already whipping past at a fair lick. The track stretched away ahead into the distance. If he had to guess, he would say they were already moving at about sixty miles per hour and slowly accelerating. It was a perfect opportunity to see something of this strange world, he realised.

'I wonder what 300 miles per hour will feel like,' Sam muttered, looking around. The view from the top of the train was great. On one side he could see across the treetops all the way to the sea. On the other side was more jungle, broken occasionally by what looked like a network of marsh and inland waterways. Even as Sam watched, a line of what looked like enormous alligators raced down a bank to slip into one of the channels. This, in turn, triggered a mass of waterbirds to launch into the air in a flurry of warning squawks and shrieks.

'Cool!' Sam breathed. 'It's like being inside the camera of a nature documentary.'

Accelerating smoothly, the train raced faster and faster until it was hurtling along at a greater velocity than any train he had ever been on. The quicker it went, the more breathtaking Sam's viewpoint became.

Aside from occasional clusters of geodesic structures and the rail line ahead, the only other evidence Sam saw of raptor technology were strange, double cone-shaped structures that funnelled into opposing ends of gleaming cylinders of shining copper. He saw lots of them during the journey, some near the tracks and others further off in the distance. It took a while for him to realise that every one of them was aligned in the same direction. He couldn't be certain, but his best guess was that they must be something to do with the energy conversion process of turning this world's enhanced magnetic field into electricity.

His theory was given a further boost when he spotted two particularly large cone and cylinder structures near a large cluster of the geodesic raptor buildings. What made no sense, though, was that there appeared to be nothing connecting the strange-looking structures to the nearby houses. Was the energy transmitted underground? He could not see any other way.

A large expanse of water opened on Sam's left and he gave a yip of excitement as he spied dozens of long necks protruding from the water. One was fairly close. What was it? Brontosaurus? Diplodocus? He did not know his dinosaurs well enough to tell. Even if he had, Sam realised these were not the dinosaurs of Earth as the fossil history showed them. Having had another sixty-five million years or so, there was no telling which dinosaurs had continued to evolve, which had remained relatively unchanged and which were extinct.

This last thought turned his mind back to his mother's fate. Was she still at the City of the Imperium? Would he recognise her? His memories of her were so vague. The only image he held in his mind was that of the picture next to his dad's bed, taken just over nine years ago. Nine years was a long time. Would she have changed much?

'Please be alive, Mum,' he breathed, looking forward at the long line of the track ahead. 'And don't do anything silly. I'm coming to find you.'

Brad had barely settled into his alcove when the burning began in his bladder. Irritated, but unable to ignore the building pressure, he realised he had not explained to the youngsters what to do if they needed to go while they were on board.

Go first and tell them afterwards, he told himself.

Pushing away from the wall, he stood up and the front walls of the tube withdrew, leaving him clear to step out of his alcove. He paused for a second outside Nipper's. Should he tell the raptor where he was going?

We've just left the station, he thought. The raptors will all be in their alcoves. *I'm only going to be a minute.*

He moved silently towards the rear of the train along the central aisle. The further he went, the more he relaxed. He had been right. There was no sign of movement anywhere. Lots of alcoves were sealed, but there were still a good number of open ones. As he reached the final partition, he peered into the compartment that housed the waste-disposal units.

It was empty. He crossed the small open area to one of the middle waste units and relieved himself into it.

Zipping up his shorts, he turned, intending to stride off back to his alcove. A hulking raptor was standing in the middle of the compartment no more than three paces away. Brad almost fell forward into it as he momentarily fought for balance. It was staring at him with unblinking eyes.

'Woah! You move quietly for a big fella!' Brad exclaimed aloud. He concentrated and in raptor language said the words, '*You quiet move.*'

The huge raptor drew back the flesh around his lipless mouth to reveal his teeth. Nipper did this when he was amused, which Brad took as a sign that the creature was in good humour. He smiled back and nodded. Keen to get back to his alcove, Brad took a step to the left with the intention of going around the raptor. The raptor immediately moved to block his way.

'*I go,*' Brad said, pointing around the raptor.

The raptor's toothy grin broadened further. Brad moved to the right. The raptor blocked his path again.

'*I go,*' Brad repeated, unable to keep his irritation from rising.

'*No,*' the raptor clicked back.

Brad looked the creature up and down. What did it want? Its scales were a darker shade than those of Nipper and his friends. Did this mean it came from a different region? Brad did not know.

Like many raptors, the creature had several scars on its shoulders, upper body and legs: evidence of past battles. Although raptor society was technologically advanced, some of the socially accepted norms appeared barbaric by human standards. It was not unusual for a raptor argument to end in a battle to the death. Looking at this beast, it looked like he had seen his fair share.

Brad's eyes came to rest on some scars unlike the rest. A diagonal line of puckered puncture scars ran across the creature's thighs. They looked remarkably like bullet wounds. But they couldn't be, could they? Brad had not seen or heard a gun in all the years since he had crossed to this world. He looked up at the raptor's face again.

'Why not go?' Brad asked.

The raptor lifted its hands to display its hooked, blade-like central claws. Opening its jaws wide, it clicked three terrifying words.

'Time . . . you . . . die.'

CHAPTER TWENTY-ONE

'Mornin', sir. Everythin' OK?' Tony called out as the FWC patrol boat pulled alongside them.

Niamh looked across at the driver. His expression was hard to read. The dark glasses didn't help.

'Yeah,' he drawled. 'Just headin' out to Monkey Island. You look like you're on your way in from there. See anythin' unusual?'

'Unusual? What sort of unusual?' Tony asked. 'We've just paddled round the island. Didn't notice anythin' weird, though – you, sis?'

Niamh shrugged and shook her head.

'Pretty keen for this time-a-day,' the officer noted. 'That's a long paddle.'

'Weather's due to close in this afternoon, so we had to come out early. Won a bet with Carrie yesterday. She's not the outdoor type. If I'd lost, I'd be readin' some dull book now, but instead, she's had to brave the water with me.'

'Good for you,' the man said, clearly not interested in the slightest. 'Listen, I'm lookin' for a girl about your age . . .'

'You an' me both,' Tony interrupted, laughing. 'Preferably a hot one.'

Niamh didn't know where to look. She tried to look amused by Tony's comment, but her smile was forced. Would it show? Her stomach was in knots, yet she could feel her face threatening to flush. Surely the man would notice?

Flashing a brief smile at Tony, the officer looked more irritated by his interruption than amused. 'Not rightly sure what this one looks like,' he said. 'Just got a call from the Sheriff's Office to come out here an' look for a boat she stole from Summerland Key yesterday. Apparently, she's English.'

'There's no boats moored at Monkey Island,' Tony offered, back-paddling to stay parallel. 'Jetty's clear. I'd have noticed if it weren't. Unusual to see boats out there.'

'Anythin' oceanside?'

'Oceanside?' Tony said, feigning surprise. 'Nope. There's nowhere to moor. S'pose it depends how big the boat is though. A small one could probably get in close enough.'

'This is a thirty-two-foot cruiser.'

'Yeah, right! Dream on!' Tony laughed. 'Only way you'd get a boat that size in close to Monkey Island on the ocean side is in about a thousand pieces. Too shallow. Reef would rip it apart.'

The man nodded. 'That's what I thought. I'd better go an' take a look anyway. Enjoy your paddle.'

Niamh gave the man a sour look, which drew a genuine chuckle from him. He eased the throttle forward and turned away. Niamh noted that he watched to ensure he had taken his boat a reasonable distance from the kayak before opening up the power and accelerating away at speed.

'Thank goodness he's gone,' she sighed.

'Yeah, but we're not out of the woods yet,' Tony replied, digging in the paddles with renewed vigour. 'If he finds the boat with no one in it, he'll be back. If he's got half a brain, it won't be hard for him to put the pieces together. We'd better paddle for home as fast as we can.'

Niamh did not answer. She knew he was right. Rather than talk, she began twisting the paddle in the rolling motion Tony had taught her, doing her best to match his new rhythm. As she added what strength she could to his urgent strokes, the canoe sped through the water faster than ever.

To Niamh it felt an impossibly long way to Tony's home beach. By the time they reached the shore near his home, she felt wrecked. Her arms were leaden with fatigue, her palms were red and threatening blisters, her back ached, her bottom was numb and her stomach and legs were so cramped that when she did find the strength to struggle out of the cockpit of the canoe, she couldn't stand. When Tony told her they would have to carry the boat back to his house, she felt tears forming in her eyes.

'I can't,' she moaned. 'Everything hurts.'

'Yes, you can,' he assured her gently. 'Don't worry, it's not far and the boat's not heavy. Come on. You can do it.'

'My legs don't want to move.'

To Niamh's acute embarrassment, Tony made her sit down on the sand and he began to massage her calves.

'Where is it hurting worst?' he asked.

'Um, that's it,' she said quickly, unable to look him in the eye. It was too embarrassing. He had taken a huge risk for her, yet all she had been able to think about the entire time was how cute he was and what sort of a boyfriend he would make. Given her thoughts about him, the very idea of Tony's hands kneading the worst areas of pain set her face flushing again.

Unlike some of the girls at school, she had never had a serious boyfriend. The most intimate she'd ever been with a boy was a bit of kissing in a quiet corner at a friend's birthday party. That boy had turned out to have a one-track mind, and Niamh had not been interested in what he wanted. She'd dumped him the next day.

'That's great, thanks. I'm sure I'll manage now,' she said quickly, pushing his hands away.

'Are you sure?' Tony asked, surprised. 'But I've not really done . . .'

'Positive,' she said, staggering to her feet. 'I'll be fine now. Thanks a lot. Now where to?'

'Hey, look!' Tony exclaimed. 'No need to worry, the cavalry's arrived. Carrie! Over here, quick!'

To Niamh's intense relief, Carrie appeared through the trees and ran towards them, hair flowing behind her like a golden cloud.

'Hi, Niamh,' she enthused. 'Glad to see Tony got to you in time.'

'Only just,' Tony said, his tone full of warning. 'Carrie, we need to get the kayak out of sight as quick as we can. You've not seen Tessa around, have you?'

'No.'

'Good,' he said firmly. 'Don't need any more complications. Gimme a hand, would you? Poor

Niamh's beat. Fisheries officer intercepted us on his way out to Monkey Island.'

'Oh, shoot! You think he might come lookin' when he finds the boat?'

'Yep. We paddled flat out all the way back, but I doubt we've got long. Let's get outta here!'

Niamh looked back out across the water towards Monkey Island and took a sharp intake of breath. In the distance she could see the fast-moving inflatable rounding the end of the island and turning in their direction.

'Too late!' she said. 'He's already coming this way. Run!'

'No!' Tony ordered, a calculating look in his eyes. 'Niamh, hide behind those bushes over there. Quickly! Unless he's got eyes like an eagle, he won't be able to see who's on the beach yet. Go with her, Carrie. Swap shirts and glasses, tie your hair back like Niamh has hers and then come back and join me. Let's see if we can't throw him off the trail.'

'That won't work!' Niamh protested. 'Carrie's perfectly tanned and gorgeous. He'll never mistake her for me!'

'You don't look that different,' he said calmly. 'Your hair is the same colour and length. You're both slim. He's wearing dark shades, so he's unlikely to pick up on the difference in skin tone. Besides, it's our best shot. Go! Quickly!'

Niamh and Carrie raced over to the nearby bushes, crouched down and exchanged shirts. Niamh couldn't believe how naughty she felt. It was strange, but creating this little deception with Carrie felt more wrong than stealing the Mitchells' boat. Perhaps it was because she was doing it with someone else, she thought.

'I need your ribbon too,' Carrie said, pointing.

Niamh untied it. 'Let me help you,' she offered. 'It's not easy to tie on your own.'

Moments later, Carrie had been transformed into as close a replica of Niamh as they could manage. Niamh looked her up and down. It was hard to imagine the man being fooled, but it was the best they could do.

'Tony gave the reason you were out early as the approaching bad weather,' Niamh said quickly as Carrie stood up to leave. 'You went along because you lost a bet. If you'd won, Tony would be reading a book today. Oh, and act like you're hurting. Believe me – I ache all over.'

'Thanks,' Carrie smiled. 'I doubt Tony would have thought to tell me any of that.'

Niamh crawled as deep into the bushes as she could and listened. She could hear the drone of the patrol boat's engine now. It was approaching fast. The foliage was dense, but Niamh could see splintered bits of the beach through the leaves. It was rather like having a selection of keyholes to look through, but not being able to get close enough to them to get a decent view through any.

Niamh tensed as the sound of the approaching boat's engine dropped to a purr. Had he run the boat right up to the beach? She couldn't see.

'Hi there again, sir,' Tony called out. 'Did you find anythin'?'

Given that he was shouting, Niamh judged the man to be holding the boat away from the beach.

'Yes and no,' the man replied. 'I found the boat I was lookin' for in a hidden inlet, but there was no sign of the girl.'

'Really? How'd she get it in across the reef?'

'Narrow channel – bloody miracle, if you ask me. Seems hard to believe that a Limey tourist girl got such a big cruiser through that channel without sinkin' it. Seems likely she had help from someone who knows the waters well. You sure you can't help me, kid?'

'Not me, sir,' Tony shouted. 'Didn't even see the boat. Maybe she left the boat so she could hide on the island somewhere. It'd be tough to find her in the trees there, but unless she's some sorta survival nut, she'd get hungry an' thirsty pretty quick. I'm guessin' if you go lookin', she'll turn herself in, if she's there.'

'What about you . . . Carrie, was it?'

'That's right, sir,' Carrie called back.

'Anythin' you can tell me?'

'No, sir. I was too busy concentratin' on paddlin' an' thinkin' on how to keep my arms from droppin' off to worry 'bout much else. Next time I think about makin' a stupid bet with my brother, I'll be sure to remember how much losin' this one hurt.'

No matter how she moved her head around, Niamh could not get a clear view of the patrol boat. Was the man convinced? The pause following Carrie's answer seemed to drag on forever. What was he thinking? Had he seen through her disguise?

'OK then,' the man called out eventually. 'Maybe you're right. I'll go get some help and have a team search the island. Thanks for your time. You kids have a nice day. An' if you see or hear anythin' of the English girl, be sure you report it to the Sheriff's Office, you hear?'

'Will do,' Tony called back. 'Good luck with your search, sir.'

At the sound of the powerful outboard motor gunning away from the beach, Niamh felt her body begin to relax. All the aches and pains, forgotten during the tension of the past couple of minutes, returned in force.

'Oh, God!' she groaned. 'I can't move.'

She heard Tony organise the lifting of the canoe and the approaching footsteps of the brother and sister as they carried it up the beach towards her hiding place. Still she could not bring herself to move.

'Niamh?' Carrie called softly. 'It's OK. He's gone. You can come out now.'

Niamh whimpered as she attempted to slither backwards out from under the bushes. The slight rustle as she moved was enough to draw their attention.

'There you are!' Carrie exclaimed. 'For a second there, I thought you'd gone an' run off without us.'

'I should have,' Niamh moaned. 'I could get you both into a lot of trouble. But I can't move. It hurts too much!'

A moment later, the brother and sister were helping her out and onto her feet. Niamh had never felt so grateful. She hugged Carrie, tears of relief and pain rolling down her cheeks.

'Thank you,' she whispered. 'Thank you so much.'

'No sweat,' Carrie replied, embarrassed. 'It was fun. Come on. Let's get you home and see about fixin' you somethin' to eat and drink. Can you walk OK? It's not far.'

'I'll manage,' Niamh replied, biting her lip against the stiffness and pain.

Mercifully, Carrie had not exaggerated. The house was no more than a couple of hundred metres away. Niamh did not notice much as they walked. It was hard to focus on anything other than the pain that was radiating throughout her body. As they approached the house, however, one thing did catch her attention. It was a tree with writing all over the leaves. Niamh had never seen anything like it before.

'We call it an autograph tree,' Carrie said, noticing Niamh's interest. 'Whatever you write on the leaves stays there for the entire life of the tree. Cool, eh?'

'It's a novel form of graffiti,' Niamh agreed, giving her a weak smile. 'I suppose the nearest equivalent back home is carving initials into the bark of a tree.'

'Yeah, that happens here too,' Carrie nodded. 'But writing on these leaves doesn't hurt the tree like carving into bark does and if you write something you later regret, you can just pull off the leaf. This one is a bit like a living journal for me.'

'Really? In what way?'

'She's written all of her past boyfriends' names on there,' Tony interrupted, laughing. 'She must have covered half the tree by now!'

'Have not!' Carrie said, sounding hurt. 'Not quite,' she added in a conspiratorial voice, giving Niamh a sly wink.

'There's a lot of names up there,' Tony said with a shrug.

'And can I help it that all the boys I've agreed to go out with have turned out to be dorks with one thing on their mind?' Carrie asked. 'I like to think of it as a visual reminder of what a bunch of losers the guys are around here. Most of them have lasted one date. Some didn't even manage that. Losers, the lot of 'em.'

They reached Tony and Carrie's home. It did not look as large as the Summerland Key house that Niamh's father had bought, but it did look nice. Tony and Niamh put the canoe into the garage and ushered Niamh through a door at the back that opened into the main living area. Carrie took her by the hand and Niamh winced. The blonde girl turned Niamh's hand over to see what had caused that reaction.

'Oh, you poor thing,' she said, looking at the line of red blistering skin across her palm and at the base of her thumb. 'That's gotta hurt.'

'No more than most of the rest of my body,' Niamh said. 'I had no idea that paddling a kayak was such hard work.'

'Well, let me get you a cold drink and then you can have a soak in a nice warm ... Niamh, get down! Now!'

Niamh didn't hesitate. She dropped to the floor, her heart suddenly hammering as the hissed warning sent a new wave of panic through her. What now? Had the Fisheries officer followed them here after all?

'Tony! It's Tessa. She's coming up the drive,' Carrie said urgently. 'Shoot! What if she saw Niamh? What should we do?'

'Damn it!' Tony muttered. 'OK, get Niamh through to your bedroom. Stay quiet, Niamh, OK? I'll deal with Tessa.'

'Stay low and follow me,' Carrie ordered.

Niamh did as she was told, crawling as fast as she could. The carpet was mercifully thick and soft against her hands, but tears tracked down her cheeks once more as she tortured her aching muscles still further. Once out of the living room and into a short hallway, she got to her feet again and stumbled along it to where Carrie was holding open a door for her.

'Feel free to lay on the bed,' Carrie whispered. 'Try to relax. I'll be back as soon as I can.'

Niamh crossed the room to the bed and slumped down onto it. Just as Carrie began to close the door, she heard Tessa's raised voice.

'She's here, isn't she?' she accused. 'You went and got her! Are you crazy, Tony? What do you think you're doing?'

CHAPTER TWENTY-TWO

Sam's first sight of the City of the Imperium took his breath away. From the crest of the shallow ridge it appeared to be a vast single geodesic structure covering many square kilometres of land. Its weird geometric shapes and interlocking structures looked so alien that he could not help feeling that he had somehow fallen into a computer-generated image of the far future. From the very centre of the city soared a vast spike of a tower, like a javelin of the gods stabbing down from the sky.

'Wow!' he breathed. 'Now that's something you don't see every day.'

There was a slight jolt as airbrakes deployed from the body of the train to begin the deceleration. They were still several kilometres from the edge of the city, but Sam had already seen how long it took to shed their momentum during their one brief stop at another station about an hour and a half earlier.

The journey had passed remarkably quickly. The exhilaration as the train had reached its amazing cruising speed had taken some time to dull, but gradually, he had adapted to the sensation of travelling at super high speed.

For more than an hour, the countryside had remained monotonously flat as they flashed up the full length of this alternate world's Florida mainland. As the train sped ever northwards, gradual undulations in the terrain began to make the scenery more interesting. Everywhere Sam looked he found new things to marvel at. He found the great herds of enormous grazing herbivore dinosaurs to be particularly fascinating. It was only when he caught sight of the fourth or fifth such herd that he realised exactly what he was seeing. These animals were being farmed by the raptors. They were the equivalent of the cows and sheep in the human world. Raptor society and values were different to those of humans, but there were some fundamental elements that seemed to have developed along similar paths.

The train decelerated slowly as it approached the edge of the city. Rather like the door to the station, the monorail appeared to run straight through the outer city wall. It was not until they were very close and a crash seemed inevitable that an enormous section of the structure opened to admit them.

Sam could barely wait to see what wonders awaited within the city, but to his disappointment, the holographic camera view suddenly vanished as they passed through the outer wall. The clamshell doors to his alcove opened and he pushed himself upright. A glance back at the wall behind him revealed the apparently solid half-tube restored to its former smoothness.

'Amazing!' he said.

'Cool ride, eh?' Callum enthused, appearing to Sam's left. 'Did you do what Brad said and watch channel three?'

'Yep. It was like a three-hour-long 3D *Disney* ride!' Sam looked past him to where Nipper and Grunt were emerging from their alcoves. 'Talking of Brad, where is he?' he added.

'In his alcove, I assume,' Callum replied, surprised. He took a few steps forward and looked into the older man's alcove. It was empty. 'No. He's not here,' he reported.

Nipper sniffed the air and growled. The boys did not need to understand raptor language to sense the ominous nature of that sound.

'Sssssam, C'umm, sta,' he hissed, pointing at the floor in front of them. A rapid exchange of clicking and growling between Grunt and Nipper concluded with Nipper disappearing along the central aisle towards the back of the train. Grunt moved in close to the boys and parked himself between them and the central aisle.

'Something's up,' Sam muttered.

'Yeah, I got that too,' Callum mumbled back. 'I hope Brad's OK.'

About a minute later, Nipper returned. There was another rapid exchange between the two raptors. It seemed to involve more growling than the usual predominance of clicks. Grunt moved aside and Nipper looked at the two boys with his big yellow eyes.

'B'ad dud,' he said.

Sam looked across at Callum. His face hung slack and the colour was draining from his complexion. He looked back at Nipper.

'No! I must have heard that wrong.' Sam gasped. 'Did you just say Brad's dead?'

Nipper nodded. It was hard to read the raptor's expression, but Sam could see the anger in his stance. Did the creature feel any regret or sadness? He couldn't tell.

'How?' Callum asked, his tone flat and lifeless. 'Why?'

Nipper made slashing motions with his claws.

Sam and Callum winced simultaneously. No words were needed to help the boys with an interpretation.

'It was a raptor?' Sam asked.

Nipper nodded again. 'Bad sssorrrrt,' he said, growling the 'r' sound. 'Come.'

At first, the boys thought Nipper was going to lead them to Brad's body, but he stopped next to the exit doors. Other raptors were emerging from their alcoves and converging on the same area. Nipper directed the boys into a corner near the doors and then he and Grunt hemmed them there, facing out at the other raptors and growling protectively.

'Poor Leah!' Callum muttered. 'Shouldn't we do something about Brad's body?'

'I don't think that's an option,' Sam replied, peering nervously round the raptors. 'Nipper and Grunt look pretty focused on protecting us. I think we'd better just worry about getting out of here alive.'

'But we can't just leave him, can we? What if he's not really dead? He might just be badly . . .'

'Dud!' Nipper interrupted emphatically.

Sam did not reply. Brad had been so enthusiastic about bringing them to the Imperium to search for Sam's mother. He had known how dangerous the journey would be, Sam was sure of it. Leah had known too. Although she had not said as much in front of them, Sam had seen the way she had looked at Brad before they left. Had she known it would be the last time she would see him?

Tears began to track down his cheeks as he stared at Nipper's back. He felt so guilty. This was his fault. If they hadn't come looking for his mum, it would never have happened. They had not been gone half a day and one of their only friends in this world was dead. It did not seem real. Sam looked across at Callum. He had put his friend in danger too. Saying something was dangerous and experiencing the deadly outcome were two entirely different things. It was bad enough knowing he was responsible for Brad's death. How would he feel if Callum became the next victim?

He noted the tears in Callum's eyes. He could find no more words to share at this moment.

Most of the other raptors ignored the two boys and their bodyguards. They waited patiently for the train to stop and the doors to open. It was at the moment the doors slid open that Sam noticed a particularly large raptor steal a glance in their direction. It was only for the briefest moment, but afterwards Sam felt sure he had not imagined it.

He played the moment over and over in his mind. The enormous creature's eyes had slid across to their corner and Sam had shivered as he contemplated the cold malice that lurked behind the raptor's gaze.

He watched as the doors opened and all the other raptors disembarked. The one that had caught Sam's eye was nearly the last to leave. He looked it up and down, noting the scars on its upper body and a line of puncture scars across its thighs. When it left, it prowled away with a loping gait and did not look back.

Nipper and Grunt kept them in the corner until the doors were totally clear before leading them off the train.

'Come,' Nipper ordered again.

The boys followed. What choice did they have? It was good that Nipper could speak a few recognisable words of English, but without their translator Sam suddenly felt more lost than ever.

'Did you see that big raptor?' Sam asked Callum in a low voice.

'Which one? They're all big.'

'Not to worry,' Sam said. 'I'm probably imagining things.'

Inside, he knew he wasn't.

The station in the city was larger than either of the two Sam had seen on their way there, but despite its size, it did not seem as busy as the others. The enormous holographic news screen seemed to be a standard feature. A difference in this station was the presence of several smaller monorail structures with lines of single cars that looked as if they would hold about six raptors at a time. As these filled and moved off out from the station along several different rails, others arrived to take their place. Seeing the vehicles coming and going reminded Sam of a taxi rank and it was to one of these that Nipper led them.

They joined a short queue that melted away in front of them with impressive efficiency. Then it was their turn. Nipper opened the side door to one of the monocars and ushered the boys inside. Grunt turned and barred entry to other raptors before climbing in last and closing the door behind them. As soon as the door was closed, a holographic image of the city was projected into the centre of the cabin and Nipper reached into the middle of it to touch a tiny icon with the tip of his claw. The holograph vanished and they were off.

The acceleration of the car as it pulled away was a shock. Sam rocked back in his seat and thumped the back of his head into the solid backrest so hard that he saw stars.

'Oww!' Callum echoed as his head made a similarly resounding impact. As the car raced out of the station along its monorail at terrifying speed, they emerged into motoring madness. 'Holy crap!' he swore, his whirl of emotions at the loss of Brad momentarily forgotten and fear taking their place. 'It's like a grand prix, but with half of the drivers going the wrong way!'

Rails converged, merged and split in a mind-twisting, spaghetti-like mass of lines, and their monocar automatically accelerated and decelerated, apparently jostling for position among the masses of other speeding cars in a mad dash for their destination.

'Makes the M25 look like a peaceful country road at midnight by comparison,' Sam gasped, wincing as they cut across the path of an oncoming vehicle. There did not appear to be any rhyme, reason or rules as to which way the cars were going.

'Oh, God! It's our turn to die!' Callum moaned, putting his hands over his glasses and then peeping between his fingers.

The two raptors began making rapid clicking noises.

'Are you laughing at us?' Sam accused, anger flaring inside him like an exploding star.

Nipper nodded, flashing his teeth at Sam in a gesture that he interpreted as amusement.

'Someone needs to introduce the designers of this crazy system to the idea of health and safety,' Callum grumbled, gasping again as another car flashed past so close that the cab was rocked by its passage. 'You could have a heart attack in one of these things.'

If Sam had been able to let go of his handholds for so much as a second, he would have thrown something at the raptors. He was so angry that even Callum's attempt at humour glanced off him. Later, Sam realised that his mind had instinctively converted his panic into anger, perhaps in some kind of defence mechanism. Whatever the reason, his rage was irrational and dangerous; the raptors could kill him or Callum in an instant. Luckily, the journey was short.

Soon the car speared off on a branch rail that took them straight towards the sidewall of the great transport corridor. When it sped through another of the heart-stopping doors that didn't open until the last second, Sam came close to vomiting.

The car came to an abrupt halt seconds later and he found he was physically shaking as Nipper opened the door and stepped outside, turning to gesture for the boys to follow.

'Quick!' Callum urged, grabbing Sam by the hand and pulling him out through the open door. 'Before it decides to mash us into a pulp against a wall or another car.'

Sam's legs felt weak as he staggered from the car. Nipper and Grunt again clicked with amusement. Sam wanted to hit them with something – anything – hard. Barely fifteen minutes had passed since the discovery of Brad's body and the two raptors were laughing as if he had never existed. Keeping his fury under check was not easy. Had they felt nothing for him? When Sam had first seen the creatures talk to Brad, there had appeared to be mutual respect between them. Could raptors feel the pain of losing someone, or were they so insensitive to death that they could ignore it as an everyday event?

'Cold-hearted, overgrown geckos!' Sam muttered through gritted teeth.

'What?' Callum asked.

'Nothing.'

The two boys followed the raptors up some steps and through another of the scary sliding doors. Inside was what appeared to be a reception area with a large central desk. A raptor in a white coat was standing behind it. He clicked a welcome to Nipper and Grunt, while eyeing the two boys with a cold gaze. Sam could see the raptor's nostrils twitching as he and Callum approached. It looked as though the creature was testing their scent. After a moment, the raptor looked directly at Sam and his eyes narrowed.

'He's looking at you,' Callum observed in a low voice.

'Yeah,' Sam said, a sudden chill cutting through the heat of his anger and shooting down his spine. 'And I don't like the way he's doing it.'

White Jacket suddenly broke eye contact with Sam, turned his head to the right and let out an ear-splitting roar. To Sam's surprise, both Nipper and Grunt began clicking and growling at once. It looked as if they were both gabbling at White Jacket simultaneously, but why?

'Call me a pessimist, but I'd say that doesn't look good,' Sam muttered.

'You a mind-reader now?'

From corridors to either side of the reception desk a stream of raptors appeared, all wearing white coats. Within seconds, they were surrounded.

'What *is* this place?' Sam asked aloud as a raptor grabbed his arm in a grip of iron. 'Nipper! What's going on?'

Nipper turned and looked at him. Although it was hard to read expressions on the raptor's face, Sam was convinced he could see a look of hopeless resignation in Nipper's eyes.

'Sssssam . . . sssssorrrrreeee.'

CHAPTER TWENTY-THREE

'Don't be silly, Tess!' Tony scoffed. 'Why would I go an' do somethin' stupid like that? Get real! She's a fugitive, for goodness' sake!'

'You tellin' me she ain't here then?'

Although her muscles were screaming at her in silent protest, Niamh couldn't lie on the bed. She could just about hear what was being said, but if they lowered their voices even slightly she would start missing things and she had to know what was happening. Forcing herself back onto her feet, Niamh crept back to the door of Carrie's room and, turning the handle with painful care, she cracked it open. The door opened the wrong way for her to be able to peep down the corridor towards the living area, but she held her breath to listen.

'Ain't no one here but me an' Carrie right now,' Tony was saying. 'Ain't that right, sis?'

Carrie strolled across the living area towards them.

'What's that, Tony?' she asked 'Hi, Tessa. Nice top,' she added, eyeing the bright, low-cut top appreciatively.

'Just us in at the moment,' he repeated.

'Yeah,' Carrie drawled. 'Mom's gone to Key West shoppin', an' Dad's at work. Why? Did you need to talk to 'em, Tessa?'

Tessa looked at Carrie with narrowed eyes as she searched for any hint of a lie, but Carrie was not giving anything away. She met Tessa's gaze and then slowly drew her brows together into a frown as the girl stared her out.

'What's with the look?' she asked. 'What's wrong?'

'She thinks I've brought Niamh here,' Tony explained.

'What?' Carrie asked, feigning shock. 'Didn't you see the *Citizen* this mornin'? Tony showed me the story earlier. Yeah, she seemed nice enough yesterday. An' I thought she was just messin' with us when she said about her dad and stealin' the boat 'n' everythin', but the paper confirms she was actually tellin' the truth. God, I feel such a fool!'

'Who do you think told Tony about it?' Tessa asked smugly.

'Really?' Carrie asked, giving a convincing performance of being surprised.

'Yeah,' Tony confirmed. 'Forgot to mention that, sorry.'

'Well, after I saw Tony this mornin', I called the cops an' told 'em where she is,' Tessa bragged. 'She won't be on Monkey Island for much longer.'

Carrie sucked in a sharp intake of breath. 'You didn't give your name, did you? Or ours?' she asked.

'Nah!' Tessa said, sticking her hands deep in her pockets. She looked so irritatingly smug that Carrie itched to smack her round the face. 'I'm not stupid, Carrie. I rang and gave an anonymous tip-off. Didn't want to admit to trespass. Still, we'd better not go fishin' over there for a few days until the heat is off the place.'

'Hmm! Sounds sensible,' Tony agreed. 'So what do you wanna do today instead?'

'Dunno.'

'I thought about catchin' a bus into Key West and takin' a wander down Duval Street. You wanna come?'

'Sounds cool,' Tessa agreed, looking up at him from under her long lashes. 'Laughin' at the tourists is better than nothin'. How about you, Carrie? Gonna join us?'

The offer sounded more of a challenge than an invitation, but Carrie ignored the tone and kept her response friendly.

'Nah!' she said, shaking her head. 'Thanks, but I've got to make a start on my summer homework project today. Sandy Perretti's comin' round in a bit. We've arranged to kick each other into doin' some work.'

'Already?' Tessa said, her voice conveying both disgust and horror. 'But there's weeks of holiday left yet.'

'Yeah, but unlike you, I don't leave stuff to the last second,' Carrie said. 'Average grades ain't gonna be good enough for me to get into the college I want.'

'Whatever you say, Carrie,' Tessa said, shaking her head with apparent disdain. 'Tony, let's go.'

'Sure thing, see you later, sis.' Tony looked back at Carrie as he followed Tessa out of the front door. He gave her a small wink.

'Later, Carrie,' called Tessa.

Niamh sighed with relief as she heard the front door close. She stepped lightly back across to the bed and flopped onto it just as Carrie came back into the room.

'You hear all that?'

'Yes,' Niamh confirmed. 'Thanks again for covering for me.'

'No problem. Tessa might be pretty, but she's an idiot,' Carrie said. 'If her mum and dad weren't such big pals with ours, Tony and I wouldn't hang out with her at all.'

'Really? I thought Tony and Tessa might be . . . you know . . . an item.'

Carrie instantly burst out laughing. 'In her dreams!' she exclaimed. 'Don't worry. Tony's got more sense than that, Niamh,' she added, lowering her voice to prevent her brother overhearing. 'He's only taking her into town to protect you. Believe me, he's got no interest in her. He's very selective about who he goes out with. I could learn a thing or two from him, but I just keep making the same mistakes over and over. Typical blonde, you could say.'

'Don't talk yourself down, Carrie,' Niamh said. 'You're better than that.' She paused. 'Carrie?'

'Yeah?'

'I can't help wondering . . . why are you helping me like this? When I think of the trouble you could get into . . .'

'Well, don't,' Carrie said. She lowered her voice to little more than a whisper and glanced back at the door. 'Truth is, Tony was pretty taken with you yesterday. Unlike me, he's always been a good judge of character. I look out for him, he looks out for me.

We banter a lot, but we're close – you understand? If he likes you, you're OK by me. Now, would you prefer a shower or a bath?'

'Bath, please,' Niamh said, trying to hide her flushed reaction to Carrie's bombshell. Tony liked her! He really liked her! It was like a dream come true. She couldn't wait to text Beth and tell her about him. There would be about a million questions of course . . .

Three-quarters of an hour later, having soaked, washed and dressed in a fresh set of Carrie's clothes, Niamh felt worlds better. Her hands were still sore and the blisters had filled out fit to burst, but the aching in her muscles had dulled to little more than a niggling irritation.

'If only I could clear my mind so easily,' she murmured under her breath as Carrie led her through to the kitchen where she had laid out breakfast.

What should she do now? The article in the *Key West Citizen* had said her dad was being flown back to England today to be handed over to the British authorities. There didn't seem to be anything she could do about that. The Mitchells' boat was effectively lost, but Niamh was sure the boys were on land somewhere, so it was not a great loss. Her transport situation seemed limited to hitching a lift in a kayak or using public transport, which was dangerous at best. Worse – now she had an added complication. She couldn't stop thinking about what Carrie had said about Tony being 'taken with her'.

What did that mean anyway? Did he fancy her or did he just think she was nice in a platonic way? It shouldn't make any difference, but it did. And this really wasn't the time to have boy issues!

Maybe she could she stay here and work out her next steps? But what would Carrie's parents do if they realised who she was? One way or another the local law enforcement agencies would find their way here eventually. Niamh would be a fool to think the FWC officer, or one of his colleagues, would not piece things together and follow her this far – especially with Tessa around. But how long had she got before they came knocking at the door?

'So what's the next step?' Carrie asked, apparently reading her mind.

'I don't know,' Niamh admitted. 'I've been acting on instinct so far, but I'm feeling pretty lost right now. Knowing Tony likes me isn't helping me concentrate either.'

Carrie smiled. 'So you like him then?'

'Yes, I suppose I do,' Niamh admitted shyly. 'But I've been going to an all-girls' school for the last three years, so I don't really know what to do around boys.'

'You've not had *any* boyfriends?' Carrie asked, her eyes narrowing as she studied Niamh's face for any trace of a lie. 'You seem so confident and outgoing.'

'In some ways, maybe. But aside from my brother, I don't get to mix with boys very often.'

'Well, you seemed to do pretty well around Tony yesterday,' Carrie observed. 'You certainly got his attention. Look, in case I'm wrong about you, I should tell you that Tony's a good brother and I don't want you to go messin' with his feelin's, OK?'

'I would never do that,' Niamh replied quickly. 'But, to be honest, I don't know what to think about Tony. He seems nice and I can't tell you how much I appreciate both of you helping me like this. If it helps, I promise I won't do anything to deliberately hurt him, but I can't hang around here to spend time with him either.'

Carrie looked at her for a moment and then nodded. 'Good enough for me.'

'Putting boy issues aside for a moment . . .'

'As should be done as much as possible,' Carrie interrupted.

Niamh smiled. 'I have no idea what to do next.'

Carrie thought for a moment. 'Well, my grandma always used to say that you should focus on the big picture. I can almost hear her voice telling me to do just that. So, what's your end goal, Niamh?'

'To find Sam and Callum and clear Dad's name,' Niamh replied, trying not to think about wanting to get to know Tony better; she had just too much other stuff to contend with. 'But I don't really know where to start. My heart tells me that my brother is still alive. I've always had a sort of invisible connection to him. And even though it feels different now – sort of thin and distant – the link is still there.'

'Finding your brother and his friend does seem to be the obvious starting point,' Carrie agreed. 'So where have you looked so far?'

'Dad flew us up and down the Atlantic side of the Keys when they first disappeared,' Niamh said. 'We covered a lot of the obvious search area, but . . .'

'But what?'

Niamh looked Carrie in the eyes. 'But thinking about it now, I didn't *feel* anything when we were up in the air searching for them.'

'What makes you think you would?'

'Like I said, I've always had a sort of sixth sense where Sam is concerned,' Niamh admitted. 'Playing hide and seek as kids was always a farce. We could never hide effectively from one another. All I needed to do was close my eyes and nine times out of ten I could turn and walk directly to where he was. Now it's as if something's scrambling that sixth sense.

Every now and then I feel faint flashes of intense emotion from him, but even then it's so distant that I find myself wondering if my imagination is playing tricks on me.'

'OK, let's assume for a minute that you're not imagining things,' Carrie suggested. 'If Sam's not in the Keys any more, where do you think he could be?'

'That's the problem,' Niamh said. 'My imagination begins running riot as soon as I start trying to follow that question through. Mostly I keep getting pulled back to Dad's ideas about the Bermuda Triangle. When Mum disappeared here nine years ago, he explored all sorts of possibilities.'

'There was something in the newspaper article about your mum going missing. That must have been terrible!'

'Well, Sam and I were only five at the time, so we don't really remember much about her, but I still miss her,' Niamh agreed. 'Dad has never given up trying to find out what happened to her though. We've grown up with his obsession about the Devil's . . . sorry, the Bermuda Triangle, so it's hard to think outside the sort of theories he's already explored. Were thge boys kidnapped? Drugged? Abducted by aliens? Taken to Atlantis? For all I know they could be dead and what I'm experiencing is some sort of ghostly mental echo effect from Sam.' Niamh gave a heavy sigh. 'Let's face it, the boys could be anywhere.'

'If that's how you feel, then why didn't you just go with the cops when they turned up?'

Niamh shrugged. 'I panicked,' she said. 'I thought I was the boys' best hope of being found. Maybe I was wrong.'

'No! Another thing my grandma used to tell me was to trust my gut instinct,' Carrie said firmly. 'I would say, go with it.'

Niamh took a deep breath and told Carrie about her experience in the pool. The emptiness that she had felt at the time did not seem so intense now. Familiarity with the space where something of her brother had dwelt inside her mind was already making the void feel more normal. The realisation of this made a hot flush of anger rise inside her. She had no desire for the emptiness to feel normal. She wanted her brother back.

'The most definite sense of him that I've had since then was when I was out on the boat before I decided to go to Monkey Island,' Niamh explained. 'I got the distinct impression that Sam was in danger and running away from something, or towards something. I'm not really sure which.'

'Well, if he was runnin', then he's not out on

the water any more,' Carrie pointed out. 'That's somethin'.'

'Yes, I suppose I should be thankful,' Niamh said thoughtfully. 'At least I don't have to try to steal another boat.'

Carrie laughed, her clear voice ringing around the kitchen area. 'What?' she began, waggling a disapproving finger. 'You mean you don't regularly go around stealin' $100,000 boats for fun on a daily basis? Oh, Niamh! You disappoint me.'

'Sorry about that,' Niamh replied, grinning in spite of the hollow feeling she had inside after reliving the experience of Sam's disappearance. 'Much as I hate to shatter my cool criminal image, I'm afraid that's just not who I am.'

'Don't worry, I know,' Carrie assured her. 'You wouldn't be here if it was. So you still haven't answered the big question. What next? Do you want to stay here for a while? I can come up with a story for my mom and dad, if you like.'

Niamh was tempted, but her instinct had other ideas. If she was going to stay ahead of the police and progress her search for the boys, she was going to have to keep moving.

'Thanks, Carrie. I'd love to, but I can't,' she said sadly. 'I need to keep looking. My intuition is telling me to head back along the Keys towards the mainland. If Sam was at Key West, I'm fairly certain I'd know it. I think I'd better catch a bus and head to Miami. Maybe I'll be able to sense if I'm getting closer to him by the time I get there.'

Carrie nodded thoughtfully. Her sparkling blue eyes narrowed. 'Tony'll be disappointed,' she observed with a knowing smile.

Niamh could feel the colour blossoming hot across her cheeks. 'Yes, well, my apologies to Tony,' she said. 'I'd love to get to know him better and I'll try to come back after all this is over, but if I can't, then I'm sure he'll get over me . . . it . . . whatever.'

'I think that's what he likes about you.'

'What's that?'

'Your modesty – you're not like the girls who live around here.'

Niamh shrugged. 'I'm just realistic,' she explained. 'Girls like me don't get to go out with guys like Tony.'

'Yeah, right! I suppose you're all too busy committin' grand theft and livin' life on the run,' Carrie said. 'Come on. I think there's one last thing I can do to help you before we get the bus times to Miami.'

Carrie got to her feet and stepped around the breakfast bar. She held out her hand to Niamh, who cautiously took it and allowed herself to be led back to Carrie's bedroom.

'Wait here,' Carrie directed. She left and returned

a few seconds later with a hair-colouring kit. 'It's Mom's,' she explained. 'I get my blonde hair from Dad. My mom's hair is much darker, but she tops up the colour every now and then to cover up her grey hairs. Let's dye your hair and change your style a bit. It should hide you from those who're not lookin' too hard.'

'But won't your mum miss it?' Niamh asked.

'Don't worry,' Carrie insisted. 'I'll replace it later. She'll never know.'

'Well, if you're sure . . .'

'Trust me. By the time you leave, you won't recognise yourself.'

CHAPTER TWENTY-FOUR

'What's going on?' Sam yelled, hammering at the door with his fist again. 'Why are you holding us prisoner? I only came here to find my mother! Is that such a crime?'

'Give it a rest, Sam,' Callum pleaded. 'They're not listening. Or if they are, they're not interested.'

'OK, Cal,' Sam replied. He rubbed at the side of his right hand, which was red from pounding the door repeatedly on and off for several hours. 'But I'm not done yet. I'm sure Nipper didn't bring us all this way just to get us locked up. He and his friends could have done that when we first beached the boat. I don't think he expected this any more than we did.'

Sam crossed the empty cell and sat down next to his friend. He felt as empty as the space they were currently trapped in. All of his hopes and dreams had drained away, leaving only anger and frustration to fill the yawning chasm inside him.

'It's OK, mate. I understand,' Callum said, placing a hand on Sam's shoulder. 'It's not your fault. Don't worry. We'll get out of here.'

Sam gave him a weak smile. Callum's words sounded brave, but they rang with the same hollowness that pervaded everything else in this place. The door was programmed with a DNA sensor like the one at the station. This room appeared to be a cell specifically designed to hold humans.

Sam looked around the empty space, studying every line of the wall structure for a hint of weakness. There were none. This structure, like everything else the raptors had built, had been constructed meticulously from very solid materials. The interlocking geodesic panels that formed the walls and ceiling were held in place by solid metal frames. Every joint was fitted to perfection, every panel – flawless. It was hard to say what material the panels had been made from. Running a finger across the surface of the one behind his back, Sam guessed they were a form of moulded dense plastic, though it was impossible to tell how thick they were. He pushed back hard against the panel, but it did not appear to flex at all. Giving up on the panels, he started to trace the joint lines of every panel around the room in sequence.

'Hey, what's that?' he asked suddenly, getting to his feet again and pointing up at a tiny black bubble in the corner of a ceiling panel towards the back of the room. 'It looks like one of those fisheye security cameras they sometimes use in department stores back home, but much, much smaller.' He waved at it and then prowled around underneath thinking.

'Do you think we might get a response if we covered it up?' Callum asked.

'Possibly,' Sam replied. 'But how are we going to do that?'

'I'm not sure yet. Give me a boost up and I'll take a closer look.'

Sam interlocked his fingers and squared his back. Callum was not heavy and as he stepped up onto Sam's waiting hands, Sam lifted him up with ease. Callum leaned against the wall for balance and then walked his hands up until he reached the ceiling. Sam tried to look up, but with Callum leaning over his head, it was hard to see what the smaller boy was doing. Suddenly, there was a flash and both boys were hurled to the floor.

Sam recovered first.

'Cal? Are you all right?'

'Owwww!' Callum groaned, cradling his right hand with his left. 'Still in one piece, I think. My fingers are a bit frazzled though. Don't think I'll be fiddling with that thing again in a hurry.'

'What happened? What is it?'

'It could be a camera, but it's hard to tell,' Callum explained. 'It seems to be protected by some sort of electric field. As soon as my hand got close, it zapped me. It was like when I nearly electrocuted myself messing about in the physics lab back in year seven.'

'Ha! I'd forgotten about that,' Sam said, his lips twisting into a wry grin. 'Didn't Mr Perry nearly lose his job over your little electricity and water experiment?'

'Poor guy underestimated the destructive power of the littlest kid in class,' Callum said, now wriggling his fingers and rubbing at the flesh on his forearm. 'What can I say? I'm just your regular bright spark.'

'Oh, yeah!' Sam drawled, 'You're a real live wire, you are! Some might even call you shocking. Now, if we could just find our way ohm . . .'

'Find our way ohm!' Callum chuckled. 'That's bad, Sam! Really bad. Ow! Don't make me laugh so much. It hurts more when I laugh.'

Afterwards, Sam could not have said what was so funny. It certainly wasn't the quality of the jokes, but for the next minute or two the boys rolled around on the floor, helpless with laughter. Perhaps it was a release of stress that triggered it, but every time one of them tried to stop, he would look at the other and they would both begin again.

The hissing noise of the door opening sobered them in an instant. Wiping the tears from his cheeks, Sam sat up and looked around. A man stood in the doorway. He was tall and slim with a receding grey hairline and glasses perched on the end of a beak-like nose. A white coat, similar to those of the two raptors that flanked him, hung from his shoulders. Despite being an immaculate white, the man managed to make it look scruffy.

'Boys,' he began, the nasal whine of his voice instantly setting Sam's teeth on edge. 'I'm Professor Winters. I work here at the Imperium's Scientific Research Facility. I've been sent to see that your ill-advised tampering did not harm you. I would also warn you against touching the monitoring device again. The shielding charge has been doubled.'

'What the hell is going on here, professor? That thing nearly fried us, and you calmly announce you've made it worse!' Sam replied, all traces of humour gone. 'Why have we been locked in here? We've not done any harm. We only came here to look for my mother, Claire Cutler.'

The man's eyes showed no compassion as he replied. 'Yes, I know. It is because of Claire Cutler that you're being held. She is a dangerous heretic and a traitor to the Imperium. The High Council of the Imperium have been trying to put a stop to the activities of the band of rebels she leads for over two years now. They are hoping that when she learns you are here, she will surrender herself to the authorities in a bid to have you set free.'

'My mother's leading a rebel group?' Sam asked, unable to hide his shock.

'And if she doesn't surrender?' Callum added quickly, steering the professor towards a more pertinent answer.

'I'm not entirely sure,' he admitted. 'The raptor council are not renowned for their patience or their compassion. If I were you, I'd hope that your mother does as the Imperium directs.'

'But she's only a marine biologist,' Sam sputtered. 'What harm could she possibly . . .'

'*Only* a marine biologist!' Professor Winters interrupted, clearly horrified by Sam's choice of words. 'You don't know what you're saying, boy. Scientists of every kind are held in the highest regard here at the Imperium. If your mother possessed any common sense, she would be using her standing, knowledge and abilities to further the magnificent work that the raptor community have achieved. Instead, she is intent on stirring dissension and malcontent. There are a few like your mother who actively seek to destroy everything the High Council of the Imperium have worked for.'

'Look, I can't claim to know my mother,' Sam said, his tone aggressive. 'I was only five years old the last time I saw her. I barely remember her, OK? From what I've seen since we arrived, upsetting a raptor isn't a good idea. Deliberately irritating the majority of the raptor race certainly isn't at the top of my 'to do' list, that's for sure. Why my mother would want to do that is beyond me, but Callum and me haven't done anything wrong. Holding us is pointless.'

The professor shook his head and turned to leave.

'Wait!' Callum pleaded. 'Please! At least tell us what sort of things she's been saying.'

'You think I would repeat her lies?' Winters sneered. 'You will not hear such nonsense from my lips. If the High Council sees fit to let you speak with her before she is executed, maybe you will learn something of her foolish beliefs, but I doubt it. Her lies are pernicious. The raptors are right to censor them . . .'

As the professor continued to rant, Callum nudged Sam gently in the ribs. Sam flicked a glance at his friend, who whispered one word at him – 'Nipper.' Sam's heart instantly started to pound. He looked back at the man in the white coat and then let his focus drift past him to the two raptors behind. Was Callum imagining things? He found it hard to tell most raptors apart. Many of them looked remarkably similar, though they no doubt felt the same way about humans.

The raptor to the right of the professor was mouthing something. It looked as if it was saying, 'Ssssaaammm.'

Callum was right. It was Nipper. And the other raptor was Grunt. How they had obtained white coats and got here Sam could not begin to guess and he didn't care. Nipper and Grunt looked poised for action. Whatever they were about to do was likely to get all of them into even more trouble with the Imperium. The two raptors would most likely become outlaws if they defied the raptor High Council. Why were they willing to risk so much to help them?

Sam got to his feet. Callum did the same. The professor was still in mid-rant when Nipper gave him a hefty shove in through the doorway. The tall man cried out as he tripped and fell across the threshold. Nipper stepped forward to block the doorway and beckoned to the two boys.

'Come,' he said clearly.

The boys did not need telling twice. They were past the professor through the door in a flash. Grunt swept Callum up and tucked him under his arm. Nipper did the same with Sam. He keyed the door and it hissed closed, sealing the professor inside. Without pause, the two raptors set off down the corridor.

Being carried across an open beach by a raptor was one thing, but Sam soon discovered that being carried along a narrow corridor at a raptor's sprinting speed was mind-blowing. Doors blurred past as the two creatures powered up to an all-out sprint. Somewhere in the building a muted warbling alarm began and Sam's heart sank. How did Nipper intend to escape? Surely they were as badly placed now as they had been in the reception hall when they had been surrounded and taken captive?

The end of the corridor was approaching at an alarming rate and Sam felt Nipper's balance shift as he began to decelerate for the turn into the intersecting passage. Grunt and Callum were still slightly ahead as they reached the junction, though Nipper had closed the gap. Sam momentarily saw two raptors in white coats appear in front of them. To Sam's amazement, Grunt didn't hesitate. The raptor lowered his head and slammed into the nearest one, cannoning it into the second and sending both to end in a tangled heap on the floor. The crunching impact sounded brutal, yet aside from slowing a little to allow Nipper to take the lead, Grunt appeared unhurt.

As Nipper passed Grunt, Sam caught a glimpse of

Callum's terrified expression. His friend was holding his glasses in place with one hand and he had a handful of Grunt's white coat twisted tightly in the other. More raptors appeared ahead and Nipper skidded to a halt. Grunt came to a stop alongside him and the two exchanged a rapid dialogue of clicks.

Some rescue plan this is, Sam thought as Nipper put him down and squared up to face the growing number of raptors blocking their path ahead. *Surely they didn't expect to just walk out with us. There could be hundreds of raptors between here and the exit.*

No sooner had Nipper put Sam down on his feet than Grunt had picked him up and tucked him under his spare arm. To Sam's amazement, rather than double back along the empty passageway behind them, Nipper let out a mighty roar and charged at the oncoming white coats. What was he thinking? There were lots of them. It looked like a suicide run. Sam wanted to close his eyes, but couldn't. Grunt had allowed Nipper to build a five-metre lead before following. Sam's body tensed as they approached the inevitable clash. What could Grunt do to help, encumbered as he was with a boy under each arm? The answer came swiftly – nothing – but to Sam's surprise, this appeared to be Nipper's intention.

Although Nipper was no bigger than any of his many opponents, he tore through them as if they were not there. All Sam could think was that life as scientists working here in the Imperium had dulled the fighting instincts of these raptors in their bright white coats. For a moment, he was reminded of a crazy martial arts movie where the hero waded into an army of opponents only to reappear unscathed, with a sea of bodies scattered behind him.

Grunt followed along behind, zigzagging around and bounding over the bodies of the fallen raptors. Some were bleeding from wounds inflicted by Nipper's deadly claws, but most were more stunned than sliced. Hammer-like blows from Nipper's feet, elbows, knees and forehead had found their targets with devastating speed and accuracy.

Given the ease with which Nipper ploughed a path along the passageway, Sam assumed he was heading for reception and intended to fight his way out of the building. Once again Nipper had a surprise in store. Halfway along the remaining length of corridor, Nipper opened a door to his right and ducked inside. Grunt followed and the door closed behind them. The room they entered was large. Sam identified a holographic projection table at one end, but throughout the rest of the space were what looked like workstations piled high with a bizarre mixture of human and raptor technology.

Grunt put the boys down and the two raptors

exchanged another burst of rapid clicking and growling before crossing the room to the far wall. To Sam's amazement, the raptors laid down on the floor with their feet against one of the larger wall panels. Nipper gave a double click and as one, the two raptors kicked out. It was hard to imagine anything strong enough to withstand that blow, but the panel did not budge. For the next thirty seconds the raptors pounded at the panel with coordinated ferocity. Their mighty leg muscles bulged with every recoil and each impact rang through the room like the striking of a gong.

Just when Sam began to think they were wasting their time and energy, a cracking sound inspired hope. The next blow drew a grating crack and the one after sent the panel clear of the wall to leave a gaping hole.

The two raptors jumped to their feet and Nipper looked out through the opening before turning to the boys and beckoning.

'Come,' he said clearly again.

The two boys ran to comply even as the door swished open behind them. Grunt swept Callum into his arms and crossed to the opening in a single bound.

'You've got to be kidding!' Callum cried, terror in every syllable. 'Ahhhhhrrrrrrgggghhh!'

Sam heard his friend's cry fade through the hole

as Nipper grabbed him and leapt to follow. Out of the corner of his eye he caught a glimpse of raptors pouring in through the open door before realising what had struck such fear into his friend.

'Bloody hell, no!' he breathed.

Leah looked out at the darkening sky from the doorway and she shivered. Her teeth ached. It was a bad sign. There was another storm coming and it felt like it was brewing for a bad blow. Lightning lanced from cloud to cloud in the distance, a momentary split in the fabric of the heavens.

Crossing her arms, she rubbed at the tops of shoulders before reaching up to rub gently at the line of her jaw. She hated sitting out storms alone. The noises frightened her. The wind whistling in the trees, the rattling of shutters and the crashing, growling thunder never failed to set her quaking. Brad normally took her to bed and cuddled her when the weather turned like this. She would miss the warmth of his chest against her back and the comforting strength of his arms wrapped round her body tonight. She hoped he was all right.

'Please look after him, Nipper,' she breathed, willing the words to hold power. Dark thoughts and dreams had haunted her thoughts from the moment he had left and it was hard to shake the feeling that something bad had happened. 'Don't be silly, Leah,' she chided. 'Of course Nipper will look after him!'

A grumble of thunder carried an ominous warning on the wind. Would this storm bring new additions to the community? It was unlikely, but possible. Sometimes the Bermuda Triangle would cause a spate of victims to be washed up on to the shoreline, but then it might be months, or even years between arrivals. Given the appearance of the two boys recently, the odds were not in favour of more new blood so quickly. However, the Triangle had no care for odds.

Leah shut the door and barred it. In a flurry of activity, she swept around the house closing and barring all of the window shutters before retiring to the bedroom. Gathering as many cushions as she could find, she piled them round herself on the bed and nestled underneath the covers. It was not the same as having Brad there, but once the bed had warmed to her body, it was not long before she began to drift towards an uneasy sleep.

CHAPTER TWENTY-FIVE

'He's falling!'

'What? Who?'

'Sam!' Niamh gasped. 'I can feel him more clearly. He's . . . OK! I can feel his relief. For a moment just then, he thought he was going to die.'

'That's really spooky, you know,' Carrie said in a low voice, looking around to see if anyone else was near enough to hear their conversation. There was no one. A car trundled past along the highway, but the single occupant did not give them a second glance. 'Can you sense where he is? Do you think he's in Miami?'

'I don't know,' Niamh said, shaking her head. 'It doesn't work that way. Mostly I just sense something of what he's feeling, especially if it's a powerful emotion like fear.' Her eyes went distant. 'I can tell he's a long way away,' she added. 'But for some reason, I can feel him more clearly than I have since he first went out on the boat and disappeared. It's weird!'

'Does Sam sense you in the same way?'

'It's hard to say,' Niamh said. 'I know from things he's said that there are times when he feels my emotions. But does he feel it the same way? I don't know for sure what goes on inside his head.'

'Did you pick up anything else, apart from the fact he was falling? Anything at all? Even the smallest clue might help.'

'No,' Niamh said slowly. 'But I think . . .' She paused and her eyes snapped back into focus. She lifted her right hand from her side and pointed at the store on the other side of the carriageway. '. . . he's somewhere over that way.'

Carrie followed the line of her finger and her eyebrows rose.

'Miami's probably a good place to look then,' she said. 'You're pointin' pretty much due north.'

'Really? That's encouraging. Thanks.'

'Do you know where you're going to go when you get there?'

'Not really, no.'

'What about a place to stay? It'll be dark by the time you get to Miami. Whatever you do, don't walk the city streets alone at night. Miami ain't the place to do that.'

'I've got enough money for a night in a hotel,' Niamh assured her. 'Maybe even two if I can find a cheap one somewhere. If I don't find Sam before my money runs out, then I'll turn myself in to the police and let them take me back to England.'

'Really? Promise me?' Carrie looked very serious.

'Yes, I promise,' Niamh assured her.

'Uh oh!' Carrie said suddenly, her eyes sliding to the left.

'What?'

'Cops inbound!'

A patrol car was approaching. Niamh could see two officers inside and the car was slowing. Running was not an option. It would just draw their attention. The car was too close for her to make a clean escape. Not far behind the car, Niamh could see another vehicle. Was it her bus? She hoped with all her heart that it was.

'Relax!' Carrie told her, sensing her immediate nervousness. 'You don't look like you, remember. They're looking for a blonde runaway. You don't look like their search profile any more. Better still, that looks like your bus. I'll talk to the cops. When the bus stops, get on and I'll wave you off. Good luck, Niamh. Stay in touch, OK? You've got my cell number.'

'I have and I will,' Niamh replied. She hugged Carrie, squeezing her tight. 'Thanks for all your help. I still don't know what I did to deserve it. You've got to come and visit me in the UK when I make it back there. You'll love it there.'

'That'd be cool. I'd love to do that.'

'Hey! Miss!'

Carrie looked round. The patrol car had pulled over and the officer in the passenger seat had wound the window down. He was beckoning to her. To Niamh's horror, she realised it was the same policeman who had chased her on foot from her house on Summerland Key. She felt sick.

The police officer glanced at her and she felt sure the game was up. To her amazement though, his gaze seemed to slide straight off her and back to Carrie. The disguise was working. She had not really believed it would, but Carrie was right. The man had not given her a second glance. The grumbling bus rounded the patrol car and its tyres crackled to a halt on the dusty gravel in front of her. There was a hiss and the door opened. Niamh bounded up the steps.

'Miami?' she asked, showing the ticket Carrie had printed out for her.

'Take a seat, miss,' the driver said, giving her a nod.

339

Niamh turned back to Carrie. 'Say goodbye to Tony for me,' she said. 'Thanks again for everything.' The doors gave another hiss and folded outwards to shut with a satisfying *clunk* and she moved back along the rows of seats until she was about halfway back along the aisle. As she settled into the seat, there was a tap at the window. It was Carrie. She was grinning and waving. Carrie continued to wave as the bus pulled away.

It looked as though she's enjoying my narrow escape, Niamh thought as she waved and watched until Carrie was out of sight. Niamh would never forget how much Carrie and Tony had helped her. Without them, she would have been caught by the police for sure.

It took a while for Niamh to settle back into her seat and fully relax. She could still feel Sam in her mind. Why were his thoughts and emotions so clear all of a sudden? It felt as though her mind had suddenly been fine-tuned to the correct frequency. The fuzzy static that had clouded her link was almost completely gone. Wherever he was, there was danger all around him. Was it the strength of his current emotion making him feel closer? She didn't think so. If anything, he felt physically further away than he had when she had been on the Mitchells' boat. It was weird . . . unless . . . unless the equivalent of a door had somehow been opened between them.

Niamh tried to think through some of the theories that her dad had told her about. Wasn't one of them based on a sort of portal? Was that it? Had Sam and Callum passed through a sort of gateway? If so, where had the gateway led? Some of the old names for the Bermuda Triangle hinted at another place – the Port of Lost Souls, the Limbo of the Lost. But wherever Sam was, it didn't feel like any sort of limbo. The Devil's Triangle – was it a trap? Was there actually some malevolent being that lured boats and aircraft into an elaborate web from which there was no escape?

A sudden revelation seemed to trap all the air in Niamh's lungs. Sam was not just afraid for himself. Niamh might have expected him to be afraid for Callum as well, but that was not it. He was afraid for . . . Mum! It felt as though someone had tied a rope around her ribcage and was pulling it tighter and tighter. Why did it feel as if Sam was thinking so clearly about Mum? Was it possible that she was still alive after all this time?

With a determined effort, Niamh drew a steadying breath in through her nose, taking in more and more air until her chest felt fit to burst. Relaxing, she allowed the pressure to expel the air gently through her mouth and then she did it again. Several breaths later, she felt the pressure on her ribs begin to relax. If it was true, it would be amazing! She had to let Dad know what she had sensed . . . but how? For all she knew, he might already be halfway across the Atlantic being escorted home by the police.

Dare she ring his mobile? The police almost certainly had it, but at least she would be able to send her father a message. Niamh looked around the bus to see if there was anyone she'd be comfortable asking to borrow a phone from. There was an older teenage boy sitting a couple of seats forward and on the other side of the aisle. He would surely have a phone, but she wasn't sure she would have the confidence to ask him. There was an old lady sitting in the seat directly behind her, four more old people sitting further forward and a young couple sitting right at the back of the bus. One glance at them and Niamh knew that she would be too embarrassed to interrupt their intimate conversation.

I can wait, she told herself. *Maybe if I focus, I'll learn more.*

She closed her eyes and concentrated, feeling for Sam's emotions and listening for his thoughts. Instantly, a sense of danger set the hairs on the back of her neck prickling. It felt as if Sam was running, but he had nowhere safe to run to. Was this really

Sam she was feeling? Niamh could not help but wonder if the feelings were simply reflections of how she felt about her own current situation.

For several minutes, she concentrated. He was travelling fast. She had the sense that he was inside, yet not inside. But that made no sense . . . Callum was with him. Yes. She could feel his presence. He was scared too. But there was someone else. Someone bigger. No. Not someone. Something. A confusing image filled her mind. Although it was unclear, the impression was of a creature that could have stepped out of *Doctor Who*, or *Star Wars*. Through the fuzzy static a face emerged, like nothing Niamh had ever seen before. At first it did not look particularly frightening, but then its mouth began to open and she saw the teeth.

Her focus was lost in an instant. Her heart was beating hard and fast. Her stomach was churning. Her eyes snapped open and the bright sunlight beaming through the windows of the bus set her to blinking away tears. Niamh had never had a waking nightmare before, but that must have been what the image was. The creature she had seen in her mind's eye could not be real. It wasn't possible, but she could not recall ever seeing anything quite like it before. So where had the image come from, if not from Sam?

With her blood hammering in her ears, it took a moment for her to register the news announcement on the bus's radio. It was the word 'coastguard' that triggered her to mentally tune in to what the news-reader was saying.

'. . . coastguard today announced they were calling off the active search for two boys who went miss-ing on Wednesday morning. Aircraft from Fort Lauderdale and coastguard vessels from Naval Air Station Key West have been combing the waters around Summerland Key for any sign of Sam Cutler and Callum Barnes, both aged fourteen and from England. The boys were on vacation at Mr Matthew Cutler's holiday home when they allegedly took Mr Cutler's boat out fishing.

Earlier today, local law enforcement authorities in Key West confirmed that Mr Cutler has been taken into custody at the request of the British authori-ties. He is to be returned to England later today for questioning about the disappearances. Suspicions have been aroused about the circumstances of the incident due to the remarkable similarities to those surrounding the disappearance of Mr Cutler's wife, American-born Claire Cutler, in 2001. No formal charges have been made, but the Sheriff's Office say they have not ruled out the possibility that the search

344

*may yet turn into a multiple homicide investigation.
A search is also ongoing for Mr Cutler's fourteen-
year-old daughter, Niamh Cutler, who was seen
running from the family residence in Summerland
Key yesterday morning. People are asked to report
any information they have concerning the whereabouts of Sam Cutler, Callum Barnes or Niamh
Cutler to their local Sheriff's Office.*

*Scientists today announced more bad news for
local fishermen as they released the latest survey
figures . . .'*

Niamh took a deep breath and let it out again in one
long, slow release. *Poor Dad*, she thought. He would
be worried sick. She had to try to let him know
she was OK. If she could get a message to him that
she was alive and well, and that Sam was still alive
somewhere, it would take a weight off his mind.
With this resolution in mind, she turned to the old
lady behind her and gave her a big smile.

'Excuse me,' she said. 'I've just realised I left my
mobile phone behind and I need to make a really
important call. You don't happen to have one I
could use for a moment, do you? The call will only
take a moment and I have a little money. I can pay.'

CHAPTER TWENTY-SIX

It was impossible! They were too high. Surely nothing could survive a leap from this height without sustaining serious injury? But Nipper didn't hesitate. He launched out through the opening and, like Callum before him, Sam yelled out in terror. The ground rushed to meet them all too quickly. As they fell, the raptor manoeuvred Sam across his chest, as a mother would cradle a baby.

In all the books that Sam had read, it was usual for a person's life to flash before their eyes in the moment before their death. Strangely, all Sam could think of was his sister, Niamh. It was almost as if she was with him, falling through the air alongside . . . no, *inside* him. It was a weird feeling. The string of bizarre events that had led to the search for his long-lost mother had been amazing, but there seemed little else left to do now than tense all his muscles and hope the end did not hurt too much.

To Sam's amazement, the impact with the pavement was not the bone-cracking, blood-spattering affair he expected. Nipper's huge thigh muscles absorbed the shock of landing with apparent ease, but even with the cushioning effect of the raptor's arms under Sam's shoulders and thighs to soften the deceleration, the whiplash effect of their abrupt arrival was severe. The pain was instant and sharp, but Sam retained consciousness and his sense of reprieve at having survived the jump outweighed any physical discomfort.

The warm feeling of relief lasted barely an instant. No sooner had Nipper landed than he was up and running again, tucking Sam back under his arm as a child might carry a doll. Lightning bolts of pain shot up and down Sam's neck and back. For a moment, he wondered if his neck was broken, but he found he still had control over his head and he could move his hands and feet, so it seemed unlikely. Grunt was a few paces ahead carrying Callum. Sam could see that his friend had his hands clamped over his eyes. Given where Grunt was heading, Sam wished he was in a position to do the same. Unfortunately, his arms were clamped to his sides by Nipper's powerful biceps.

347

The two raptors ran like the wind towards the terrifying mass of traffic that raced with chaotic precision around the main hub of the Imperium. Sam saw Grunt leap an instant before he felt the bunching of Nipper's muscles.

'Noooo!'

The word emerged from between Sam's lips as barely more than a whimper as Nipper sprang. If Sam had thought the jump from the building was terrifying, this was worse. The two raptors launched high into the air straight into the crazy mess of speeding traffic. The sudden acceleration as Nipper landed on top of one of the vehicles was almost as abrupt as the deceleration on landing from the long fall a few seconds earlier. Sam could feel the raptor's muscles straining as it fought to maintain its fragile purchase on the roof of the high-speed cabin car. The screeching of Nipper's claws on the polished metal surface as he tried to keep his balance sent shivers down Sam's spine. The sound was more piercing than fingernails running down a blackboard. Nipper leapt again and they landed on another roof heading in the same direction.

The mad transportation system of the Imperium had been terrifying enough inside one of the mono-cars, but that fear was as nothing compared with how it felt to be carried from roof to roof across the seething mass of vehicles. How Nipper timed his jumps, Sam would never know. The raptor seemed to know instinctively which cars were changing lanes and accurately predicted where his chosen target car would be with every leap. In a terrifying sequence of death-defying leaps, Sam was carried away from the heart of the Imperium.

He could no longer see Callum and Grunt. But Sam could only hope they were elsewhere on the superhighway, clinging to the roof of another car. The alternative did not bear thinking about. A *thump* made Sam look left. A large raptor had landed on the roof of a nearby car and was preparing to leap again. To Sam's horror, he realised it wasn't Grunt.

From the moment they had leapt out of the hole that Nipper and Grunt had kicked in the side of the Imperium building, the idea of their being followed had not entered Sam's mind. He was struggling enough to cope with the danger and fear of the crazy things Nipper was doing. Pursuit seemed beyond impossible, yet the reality was literally staring him in the face.

'Nipper! Look out!' Sam yelled as the incoming raptor sprang into the air towards them.

Apparently, his warning was redundant. Rather than leap away, Nipper twisted and met the incoming attacker with a kick that sent his assailant over the side of the car. There was a short screech of claws on metal and a car travelling in the opposite direction hit the raptor with a sickening *thump*. It was gone.

Sam was so tense with fear that he could taste the bitterness of it on his tongue. Nipper coiled and sprang again and Sam could only brace himself as cars flashed past beneath him before another car appeared, as if by magic, for them to land on.

'Oh, God! There's more of them coming.'

Sam could see several now. Seeing them leaping from car to car was both breathtaking and horrifying. These were no raptor scientists in their pristine white coats. These raptors were every bit as big and as fast as Nipper and Grunt. *Where are they coming from and how have they followed so quickly*, he wondered.

The monocar that Nipper and Sam were piggy-backing did an abrupt turn to the right, spearing off along a branch rail that took them away from the madness of the central hub. Looking over his shoulder, Sam watched as two further cars, both toting unorthodox passengers on the roof, swung right to follow them.

'Grrrrrrr!'

The growl from Nipper said it all. Sam had no idea how, but it appeared that the following raptors were somehow controlling the direction of the cars. They were being shepherded and now that they were away from the hub, it was impossible to make a quick switch and throw them off track again. Sam looked left and right as the car zipped along a narrow alleyway between two buildings. Where were they going?

Another alley merged from the left and to Sam's amazement, a car carrying Grunt and Callum sped out to join the rail just in front of them. More cars followed, some with raptors clinging to the roof. Looking back, Sam watched with dismay as one of the trailing raptors made an incredible leap forward to a closer car. It did not land cleanly and spent a second or two scrabbling for balance, but it did not fall. He could see others preparing to follow suit. There was no way that Nipper could make a similar jump carrying him. The gap to the car ahead was far too great.

Nipper called out a series of penetrating clicks, followed by a long, loud growl. Grunt acknowledged from the car ahead with the sound for which he had been named. Sam had no idea what they had agreed, but he could feel Nipper's muscles bunching again, so he braced himself for another leap. Surely he was not planning to try to jump forward to join Grunt on his car?

At an unspoken signal, both raptors simultaneously threw themselves sideways from their respective cars. Even hitting the ground at a sprint was not enough for the rapotrs to keep their feet under them. They tumbled, rolling so quickly that Sam was too disorientated to tell how Nipper shielded him from the impact. His head was still spinning when he realised the raptor had somehow rolled upright and was running again with Grunt matching him stride for stride.

The two raptors were racing along at an insane speed, but still it was not fast enough. The trailing raptors, having jumped to follow, were unencumbered and gaining ground all the time. Nipper angled left and headed for an alleyway between two buildings. He appeared to be heading for the outer wall of the city, but no sooner had he turned into the alley than Sam's heart sank. It was a dead end. They were trapped. The two raptors slowed as they reached the end wall. There was no time to break any panels. Their pursuers were too close behind. Nipper came to a halt and carefully placed Sam down on the ground before turning to face the pursuing raptors.

The light in the alleyway was slightly dimmer than it had been out in the wider spaces between the buildings where the rail cars ran, but it was bright enough for Sam to see that these raptors all had a darker shade of scales than Nipper and Grunt. There were five of them blocking the way back out into the open. Seeing that their prey was trapped they slowed and formed a line, advancing side by side, a walking wall of muscle and teeth. Behind them, another raptor entered the alleyway and paused at the entrance.

At first, Sam was not sure, but when the wall of raptors stopped and parted to let the leader through, he saw the scars and knew instantly that it had to be the same one.

'It's the scarred raptor from the train,' Sam gasped, looking at Callum. 'Look at the line of marks on his legs. I think he's the one who killed Brad.'

The incoming raptor bared his teeth in a wide grin and nodded.

'He understood you,' Callum muttered. 'Careful what you say.'

Nipper suddenly hissed and the scarred raptor stopped his advance. Two paces behind him his five followers also stopped. Scar and Nipper faced one another for a moment and both bared their teeth. It was hard to tell whether this was a display of defiance, aggression or contempt.

Scar spoke first, firing out a staccato sequence of clicks that echoed in the enclosed alley. Nipper responded in kind. Despite not understanding anything of the language, Nipper's posture and deep-throated growling response were not hard to interpret. He was not going to back down.

'If I was a betting kind of guy, I'd say that the big old raptor over there just asked Nipper to do something and Nipper told him to go to hell,' Callum whispered.

'No bet here,' Sam replied. 'That's how I read it too.'

There were another couple of exchanges, but the tone and posturing remained the same throughout. Suddenly, Scar roared, causing Sam and Callum to jump. Nipper and Grunt visibly tensed, but neither of them backed down one iota.

'They can't fight all six of them,' Callum muttered. 'They'll be slaughtered.'

'You saw what Nipper did to the scientists,' Sam said, trying to sound optimistic.

'Yeah, but those were highbrow scientist types. These look like a bunch of skinhead thugs by comparison.'

Sam had to admit he was right.

It appeared Scar had made his final point. He turned and walked back through his line of followers, who instantly closed ranks and stepped forward as one. Nipper growled so deeply that Sam could feel the sound vibrating through his chest. Grunt added his voice and the two leaned forward, bunching their muscles in preparation for the inevitable attack.

It was not to come.

To the boys' amazement, Nipper and Grunt suddenly spun and crouched over them, shielding the boys' bodies just as a shocking sequence of minor explosions went off all around them. The rattle of shattered plastic panels raining against the opposing walls was followed instantly by the unmistakable sound of gunfire. Sam tried to wriggle into a position to see what was happening, but Nipper held him down and gave him a warning growl.

'Take them down!' yelled a woman's voice. 'Don't let them get away!'

More gunfire.

'The leader. Take out the leader!'

Further shots. A pause.

'Hell and damnation!' she cursed. 'That's twice he's given us the slip! No, don't go after him. There'll be more of them here any minute now. We need to make ourselves scarce. Come on, guys. Get the kids and let's get the hell outta here before we have a real fight on our hands.'

'Yes, ma'am!'

Nipper got up and before Sam had a chance to move, a man grabbed him by the hands and dragged him to his feet. The man looked at him and grinned. He looked like a modern-day pirate. His dark beard and moustache were flecked with grey, and his teeth were yellowed and crooked.

'There's no mistaking it,' he announced. 'This has to be your boy, Claire. He looks just like you.'

Sam's heart threatened to stop altogether. Claire? His mother? Here? He looked around and there she was, unmistakably older than the woman in the photos that Dad held so dear, but definitely the same person.

'Mum?' he said.

'Sam!'

Sam wanted to say more. A million questions crowded in his mind, but he suddenly found he could scarcely breathe as his mother swept him into a crushing hug. The unmistakable outlines of several weapons pressed hard against his body, including what felt like a pistol in her right hand. This was not quite the reunion he had imagined, but he didn't care. Against all odds he had found his mum. Nothing else mattered at that moment.

'Are Matt and Niamh with you or did you cross alone?' she asked urgently.

'No,' he answered. 'Just me and my friend, Callum.'

'Claire, I hate to break up the party, but we need to get out of here,' the bearded man announced, scanning the alley with worried eyes.

'Sorry, Sam, but Nathan's right,' his mother said softly, giving him an extra hard squeeze before letting him go. 'Bring your friend and follow me. Stay close. I don't want to lose you again. As soon as we're in safe territory, I want you to tell me everything. Don't leave anything out. Oh, and I've got nine years of hugs to catch up on,' she said, giving him a warm smile. Even as she spoke, she was simultaneously flashing hand signals at the men and raptors around her with her left hand. From the pistol in her right hand, a thin coil of grey smoke was curling from the barrel. 'For now we've gotta concentrate on getting away from here or we'll all end up dead.'

'Sure, Mum,' Sam said, holding his voice firm; it felt so bizarre to say that word after so many years. He looked at her alert posture and the other gun holstered at her right hip. Her hair was tied back in a functional ponytail. She looked fit and dangerous. It was fair to say that she was about as different as she could be from the person he had been expecting to meet.

'Hey, Sam!' Callum whispered. 'You never told me that your mum was a Sarah Connor clone. You know – Sarah Connor from the *Terminator* films.'

Sam looked him in the eye as he replied. 'Believe me,' he whispered back. 'I had no idea what she was like. No idea at all.'

CHAPTER TWENTY-SEVEN

'Hello? Who's this?' Niamh asked, keeping her voice low and leaning forward to prevent the lady behind from listening in.

There was a slight pause.

'Hi there, Niamh. This is Niamh, isn't it? I'm afraid your father can't answer the phone right now, but he's very concerned about you. We all are. Can you tell us where you are?'

Niamh knew instantly that she was talking to a policeman. She had seen enough films to know that the police had the technology to track incoming calls. They were probably tracing the signal so she needed to keep the call short.

'Just tell my dad that I'm fine and that Sam is alive. I'm going to bring him back,' she murmured quickly.

'That's great news, Niamh,' the voice assured her smoothly. 'I'll be sure to pass on the message. Have you heard from Sam? Do you know where he is?'

How much to say? The policeman would not take her seriously if she told him she had a telepathic bond with her brother. Anything along those lines would make her sound crazy. *He's stalling you*, she told herself. *Keeping you on the line to get a lock. Get off the phone now.*

'In a manner of speaking,' she said softly. 'He's gone north.'

She punched the disconnect button. North – why had she told them that? Something inside her had felt an irresistible need to justify her inner knowledge that Sam was still alive. The whole of North America was north of the Keys, but Niamh couldn't help feeling annoyed with herself. Had she been quick enough to avoid them tracking her? The phone call had only lasted a few seconds – less than thirty for sure. She didn't know how she could check the length of the call on this sort of handset. She turned to the old lady from whom she had borrowed the mobile and handed it back.

'Thanks,' she said. 'Here's a couple of dollars.'

'Oh, don't worry about that, honey,' the lady said, closing Niamh's fingers round her money. 'You were only a few seconds. Did you get through

OK? The signal comes and goes a bit around here sometimes.'

'It was perfect, thanks.'

Niamh gave the lady another smile before turning around again to avoid being drawn into an extended exchange. They were approaching Marathon Key now. It was one of the more densely populated islands and Niamh spent several minutes looking out of the window at the houses and the shops. There were a few people walking around, but most had more sense than to take a stroll in the intense heat of mid-afternoon. She saw another Munroe County patrol car parked up in front of one of the real-estate offices. There was no sign of the officers though.

The deceleration and the crackling crunch of the bus's tyres on the grit as it stopped took Niamh by surprise. She had not thought about the bus stopping before Miami. Her stomach tightened as she craned her neck to see who was going to get on. What if there were patrol officers at the bus stop?

Three passengers climbed aboard. None were in uniform and none so much as looked at her. The doors hissed closed and the engine of the bus gave a guttural growl as the driver eased them out onto the highway again. Niamh leaned forward and ducked her head down into her hands. She could feel her face flushing and her heart was still racing.

Don't go getting paranoid, Niamh, she told herself, rubbing at her cheeks with the palms of her hands in an effort to disperse the heat she felt there. *You're being ridiculous!*

A mobile began to ring behind her. As the old lady in the seat answered, 'Hello?', Niamh's heart leapt again. Ring-back! Niamh had not thought to try to block her number to the receiving phone. The police only had to look at the incoming number on her dad's mobile and call it back to find out where she was. Ears pricked and concentrating intently, she listened.

'Oh, yes! No, that's fine. Now's as good a time as any,' the old lady was saying. 'Yes, it's working fine now, thank you . . . No, there's been no recurrence . . . Yes, he was very efficient and polite – a very nice young man, I thought . . .'

Niamh sighed with relief. It sounded like a customer-satisfaction survey or something.

'Thank you, no. I'm sorry, but I'm headin' up to Miami for a few days, so that'll be impossible . . . No problem . . . Too far! Just passin' through Marathon, so there's a long old haul to go . . . Thanks . . . You're welcome. Goodbye now.'

Why had the old lady told them where she was? Perhaps it had been the police after all. What sort of information could they access about the owner of the phone number? Would they role play in order to obtain information with more subtlety? It sounded far-fetched – the sort of thing that happened in spy films. Niamh had a sour, sinking feeling in the pit of her stomach. Could she take the risk that she had compromised her position? No. She had to get off the bus and find another way to Miami. If the police were on to her, they would not take long to catch up. Why had she made that call! With hindsight, it had been a stupid thing to do. Just because the phone wasn't hers had not made it safe.

Niamh grabbed the top of the seat in front of her and half rose. She had another problem, she realised. They were just leaving Marathon Key and the seemingly endless Overseas Highway stretched ahead. She had no idea where or when the bus would next stop.

I'll get off at the next island, she told herself. *Maybe if I hitch a lift in the opposite direction for a bit, it'll confuse my trail.* She sat back down. 'Think!' she muttered. 'Think!'

Never had a vehicle seemed to trundle along so slowly. The long bridge crawled past at a painfully pedestrian pace and Niamh ground her teeth in frustration and clenched her fingers into fists as she willed the bus on. Seconds ticked by with interminable slowness as they dragged into minutes and she could not help feeling that every one was vital if she was to avoid being captured.

The next island was not far away now. It was a fair-sized one, but it could have been tiny for all Niamh cared. She got to her feet and began to make her way forward, intending to ask the driver to pull over and let her off. It was about halfway to the front that she saw the flashing lights of the police traffic control point ahead some way ahead. A uniformed officer was standing in the road directing the cars through. Even at this distance she could see that his focus was on the approaching bus.

'Oh, God, no!' she muttered as a shroud of panic tightened round her.

She was trapped. She looked around for a way out. An emergency exit sign at the back of the bus caught her eye. Could she get out through the back door without being noticed? It looked like her only chance.

The bus began to slow. Yes, it was being flagged down and directed into a special lane. Niamh kept her head down as she moved to the very back of the bus. She could feel the other passengers watching her with a mixture of curiosity and the beginnings of suspicion.

'Excuse me,' she said politely as she eased past the young couple at the back of the bus and into the corner seat next to the exit. They shuffled aside without question, still ensconced in their conversation and oblivious to anything unusual about Niamh's change of seats. Taking her seat in the corner, Niamh could see some of the other passengers casting sneaky glances over their shoulders at her.

As the bus slowed further, Niamh picked her moment and threw her weight against the bar-style handle of the emergency exit. A high-pitched warbling alarm sounded at the front of the bus as the door swung open, but she barely noticed it.

'Hey! Whaddaya think you're doin'?'

Niamh ignored the driver's shout. Instead, without hesitation, she jumped. It was quite a drop and she hit the tarmac hard. Her feet went instantly from under her and she tried to tuck into a roll. It was not a good landing. A burning sensation across her left side and back, and a sharper pain in her left ankle were instant indicators that she had hurt herself, but there was no time to consider them.

On her feet and running in a limping gait across the road, there was a sudden squeal of tyres to her left. Her head snapped round and she gasped. The car was virtually on top of her. Instinct made her jump, and for the second time in a matter of seconds, her feet were swept from under her. Fortunately, having slowed for the police check point, the car did not hit her hard. Niamh rolled across the bonnet, not even reaching the windscreen before falling off the other side of the car and landing on her feet.

People were shouting, but she ignored them. She clambered over the first of the two barriers in the middle of the carriageway. There was a fair bit of traffic on the opposite side, but there were gaps between the cars big enough for her to dart through if she was quick.

Someone was coming after her. A glance. A uniform. It was all she needed to see. She scrambled over the second barrier and hesitated. Cars honked horns, some swerving slightly within the fast lane to give her more clearance as they passed. This was crazy!

A hand grabbed Niamh's shoulder and she screamed. She had not realised the police officer was so close. She twisted and squirmed, trying to get free, but the hand had grabbed a fistful of her T-shirt and try as she might, she could not wrench free.

'Stop fighting me, Niamh! You are Niamh Cutler, aren't you? You don't need to run. I'm not going to hurt you.'

Defeated, she slumped against the central reservation barrier and burst into tears.

'Don't do this!' she sobbed. 'Let me go. I have to

find them. You won't do it. No one will. I'm the only one who can.'

'Your brother and the other boy, Callum?' the policeman asked. 'Niamh, we've got most of the Monroe County force lookin' for 'em. Don't worry. We'll find 'em. Of course, if you know somethin' about their whereabouts, we'd be most grateful for the information.'

He paused. Niamh said nothing.

'Come on,' he continued, climbing over the barrier and sitting down beside her without once releasing his grip. 'We can talk about that later. Come with me. Let's get you cleaned up. Looks like you took some nasty scrapes jumpin' from that bus. You're one crazy young girl, you know! I thought you were gonna be flattened for a moment there.'

The burning sensation on Niamh's back and side began to pulse as she allowed herself to be led back over the barriers. She had failed them. After all her efforts and running, it was over and the boys would have to find their way back without her help. The distant sound of a wailing siren sounded. A patrol car was approaching at speed from the Marathon direction. Cars were slowing on both sides of the carriageway to see what was happening and a cater-pillar effect was forming that looked likely to create a jam.

The officer held out his hand and stopped the traffic so that they could cross back towards the bus and the other officers at the checkpoint.

'It was the phone call, wasn't it?' Niamh asked, looking up at him. His eyes were hidden behind dark glasses.

'Phone call?'

'The call I made from the old lady's mobile on the bus,' she explained. 'That's what got me caught, wasn't it?'

The policeman looked at her and smiled.

'I don't know anythin' about a phone call,' he said. 'I saw you jump from the bus and it wasn't hard to put two and two together.'

'You mean I could have slipped past you if I'd stayed on board!'

'Possible, but unlikely,' he said. 'Unless you've picked up a very good false ID from somewhere. You changed your hair and clothes. I wouldn't have picked you out straight away, but my colleagues and I have been stopping all buses, vans, lorries and any vehicles carrying teenage boys and girls of about your age. That's the good thing about policin' the Keys. With only one main road and the rail line in and out, unless your mark has a boat, setting a net to catch the folk we're lookin' for ain't hard.'

The approaching patrol car forced its way through

the traffic and up to the checkpoint. The officers inside jumped out.

'Is that her?' the driver called. 'Is that Niamh Cutler? We radioed ahead to tell you she was on the bus, but got no response.'

'Yeah, this is Niamh Cutler,' the officer called back. He turned back to her. 'Seems the boys were on to you anyway. Don't feel bad. You're not in any trouble that I know about. The family you stole the boat from don't want to press charges.'

'They don't?' Niamh said, surprised. 'Mr Mitchell looked furious.'

'Oh, I don't doubt he was at first. But it seems they care about you, Niamh. Lots of folk do.'

'So what happens now?'

'We'll get you cleaned up and you'll be sent home on the next available flight,' the policeman said. 'Your father's due to take off shortly, so I'm afraid you won't be able to fly back with him.'

'And what about my brother?'

'As I said, the Monroe County force have all been alerted to look for the boys.'

'But I heard on the news that the search had been called off.'

'That's just the coastguard's active search,' he replied. 'We'll keep lookin'. Don't you worry. We don't give up so easy.'

Niamh looked up at the man. He looked and sounded genuine, but she could not help feeling that he was almost reading from a script.

'You won't find them,' she said softly. And she knew that that was the truth of the matter. Wherever the boys were, they were not in Monroe County.

CHAPTER TWENTY-EIGHT

Sam couldn't help but feel a little guilty. For several years now he had viewed his father's obsession with the circumstances surrounding his mum's disappearance as a weakness, yet here she was, very much alive and larger than life. His dad's tenacity and refusal to just walk away and accept her death suddenly looked very different in the light of Sam's reunion with his mother.

He and Callum were led through one of the holes that had been blasted in the side of the alley. The majority of Claire's party were human, but there were also several friendly raptors waiting on the other side of the wall. Claire led the party left towards the nearby outer city wall where they began to descend in quick succession through an open trapdoor in the ground. She paused a moment and spoke with some

371

of the raptors in their own language before dropping down through the hatch. The strange stream of sounds appeared to flow naturally from her mouth and it was clear to Sam that she was far more fluent than Brad had been.

Thinking of Brad made him think of Leah. What was she doing now? Was she OK? How was he going to get word to her about Brad? It was not a pleasant train of thought.

The pirate-faced man called Nathan went immediately ahead of the two boys, with Nipper and Grunt following close behind. Two more men with guns, together with another raptor formed the rearguard. The drop through the trapdoor was a little less than two metres into a dark passageway that appeared to run parallel to the outer wall of the city in both directions. Sam and Callum were led to the left where several glowing torches were already lighting the way with a soft white glow. As they looked back, Nipper, Grunt and the two men with guns all dropped into the tunnel behind them. Once inside, their two raptor friends had to stoop as they were far too tall to walk upright. The final raptor shut the trapdoor without entering the tunnel.

'What about him?' Sam asked Nathan, gesturing upwards.

'Don't worry about . . .' the man made a sound in his throat that sounded a bit like 'Krrrick-crack'. 'He's a born survivor. He'll cover our tracks and lead the Imperium scum a merry dance before losing them. Come. We'd better get as far away from here as we can, just in case. Watch where you're placing your feet and try to move quietly. Raptors have acute hearing. Let's not give them any easy leads.'

Sam could not see his mother. There were too many bodies ahead of him in the narrow passageway. He could only assume that she was somewhere at the front of the party leading the way. It was hard to believe that he had actually found her after all these years of thinking her dead. Sorting through his feelings was difficult. He was excited, but also shocked to see her wielding guns and ordering men around like a general. Sam had always had the impression from the photos that she was a gentle, inquisitive sort with a love of nature. It was hard to reconcile that image with his first impression of the reality.

The party moved silently along the passageway for some distance before turning left into an adjoining tunnel. As they moved, Sam noticed many other branching passageways. It appeared there was an entire labyrinth of them running below the city. *What are they for?* he wondered. *There's no smell of sewage and they don't appear to be conduits for cables, or pipes.*

He looked carefully as they went, searching for clues without success. There were markings on the walls of the tunnels by which they were apparently navigating, but nothing to indicate the purpose of the maze of passageways.

Taken by surprise, Sam walked into Nathan's back as he stopped without warning. He began to whisper an apology, but Nathan placed a finger to his lips in a clear signal for silence. There was a slight scraping sound and a rectangle of light appeared in the ceiling ahead. The tension in the air was palpable as someone was lifted up through the open hatch.

'All clear,' Claire confirmed in a low voice.

One by one the group climbed up into the room. Nipper and Grunt lifted Sam and Callum up through the ceiling and leapt up into the room after them with ease. Claire was waiting. Nipper had barely put Sam down when she pulled him into her arms and held him close. She was strong, he realised, as she all but crushed him with the hug.

'Easy on the ribs, Mum!' he squeaked. 'I've picked up a lot of bruises today.'

'Sorry!' she apologised, easing off the pressure. She had tears in her eyes as she spoke again. 'It's just so good to see you. Once I realised what had happened, I never thought I'd see you again. But how did you get here? Where are Matt and Niamh?'

Sam felt his face redden as he answered.

'Me and Callum here sort of borrowed Dad's boat to go fishing . . .'

'What do you mean, "sort of borrowed"?' she interrupted, holding him at arm's-length and raising an eyebrow. 'Don't tell me your father has let you turn into a thief?'

'No, Mum! Don't think that. Dad's been great. It's just . . . well, he kept disappearing off and leaving us on our own while he looked for . . . He's never given up on finding you, Mum. I was bored, so I thought I'd take Callum out fishing. We were only going to be out for a couple of hours and I planned to get us back long before Dad got home. There was a strange-looking patch of water and . . .'

'. . . you crossed over to this place,' Claire finished. 'Poor Matt! First me and now you as well! He must be beside himself with worry. The damned Imperium have a hell of a lot to answer for.'

Sam thought about that for a moment. From what little he knew, her accusation didn't make any sense. Claire saw his confusion and laughed. She drew him into another hug. He didn't mind at all. Hugs had never felt so good.

'To be fair, Sam, it's not really the fault of the current crowd,' she admitted. 'But they're as bad as the original culprits for closing their minds to what is happening. The Bermuda Triangle phenomenon is the fault of the raptors and it's not limited to that region. The effects of what they've done are most concentrated there and in the waters off the Japanese coast that some have dubbed the Devil's Sea, but there've been incidents right across the globe. And it's getting worse.'

'Sorry to butt in, Mrs Cutler,' Callum interrupted. 'Before he was killed, our friend Brad told us about the raptors pumping radioactive waste into the Earth's core causing the crossings, but he said it was just a rumoured theory.'

'Mum, this is my friend Callum Barnes,' Sam offered by way of introduction as he eased free of her embrace.

'Nice to meet you, Callum,' Claire replied, giving him a warm smile. 'I'm not sure what your friend told you, but we believe we've got enough evidence now to prove to any who are willing to listen to the facts that the magnetic storms are to blame for the rifts forming between dimensions. As far as we can tell, at the heart of the most intense storms magnetic disturbances form that are so strong, they literally slice through the fabric between universes.'

'So do the rifts work both ways?' Callum asked eagerly. 'Do you think we could get back to our world through one of them?'

'We don't know for sure,' Claire said carefully. 'People have tried, but to our knowledge no one has successfully managed to penetrate safely to the eye of a storm at the peak of its strength. That's when the rifts form. As far as we can tell, the rifts are normally short-lived. To make a successful crossing would mean getting to the eye of a seriously powerful storm, locating the rift and crossing through it during a relatively tiny window of opportunity. Don't think I haven't considered trying. I would have given anything to get back home to you, your sister and your dad, Sam. Believe me, I would. But the storms are so unpredictable and to try in any of the boats we've built here would be suicide.'

Sam looked at his friend. Callum looked thoughtful, but Sam could see that he had not been put off the idea by his mother's explanation. Callum was still in information-gathering mode.

'Come on,' she said. 'This is our current headquarters. We should be safe here, so we might as well get comfortable as I try to answer some of your questions. It might take a while. There's a place to sit through here.'

She led the boys away from the trapdoor, which had now been sealed again. The raptors and men had dispersed through three different doors. Claire walked into a room that had been furnished for human comfort. There were several seats of varying size and design, a large central table and several smaller ones. A large bookcase on one wall was full to overflowing with a mixture of hardback and paperback books in several languages. Some of the books appeared leather-bound and very old. Others were very recent. Pictures adorned the walls, two of which looked to be from Earth, but most appeared to have been painted locally.

The boys sat together on a bench-like seat covered with cushioned material that was surprisingly soft.

'Would you like a drink, boys?' Claire asked, opening a cabinet to reveal shelves of cups and bottles. She picked up an earthenware flagon. 'This is a local cordial that's tasty.'

'Yes, please,' they answered together.

'Here you go then,' she said, pouring two cups and passing them across. She sat down next to Sam. 'Now where to begin? Tell me everything you can about the last nine years, Sam. Which school are you in? How're Matt and Niamh?'

Sam did his best. He had never been a particularly good storyteller, but prompted by frequent questions, he spoke for quite a long time before he was finally allowed to ask some questions of his own.

'What about you, Mum?' he asked. 'I think Dad might have a fit if he saw you carrying all those guns. What happened after you crossed into this place?'

'Well, you've crossed, so you know what that bit was like,' she said. 'The storm we emerged into was terrible. My work colleague, Jane, didn't make it to shore. She was swept overboard by a wave, but I couldn't even say when it happened. At the time, I was so focused on keeping the boat afloat that I didn't notice her go. I felt terrible when I realised that she wasn't onboard any more, but I didn't dare turn the boat round and look for her. Starting my life here with her death on my conscience wasn't a great way to begin.'

Sam placed a hand on her arm and she squeezed it gratefully.

'When I finally beached the boat, I found myself in the Reserve. A couple took me in and looked after me until the storm passed. They told me enough to prepare me for my first encounter with the local raptors. Initially, I was frantic with worry about you all. I was desperate to try to get back, but by the time I got back out to my boat, the raptors had stripped it so thoroughly that it was no longer seaworthy. I had no way of going out, which with hindsight was probably a good thing. I tried to convince some of the other humans in the Reserve to help me build a boat, but they all said the same thing – it was hopeless. There was no way back. When the raptors realised I was a scientist, they were very keen to get me here to the City of the Imperium to work alongside their people looking for solutions to the problems they're facing with their ecology. To begin with, I was naïve. I thought they wanted real answers and I worked hard to find them. Turns out what they really wanted was to find a way to blame us humans for what was happening.'

'Figures,' Callum said, nodding.

Claire perched on the edge of a nearby chair and thought for a moment. 'You can't have failed to notice by now that the raptor civilisation is highly technologically advanced. In many areas, their scientific knowledge and engineering skills are significantly ahead of our own. From what I've learned, raptor scientists first developed nuclear power about eight centuries ago, but they made many mistakes and suffered several catastrophic disasters.'

'Brad didn't mention nuclear disasters. That's not good,' Callum noted.

'Sure isn't!' Claire agreed. 'But they were unwilling to give up such a powerful source of energy and so they persisted. Eventually, they not only overcame the more obvious problems, but they expanded their use of nuclear energy until it was in everyday use throughout raptor society. There was a price though.'

'Nuclear waste,' Sam said.

'Precisely! They've generated vast quantities of it over the years. To begin with, they dumped it in the deepest parts of their oceans, but soon they began to notice strange mutated creatures appearing. Some proved incredibly dangerous and so the raptor scientists, terrified that mutations might somehow begin to spread through their own population, began to look for alternative solutions. So, as your friend told you, they started to pump the waste into the Earth's core. The idea was to reduce the raptor dependence on nuclear energy, safely dispose of the nuclear waste and develop a clean, new energy source – the Earth's natural magnetic field – all in one fell swoop.'

'That's how they have such advanced technology like the train we travelled on to get here?' Callum asked, frowning.

Claire Cutler nodded. 'Spot on. Clever lad, isn't he?' she noted, giving Sam an approving smile.

Sam nodded. 'But the scientists couldn't have achieved that overnight.'

'No. It took centuries. That's part of the problem. The raptors have invested so much time and energy into creating this supposedly clean energy system, that they've closed their eyes to the ongoing and increasing catastrophe that makes our global warming problem back home look like a storm in a teacup.'

'Wasn't it dangerous, pumping the nuclear waste into the magma?' he asked.

'As it turned out, yes,' Claire answered. 'But not as directly dangerous as you might imagine. The one scientist's plan to despose of the waste worked exactly as he had anticipated. Unfortunately, what he hadn't predicted were some of the nasty side-effects. He had expected increased vulcanism. That was an obvious one really. Heat the magma, it expands and the pressure has to go somewhere.'

'And volcanoes began erupting all over the world. Brad mentioned that too,' Callum replied, shaking his head. 'I'm guessing that was easy enough to dismiss as a natural phenomenon.'

'Right again,' Claire said, giving him an approving smile. 'That's exactly what the Imperium did, but it wasn't the worst of it by far. What the raptor scientists failed to anticipate was that the increased magnetic field of the Earth is accelerating the mutation process among their population just as surely as dumping nuclear waste into the ocean or trying to bury it in remote sites, maybe even more so. Oh, it's not as dramatic or as quick, but it's happening. And worse, it's happening right across the globe, not just in localised areas.'

'So how are the raptors combating it?' Callum asked. 'Surely they know what's happening.'

'Yes, they know,' Claire confirmed. 'They've known for centuries. That's why the bulk of raptor society lives in these especially designed geodesic structures. Another of their scientists worked out that within a structure like this the inhabitants are protected from the effects of the increased magnetic field. It acts like a sort of protective cage, channelling the magnetic effects through the structure.'

'But not all of the raptors live under the domes?'

'Correct.'

'And the storms?' Sam asked.

'Are the other major side-effect,' Claire confirmed. 'The raptors' historical records show that the level of storm activity around the globe has been steadily increasing ever since they started pumping the waste into the core. In turn, the number of rifts forming between dimensions is increasing too. The Imperium has chosen to blame the storms on the unfortunate humans who have crossed here because they are stubbornly refusing to lose the benefits of the blend of nuclear and magnetic energy. They keep the general population in the dark about what is actually happening, but they know.'

Callum and Sam looked at one another for a moment, but neither said anything for some time. It was an amazing situation.

'At least in our world people are doing something to combat global warming,' Callum said eventually. 'All right, it might not be much and it almost certainly isn't enough, but they are doing something.'

'It all comes down to political will,' Claire said firmly. 'When I delivered the findings of my joint study with the raptor scientists, the Imperium decided to ignore them because the truth was too bitter a pill to swallow. I quickly discovered that my work was being swept under the carpet and I questioned why nothing was being done. This turned out to be less than wise.'

'What happened?' Sam asked.

'A series of attempts on my life followed,' she replied, her blue eyes narrowing with cold anger as she momentarily relived the experiences. 'But I was lucky. Two of my fellow researchers were raptors who had recognised the truth in my findings. They protected me and risked their lives to help me escape. We three became the founder members of AIM – the Anti-Imperium Mob – and we've been fighting the Imperium and its agents ever since.'

'Nice . . . I think.' Sam looked at his mother's face. She was clearly passionate about what she was doing. 'So were those raptors who chased us here Imperium agents?'

'Maybe, but not necessarily,' Claire answered, frowning. 'Raptor politics are perhaps more complex than those back home. Take that scarred raptor who led the chase. He's an officer in a sort of secret police force allied to one of the many Imperium subfactions. I've run into him a few times before.'

'We think he killed our friend Brad,' Callum said.

She nodded. 'That wouldn't surprise me at all,' she said. 'There is always a good number of his organisation monitoring the Reserve and quietly killing off humans whenever possible. He and his group seem to have an irrational hatred of us and of raptors who are sympathetic to our welfare.'

'So what exactly are you doing?' asked Sam. 'Assassinating Imperium members and their agents? That's pretty radical.'

'No! We try to minimise the use of violence,' Claire said quickly. 'The problem is that whatever peaceful protests we make are met with violence. It's the raptor way. As they're so fast and strong, we humans stand little chance of survival without the advantage of advanced weapon technology. Guns are the obvious solution to protect ourselves when we have to. Raptors don't use them, but they've come to recognise their potency. What we try to do is to get messages broadcast on the public networks, interfering with the Imperium channels at peak times. Or we sabotage pumping stations and magnetic conversion units, forcing them to shut down.'

'And does that work?' Callum asked.

'Sometimes . . . for a while,' she answered. 'But the Imperium are always quick to cut off our broadcasts and repair any damage we manage to do. Our efforts to date appear to have had limited impact. We have agents working in several Imperium departments. Today, for example, we knew you had been taken prisoner within minutes – long before the Imperium began broadcasting their ridiculous demands. I arranged for your two raptor friends to infiltrate the building and they agreed to bring you to our ambush point.'

'So that's how you managed to be waiting for us!' Callum exclaimed. 'Neat.'

'So what else have you tried?' Sam asked. 'What about getting word through to our world? If what the raptors are doing here is going to have a long-term effect on Earth, surely one of the top priorities of your organisation should be to let the people there know what is happening. The Devil's Triangle, as Dad insists on calling it, still has a reputation as an unsolved mystery. You've got the answers. The Devil has a face – the face of a raptor.'

His mother shook her head. 'We don't have enough people to expend lives on a one-way trip into the middle of one of those storms,' she said firmly. 'It's a nice idea, but what would it achieve?'

'Getting our family back together,' Sam suggested pointedly. 'Dad and Niamh will be frantic by now. We should at least try, Mum.'

Claire turned and took his cheeks in her hands. She looked directly into his eyes as she answered. 'Sam, the most likely way our family is going to be reunited is if your father and sister cross to this world, do you hear me? Attempting to go back will only get us killed.'

'But how do you know that for sure?' Sam insisted. 'There are times when I can sense Niamh, Mum. And she can sense me. We have a sort of invisible link between our minds. It must be something to do with us being twins. She's more sensitive than I am. I'm fairly sure she knows I've found you and I'm sure she'll tell Dad.'

Sam stared into her eyes. He didn't like what he saw there.

'He kept looking for you for nine years, Mum,' he continued. 'Once Dad knows we're both alive, there's no way he'll ever give up. Think about it. If they cross, they won't know to expect a storm. Dad and Niamh could both die trying to reach shore. Don't you think we should do something about that? We need to reach them before they make the mistake of coming here. Maybe we can use the link somehow.'

'How?' his mother asked.

'I don't know,' Sam admitted. 'But there must be some way we can use it.'

Claire sighed and shook her head. 'I'd love to think there was a way,' she breathed. 'But I can't see it. We would still need to get to the eye of a powerful storm on a hostile sea. Without a sturdy ship, our chances of survival would be minuscule, mental link or no mental link. No. The logical thing to do is to stop the raptors in this world from making matters any worse.'

'But . . .'

'No buts!' she said firmly. 'Think. Assuming for a moment we did succeed in getting back to our world – what then? There would be nothing we, or any government in our world, could do to stop the effects of what is happening here. Unless we can stop the raptors from making things worse in this world, more and more people will end up crossing here. That means more families will be split and more people will die, Sam. It's down to us to do something. And even if, by some miracle, we do manage to stop the raptors from pumping any more nuclear waste into the core, it's likely to take centuries to reverse the effects of what they've done.'

'That sounds like Claire Cutler the scientist talking,' Sam grumbled angrily. 'What about my mum? What does she think?'

'That's harsh, Sam,' Callum commented, frowning. He made a subtle calming gesture with his hands.

'No, it's OK, Callum,' Claire said quickly. 'Sam has a right to say what he thinks. It's better to have these thoughts out in the open. I don't want to put any of my family into unnecessary danger, Sam. You say that Matt has searched for nine years, but he's not stumbled into a rift in that time. I think it's safe to assume it's unlikely that he's going to change that record in the next few days. Let's all take some time to think things through before we make any firm plans or promises, shall we?'

'OK. I suppose that's fair,' Sam conceded grudgingly. He leaned across and hugged her again. As he did so, he closed his eyes. In that special corner of his mind's eye he momentarily sensed Niamh. The sense of her presence was fading. She was hurt. He concentrated harder. He could feel her pain pulsing through his ankle, side and up his back. But from what he could tell, she was remarkably calm.

I'll get home, Niamh, he thought, trying with all his might to direct the words at her. *I'm with Mum now*, he added, forming a picture of Claire Cutler in

389

his mind and concentrating hard on keeping it firm as the sense of contact weakened to a whisper. *I'll find a way home and I'll bring Mum and Callum with me.*

As she approached the police car, Niamh reached inside her mind to where Sam's presence had been so strong earlier. It was still there, but it was as if the static was building again, obscuring her view. A fuzzy image entered the space in her mind. It was faint, but unmistakable. 'Mum!' she breathed. 'You found Mum!'

'What was that? Are you OK?' the policeman asked.

Niamh shook her head and smiled. Sam had found their mother! Niamh realised there must be substance to the stories surrounding the Devil's Triangle. Sam must be somewhere that was difficult to return from: somewhere so remote that their mother had been trapped there and not managed to escape in over nine years.

She had to talk to her father. Perhaps it was a good thing that the police were planning to return her to England. If Sam and her Mum were trapped somewhere that remote, what hope had she got of finding them alone? Matthew Cutler knew just about everything there was to know about the legends surrounding the Devil's Triangle. If anyone could make sense of the strange things Niamh had sensed from her brother, it was her father. He was their best hope now of getting Sam and their mum back where they belonged and finally ending the heartache that had started nine years ago.

Niamh tried hard to focus on the connection with Sam. *It's going to be all right. Dad and I will find you – both of you!*

She looked up at the policemen. 'I'll be fine,' she replied. 'It's all going to be fine.'

She just hoped she was right.

Acknowledgements

This book has been enriched by the input of many people. In particular I would like to thank: Cheryl Smith and Mark Howell, reporters at the Key West Citizen, Mr James E. Brooks, Public Affairs Officer at Naval Air Station Key West, LTJG Matthew Meinhold of the United States Coast Guard, Mr David E. Vaughan, PH.D., Executive Director of MOTE Marine Laboratory on Summerland Key, Mr John Hunt, Captain Patrick Langley and Officer Robert Dube, from the Florida Fish and Wildlife Conservation Commission, Marsha Martin at Schmitt Real Estate, Marathon, and Thomas L. Hambright, Monroe County Historian at the Key West Public Library.

A special thank you also goes to fellow author, Ian Watson, for the idea on how to make the earth's magnetic field stronger, and to pilot, Simon Ludlow, for his knowledge and insights on flying the Piper Cherokee (which is one aeroplane I've never flown!).

Although there is a 'Monkey Island' in the Florida Keys, my geography of it in this story is totally fictional, as I did not get the chance to visit it during my research trip.